By Lee Ohlson

Ashford Hall
A Shadow Comes Darkly

Published by DREAMSPINNER PRESS
www.dreamspinnerpress.com

# Ashford Hall

LEE OHLSON

Published by
DREAMSPINNER PRESS

8219 Woodville Hwy #1245
Woodville, FL 32362 USA
www.dreamspinnerpress.com



Ashford Hall
© 2025 Lee Ohlson

Cover Art
© 2025 Nenad Serac
Cover content is for illustrative purposes only and any person depicted on the cover is a model.



Trade Paperback ISBN: 978-1-64108-839-8
Digital ISBN: 978-1-64108-838-1
Trade Paperback published July 2025
v. 1.0

# Part One—Summer, 1851

# 1

IT WAS by dint of my upbringing that I had spent scarcely any time beyond the limits of London at the age of twenty-eight, aside from the Eton schooling that a scholarship had paid for and the Cambridge education that had precipitated my career as a lawyer. The son of a retired English colonel and a woman from Karachi he had fallen in love with, I enjoyed a comfortable, but not lavish childhood, a middle-class existence that was nonetheless far less than I thought I deserved.

Having finished school nearly three years prior, I had been gainfully employed as a lawyer since. I had seen no reason to leave London, my cozy flat, my familiar haunts, for any considerable amount of time. A few days in France, a week or two in a country pile owned by some colleague or distant friend—neither of these constituted a true vacation from London, and as another sweltering summer approached, I found that for once I was struggling to imagine another three months hunched over the desk of my crowded law firm. It was barely June, and I could already taste the heat, feel the human crush of the city.

Most of the cases I had wouldn't go before a judge until August at the earliest, and the paperwork could all go where I went. There seemed little point in the years of work I'd done to become financially stable if I couldn't take some time away from the office to gallivant during the summer months, but as my desire to go away intensified, my uncertainty regarding where to go did the same. Leaving the country was my favorite choice, a little jaunt down to the continent within my grasp… and then the letter came.

For years after, I would wonder at the fact that the letter from Charles came at the same time my need to escape London turned into a full-blown obsession. My daily routine was the same—breakfast, work, a hansom cab home—but that day it had simply been too much. The heat was suffocating, the smell coming off the Thames stronger than usual, a shirt that had been comfortable when I'd left home now scratching the back of my neck where it met my skin. The thought of subjecting myself to this until the fall chill set in was unbearable, and by the time I returned home I was in a truly foul mood.

"A letter's come for you," was the first thing my landlady said as I stepped inside. She held a small cream-colored envelope in my direction. "It'll be that Ashford boy, I reckon."

A letter from Charles was a balm I hadn't known I'd needed. Charles and I had been friends since Eton, and our communication was both regular and lengthy, to the extent that the letter I held in my hand felt measly compared to the letters I'd grown accustomed to. However, Charles had an excellent habit of visiting me when he was in the city, and a short letter from him, perfectly timed at the beginning of June, was hopefully an indication that he cared to do just that. "Thank you," was the only thing I could say to avoid a deeper conversation, taking the letter from my landlady before running my thumb over my name written in the deep blue ink Charles favored.

I headed up to my flat on the top floor, a small and comfortable apartment that had once belonged to my landlady's son, and walked over to my desk under the window. The seal on the reverse of the envelope—a simple "C.A" in the same dark blue wax as his ink—came away easily against my ivory-handled letter opener and I was soon holding Charles's letter, written in a looping script I knew so well.

> *June 1, 1851*
> *Dear Tom,*
> *I hope this letter finds you well. I write from*
> *Ashford Hall, a place I am sure you are familiar with*
> *through numerous stories regarding my childhood home.*
> *I realized a few days ago that despite these years of*
> *friendship, I've never once thought to invite you here. I*
> *know your practice in London is busy, but the summer*
> *months are never pressing for the courts, and I am*
> *missing you terribly. My brother is a bore and a man can*
> *only ride his horse around the grounds so much before*
> *he tires of being alone.*
>
> *If it isn't too much to ask, there is a room for you*
> *here, along with a balcony where you can work on your*
> *cases if you'd like. I think it would make both of our*
> *summers far more entertaining if we were to spend it*

*together rather than apart. I await your response, and*
*if you decide to say no, just realize that I will spend the*
*hottest months of the year in abject misery without my*
*best friend.*
    *Love,*
    *Charlie*

I could only smile, setting the letter down on the desk, leaning back in my chair, and looking out the window at London sprawling before me. At that time I was living in a fairly nice part of London, better than the neighborhood in which I grew up, but even there I felt innately smothered; as culturally vibrant as the city was, the idea of passing up the opportunity to spend a few months in the country, the air fresh and the company pleasant, was utterly unimaginable. I penned my response quickly in the spidery cursive that had served me well when taking copious notes in school but now meant I struggled to have my writing understood. I, of course, gave Charles a hasty yes, with the promise that I would be in Somerset no later than the following Monday after having the opportunity to tie up some loose ends in London.

Luckily, there was something about summer that made people amenable to requests they wouldn't have granted had they been made in the more oppressive winter months. By Friday at the end of work, myself and a carriage filled with various boxes were on our way to Somerset. The journey was, thankfully, not a particularly onerous one, although it was long compared to what could have been accomplished by train, and by the time the sun was setting over the country estate on Sunday evening, I was crossing the threshold into the esteemed Ashford Hall.

The stories Charles had told me over the years did not do the place justice in the slightest. As the estate was in the center of a massive forest, it took nearly half an hour to make it from the front gate posts to the inner walls, great stones meant to keep out whatever ancient enemies the Ashford family had stood against—although if I was being quite honest, I didn't believe there were any. The house was older than I could place, but there were more modern bits built onto it, including a cottage that sat at the edge of the woods for the deceased lord's former manservant and his family, the construction of which an undertaking I remembered hearing about my first year at Eton with Charles. Ivy sprawled up the stone facade of the house, including the roof of a large greenhouse attached to the manor that was currently reflecting the setting sun, and the sight of the manor home left me positively breathless. It brought to mind some great French palace, sprawling and beautiful, and for a few moments I was certain I had been brought to the wrong estate. I had never doubted that Charles had come from wealth, but this seemed an impossible home for a man like my friend to have been raised in.

The carriage driver stopped in front of the dual stone steps that led up to the home and before I could even dismount, Charles had thrown one of the great oak doors open and was hurrying down towards me. Knowing him, he had undoubtedly been hovering by the front door awaiting my arrival, and the idea that someone had been so eagerly anticipating me was enough to bring a lump to my throat, the loneliness of London having been endured for too long. I pushed the carriage door open, much to the chagrin of the driver, and stepped out onto solid ground for the first time since leaving the inn that morning. There was no time to recover from the rumbling of the road before Charles had me in a bone-crushing embrace.

It was rather like being smothered by an oversized blond dog. Charles had always been bigger than I was, my own good looks attributable to a slim build and dark, curly hair and no great robustness. Six feet and two inches, Charles was ash blond with wide green eyes and broad shoulders that had served him well when we'd been at school and other boys had been particularly mouthy about Charles's lack of a mother or my lack of a title. I'm embarrassed to admit that despite how ungentlemanly the hug was, I rapidly hugged him back, tangling my fingers in the fine fabric of his white shirt. It was nice to be greeted with so much excitement. This sort of affection was rare, my friends in London newer, posher, less prone to physicality like this, and I couldn't help but soak it in until Charles held me at arm's length. "You're far too thin, Tom."

"You saw me in April, you liar," I said, laughing as I finally removed myself from Charles's grasp. The carriage driver had already begun to unload the boxes, one of the stable boys assisting him in carrying them inside, and I realized for the first time that this was actually happening, that I was here for the summer. A true country estate, something out of an Austen novel, and it was mine to explore. "You're sure that this isn't an imposition?"

"Positive," Charles said. "Come along, I'll give you the grand tour and show you to your suite."

"Suite?" I asked, following Charles up the steps and pausing briefly to thank the carriage driver; I knew the man wouldn't expect it, but after traveling with someone for nearly three days, it felt like the correct thing to do. "I hardly need an entire suite."

"It's simply a bedroom and a sitting area with a desk. But you're on the same side of the house as I am, so we can bother each other as much as we please." He held the door open and I stepped inside; even in the summer heat the great hall was nice and cool, two large staircases mimicking the stairs out front and leading to each wing of the house. The great hall itself was lofty, the ceiling so high that it was difficult to make out the undeniably beautiful details that had been etched into place when the estate had been built centuries before.

Each subsequent room was just as stunning as the great hall; from the dining room to the ballroom to the parlor, everything was impeccably decorated and perfectly maintained. I do not mean to insinuate that I was raised in a home without means, for even retired my father boasted a fair salary, but our house had been small, and my mother had kept tenants, which made it feel even smaller. Compared to the wealth of Ashford Hall and the life I knew Charles had been raised in, my upbringing paled. I could see the ghosts of Ashford men wandering these halls, holding elaborate balls and hosting important members of parliament, and the history of the place captivated me from the first.

Finally, we came to rest on the eastern side of the house, a lavish hall decorated with art that seemed to have been plucked from master studios across Europe, and Charles indicated a beautifully carved door. "This is yours," Charles said before pointing down the hallway to another door on the opposite side. "And those are mine, so if you ever need anything, I'll be within shouting distance. Come along."

He pushed into the suites that would be mine for the summer, and despite his modesty at the front steps, I could tell that he was pleased with his choice for where I would be staying. I couldn't fault him as our lengthy friendship had ensured that Charles knew my tastes as well as I knew them myself. The room was light and airy, a balcony overlooking the massive gardens that lay to the east, a pond glimmering just beyond them. Clearly the maids had been working to air out the room, the linens freshly changed, the curtains pulled back, and the balcony doors flung open. "This is too much, Charles."

"That is simply not true," Charles said. "These rooms were where my mother hosted guests when she was still alive. I knew you'd be most comfortable here. The view was always her favorite, and you've always reminded me of her."

"Ah, your fondness for me is finally explained," I said, and he laughed, that bright clear sound that I had so loved as a boy. Charles was then, and had always been, the best of friends to me, and if I had known then the sort of peril that summer at Ashford Hall would put that friendship in, I would have turned heel and run back to London at that point. But I didn't, and the events of the summer did not, inevitably, tear us apart the way I once fathomed they would. Then, in that evening light, I believed that the secret I had kept from Charles since we had been boys was a secret that our friendship could not withstand.

"Even if you weren't like her, you would still be my friend," Charles said, leading me into a bathroom that led into the actual bedroom, set back away from the door so I would have some privacy. "Dinner is in an hour, time enough for you to freshen up. I've instructed Felix to bring your documents to your parlor here, but if I catch you going through them before the weekend is over, I will be quite disappointed. Remember, you've come here for pleasure as much as anything else."

"No law until at least tomorrow morning, I promise. I recall you mentioning a Felix you played with as a boy, but who is he now?"

"My brother's manservant, but he has temporarily taken over duties of head butler while our butler is visiting his daughter in Essex," Charles said. "You'll meet him soon enough. Don't be alarmed by his, uh, modern interpretation of his duties. As you know, Felix was raised alongside myself and Arthur and has always benefited from a rather elevated relationship with us compared to what you may have seen from other servants."

I smiled at this, shaking my head. "So you're warning me he has a penchant for argument? I am not so bothered by that as others in your stratosphere, Charlie. My profession means I frequently cross class lines."

"I know, I know. I just wanted to warn you. He offended one of Arthur's friends last time my brother had some lords down. You would have thought he'd called for the assassination of the queen, the way they reacted."

"Then Felix and I will get along quite well," I said. "I'll see you at dinner if I don't get lost on the way. And Charles, thank you. I can't imagine spending my time in London after seeing this place."

"You're always welcome," Charles said, pulling me into another brief one-armed hug before leaving me alone in the suite. As soon as the door snicked shut behind him, I wandered to the balcony, leaned against the railing, and peered out over the gardens. They were masterfully maintained, a sea of green with flowers and trees visible at intervals, and the fresh smell coming up off the plants was so refreshing I thought I could stay there for hours, simply breathing it in.

I was so taken by the scenery that I did not notice the man walking through the garden until he was nearly beneath my balcony, and when I finally spotted him, I found that I was looking at someone as exceptionally beautiful as Ashford Hall itself. He was tall, with broad shoulders and dressed in a perfectly tailored shirt and trousers, and I may have mistaken him for a well-dressed guest if not for his more than passing resemblance to Charles. While Charles was an open book, this man—Arthur Ashford, if my instincts were correct—had his brother's good looks with none of his easy charm. Rather, from my perch on the balcony, he seemed to hold himself with a haughtiness that was rather startling.

I had heard of Lord Ashford, of course, and Charles had always sung his praises. Arthur was said to be kind and effervescent, a sort of quasi-hero to Charles, who was three years younger and who had followed as closely in Arthur's footsteps as a second son could at that time. I had anticipated a copy of the younger Ashford, and to find myself now looking down at a man who could have been sculpted by Michaelangelo and easily landed among the most beautiful artwork known at the time was both unnerving and a fright.

Charles had never known the sort of man I was, the sort of man I *truly* was, the sort of attraction I had always harbored. There was a reason I was unmarried at my age, despite my profession and my looks, and it had nothing to do with a lack of interested women but everything to do with a lack of interest on my part. I had realized as a teenager that I had no use for women as anything more than friends, that men held for me the sort of beauty that I assumed I should have found in the fairer sex, and I had hidden this from Charles for good reason, unable to believe that my friend would accept this truth about me.

Seeing Charles's brother for the first time, I felt that untethered attraction rise like a snake coiling in the pit of my stomach. It was a moment of unguarded hunger and I paid for it dearly, because just as I became aware of my attraction, Arthur Ashford raised his head and met my eyes. He was terribly handsome, his face more hawk-like than his brother's, his eyes a piercing green framed by ash blond curls, everything about him screaming of pride. It was his expression, however, that sent fear lancing through me. Arthur studied me for the briefest of moments and seemed to read my mind, his lip curling in the slightest sneer before he turned away and continued on his walk.

I was discovered before I could even properly meet the man, and it was my own damnable fault.

2

Filled with a sense of foreboding due to my own carelessness, I left the balcony and returned to the parlor room, busying myself in growing familiar with the place while also trying to calm my racing pulse. The odds that Arthur had truly intuited my expression were thankfully low, but at the time I was convinced that I had been caught out as an invert before I was even able to properly introduce myself to the man. I had always been easily read, a man who I'd had a few dalliances with in London having once told me that he'd known before he'd even approached me that I would be amenable to his advances, but what I was failing to take into account at Ashford Hall was that Arthur was undoubtedly not accustomed to looking another man in the eyes and finding attraction there. He must have misinterpreted it.

Distracted and nervous, struck both by the beauty of the man I had just seen and my fear that I had inadvertently destroyed my holiday before it had even begun, I was in the midst of rearranging the desk Charles had provided for my use when a swift knock came at the door. It startled me so badly I nearly knocked over an ink bottle, steadying it before it tipped off the edge of the desk and glancing towards the door. "Come in," I said before I could overthink, although some overactive part of my mind was convinced that it was Arthur come to reprimand me.

Instead, the door opened and a man perhaps a little younger than myself entered, holding my luggage and smiling at me. I instantly realized this must be Felix. Shorter than I was by a few inches and red-headed, he had an air about him that oozed friendliness, but it was a facial scar that gave his identity away, a pale pink stripe that reached from his chin to just below his right eye. Charles had told me the story many times, he and Felix playing in the woods of Ashford Hall as children who did not seem aware yet of the social class that would divide them. Felix misstepped, falling a good twenty feet down an embankment and nearly into the river that ran through the far end of the property. It was a tale that always got laughs from the audience he was telling it to, and it doubled now as a perfect identification of the man standing in the doorway. "Hullo, Mr. Whitmore."

"Felix, isn't it?" I asked, and Felix grinned at me, stepping into the room before setting my luggage down next to the chaise longue that took up the wall opposite my desk, no doubt so Charles would have a place to lie when he came to interrupt my work during the summer. "I suppose Charles warned you about me."

"Warned me? The man has spoken of nothing else since we received your letter, sir. He's been quite excited. It's rare that Charles gets to bring his friends here, so we're all quite pleased about the opportunity to meet you."

"You mean you're pleased that he has someone else to bother," I said, and Felix laughed. Restored from the panic I had given myself minutes earlier, I ventured a question I would not have dared had I still been rattled. "Is Lord Ashford currently in the garden?"

"He walks there in the evenings before dinner to improve his digestion," Felix said. "I suppose you saw him?"

"I did," I said, glancing back at the balcony and recalling the look Arthur had given me. "Does he normally look so—"

"Unfriendly?" Felix offered. "Disgusted? Angry?"

I laughed, already charmed by the man; I could see why Charles had immediately assumed I would be friends with him. "Yes. Is that just the nature of his countenance?"

"Unfortunately, yes. His father was the same. They used to call him Lord Stoneford behind his back, and I fear they'll do the same to poor Arthur. He really isn't as terrible as all that. Just tends to be unaware of how he looks when he's deep in thought. Did he give you a dirty look?"

"He did," I admitted, not wanting to tell Felix that my assumption had been that Arthur had read the look in my eyes and realized exactly what it meant. I would have to get better at masking my attraction, and hoped in that moment that I would be able to do so by reminding myself that Arthur was my closest friend's brother, and not some man who might be amenable to my flirtation. "To be fair, I was trying to figure out who he was and was looking at him with more scrutiny than was perhaps polite."

"I assure you the look wasn't personal," Felix said. "He most likely was trying to figure out who you were in return. Although admittedly, Charles's description of you is perfectly apt."

"Oh, I simply must hear how Charles describes me," I said, glancing at the door as the stable boy who had been roped into assisting with my boxes appeared, giving me a desultory bow before setting the first of many boxes next to my desk. I smiled at him before Felix's next words distracted me.

"Dark and handsome, with big brown eyes and a rather outdated sense of style," Felix said, grinning. "All of which describes you to a tee."

"Outdated sense of style?" I plucked at my shirt, sighing softly. "I suppose that's not entirely off the mark, but to be honest I've never concerned myself with the latest fashion. It's not much needed in court."

"I'm sure Charles will take the summer to rectify that," Felix said, tapping the top of the luggage he'd set down. "Now, I'll leave you be so you can wash up for dinner. All your clothes should be here, and I had one of the maids put hot water in the tub before you arrived. It should still be warm."

"Thank you," I said, relieved to finally have a chance to wash up after the journey. "I'll see you at dinner?"

"I'm sure I'll be around," Felix said, giving me a bow that was solidly mocking before leaving the room. I had liked him from the start, Felix's comfort with me clearly speaking to how the Ashfords had treated him, and I was pleased to discover that his quick wit did nothing to detract from his thoughtfulness in running the household and ensuring the comfort of the guests. My first night at Ashford Hall was a pleasant harbinger of the summer to come, the water in the washroom basin the perfect warmth to wash the dust of travel from my face and to spruce myself up before the inevitable call for dinner came.

While the stable boy unloaded boxes in the main parlor of my room, I washed and dressed in a shirt that Charles himself had purchased for me on one of his not-infrequent jaunts to London. Ostensibly my "opera" shirt, it seemed as good as any other for dining with a lord, and by the time I was ready for dinner, I had convinced myself that I was as presentable as I was going to get.

I knew, without sounding too preoccupied with my own looks, that I was considered handsome, although not in the pale way that was in fashion at the time. I had inherited my mother's curly black hair and dark eyes, my skin a deep brown that complemented the rest of me, and I had never struggled to be found attractive as a result. Charles, in particular, valued my looks in our friendship, as we were almost always guaranteed to be the best-looking pair of men at any ball that we attended, a combination that made for easy first dances and pleasant conversation.

Still, even as I prepared for dinner, I knew why I was making myself look good, and it wasn't because of Felix's words or Charles's usual expectations of me. It was the recollection of those green eyes looking up at me from the garden, the strange look in them, the almost- judgmental gaze. I had to prove Arthur wrong, whatever it was he thought about me. I had to be more handsome, more intelligent, more charismatic, to change his mind. At the time, I suffered from a near destructive desire to have people like me, and the idea that the brother of my best school friend thought negatively of me was so entirely repulsive that I would have done anything to ensure that he changed his view.

By the time the dinner bell rang I had primped and polished the most I could within a single hour, and I emerged from my room with as good a temperament as one could be expected to have after a journey of a hundred and thirty miles. Charles met me in the hallway, and I don't recall much of our conversation on the way down to the dinner table except that it was most likely mind-numbingly dull, a dozen different questions asked and answered about mutual friends we had scattered across the country. We had never felt the pressing urge to be particularly formal with one another, having known each other first as rowdy teenagers, and this comfort meant we could slip from casual conversation to the deepest, most heartfelt screeds within moments. The walk to dinner just didn't seem like the time to bare our souls to one another after a few months apart, so we kept it light and boring.

Because I was barely paying attention to the conversation and was instead soaking up the atmosphere of the magnificent rooms we passed through on our way back to the staircase that would take us closer to the dining room, I was unprepared for the moment when, the hallway opening up to the great hall, Charles and I found ourselves on the opposite end of the stairs from Arthur. Still dressed in the same clothes he had been wearing while wandering in the garden, dappled sun from a nearby window painting him in the palest last rays of daylight, he looked for all the world like something taken right out of a Renaissance oil painting and placed in the hall before us.

To say I was caught off guard was an understatement of the highest order. Whatever Charles had been saying was lost on me, and it took all my strength not to stop dead in my tracks at the sight of Arthur, who was regarding us with that same haughty look as before. I remembered what Felix had said, that it was a product of nothing more than an inherited mien, and considered that perhaps this was the truth before I was immediately proven correct in my first impression. After surveying us for a few more moments, Arthur turned and went down the far set of stairs on his own, a clear lack of friendliness in his actions.

"Is he usually so rude?" I asked, looking at Charles, and not bothering to keep my voice down, half hoping Arthur heard me. Charles was watching his brother walk down the stairs and I could read the confusion on his face, which was answer enough to my question. "Does he have a reason not to like me?"

"Not that I know of," Charles said, looking back at me briefly before walking towards the stairs on our side. "Unless… he does know that you're, well…."

"Lower class," I supplied, knowing perfectly well that it was how Charles was going to end his sentence. "But presumably he's always known that?"

"He has, and he's never acted as though it was an issue before," Charles said, dragging his thumb over his chin. "Have you been in the papers lately?"

"Not recently," I said, thinking back over the cases of the last few months. My time in court was hardly revolutionary, mostly small criminal cases, the very occasional murder. Rarely did I make the papers, and even then it was mostly just reporting on whatever case I had managed to win or lose, hardly even mentioning my name. "I haven't done anything of note, either. Nothing to offend his lordship."

"Well, maybe don't call him 'his lordship' to his face," Charles said, stopping at the bottom of the stairs and turning to look up at me. "We'll figure it out, Tom. If he hates you, well… we can go to Brighton for the summer."

I laughed despite myself and followed him into the dining room, finding that the table was set and laden with every sort of summer dish you could possibly desire. It was clear that even if the lord of the manor was not a fan of mine, Charles had done everything he could to make my first dinner in the house an amazing one. Arthur was standing near the fireplace at the far end of the room, talking animatedly with Felix, and for a moment I recalled that before being head butler Felix had been Arthur's manservant, a position that no doubt meant they were closer than I could have anticipated. Still, I was once again caught off guard when Arthur looked at me, that almost revolted look in his green eyes, and then said something to Felix, who bowed his head and left the room.

"Have a seat," Charles said, settling into the plush chair to the right of his brother's at the head of the table. The only other seat with a place set was at Arthur's left side, a position that put me in terribly close proximity to the man, and for a moment I considered how rude it would be to drag my chair to the far end of the table across from Arthur before deciding that it had never been in my nature to run before, so I certainly wouldn't do it now. Instead, I sat where Charles had indicated, carefully unfolding the cloth napkin to the side of the plate and laying it across my lap. "What were you telling Felix?"

Arthur hesitated near the fireplace before moving to his seat, sitting down and looking as prim and proper as I expected a lord to be. Even in the dim light of the dining room with only gas sconces to see him by, even after the way he'd been looking at me all evening, I couldn't help but be aware of his beauty. It was a damn shame that he had such a haughty expression, because he was a genuinely wonderful man to behold. His lips were full and rosy, his jaw well-defined and sporting the late-day stubble that spoke to a sort of virility that I enjoyed in a man. His blond hair, perfectly curly, was exactly in the fashion of the time, cut close to the nape of his neck but still with that delicate wave that was sported by so many of the actors who graced the London stages. In the soft light, his green eyes were so dark they were nearly emerald, and I found myself wishing he would look at me despite knowing I would find at most disdain there.

"I was informing him that I would prefer it if our guest's papers were not placed in *my* library," Arthur said, and to hear him speak was just as conflicting as the desire to have his eyes on me. The disregard in his voice, the sheer disinterest, filled my heart with a sort of ire I rarely succumbed to, but the *sound* of it…. Melodic, perfectly polished, a timbre that would undoubtedly thrill me to the bone were it to whisper my name in my ear. That was the first night I had to force down the hunger that threatened to consume me, and while I have at times wished I had done a better job at it, I have no complaints now.

# 3

ARTHUR'S VOICE left me so inflamed, both in anger and in heart, that I was momentarily stricken dumb. It was only Charles, leaning back in his chair to provide room for the maid who had appeared from some door and was pouring his wine, who roused me from my stupor. "Did some boxes end up there by accident?" he asked, seemingly unperturbed by the tone his brother took. "I put him in Mother's old suite and told them to put the boxes in his parlor. Felix was well aware."

"And yet someone decided my library was a better home for two of them," Arthur said, shrugging one shoulder, and the animal part of my brain posed the question of how that shoulder would look unclothed. "I thought I informed you when you had the idea to invite a guest that I wouldn't appreciate my space being impinged on."

"He's hardly a guest, Arthur. It's *Tom*," Charles said, as though Arthur had any reason to believe that freed me from the usual bonds of guestdom. "We'll move the boxes after dinner, and no harm will be done."

"You're the lawyer?" Arthur asked, and he was neither looking at me nor using a tone that seemed to be particularly friendly, so it took me a moment to realize he was speaking to me at all.

"Yes," I said, watching as the maid poured me a glass of wine and wishing I could ask her to bring me something stronger. "You're not a fan of that profession, I take it?"

Arthur looked at me then, his face impassive. "Why do you say that?"

"I have eyes, Lord Ashford, and ears," I said, and normally I would have watched my tone but decided, somewhat impetuously, that if I was just *Tom* I could use the same tone that the lord was using with me. "It's fairly obvious you think little of lawyers, unless you perhaps just think little of me."

There was something almost like amusement in Arthur's eyes, but I passed it off as a trick of the light; it seemed impossible to believe that a man with such a poor attitude could be getting any sort of entertainment from my clear attempts to prompt an argument with him. "You're correct," he said. "I have little use for lawyers."

"Most people have little use for us until they find themselves in need of our services," I said, taking a sip of my wine as the maid returned and began to serve our plates. I was not so low class as to be entirely unaccustomed to being served at the table, but I disliked the feeling of being waited upon and had to remind myself not to step in and assist. I had grown up with servants, but their presence was minimal, and my mother had been far more involved in our regular meals than I supposed Lady Ashford had ever been. "And I'm sure a man like yourself has had few dealings with us. But I'm not here as a lawyer. I'm here as Charles's friend."

"You really have no inkling of why I might dislike you," Arthur said, giving the maid a brief nod as she finished his plate and moved away from the table to wherever she was expected to wait. "That's quite interesting."

At this, I racked my mind. I had never met Arthur before and had only met the late Lord Ashford once when he had been gracious enough to take Charles and I out for dinner after we had graduated from Eton. All I recalled of the man was that he had been stern yet warm in a way that I had respected, and I could think of nothing in our brief interaction at the time that might have led any of the Ashfords to dislike me. Certainly, Charles had given me no reason to believe that his family had such strong feelings against me, and as I sat there, looking at the roasted chicken on my plate and trying to think of any situation which might have given Arthur misgivings, I landed once again on the first thing I had feared when I had met his eyes from my balcony.

He knew.

He knew who I was, beyond Thomas Whitmore, respected lawyer. He had seen me, or had heard of me being seen, at one of those gentleman's clubs known to be frequented by men like myself in London. Perhaps he thought I had designs on his brother or that I was some force put into their home to lead them into future gossip among England's noble families. I was once again struck so forcefully by this imaginary persecution that I almost said as much, but Charles spoke before I had a chance to embarrass myself. "Is this about Louis Garretty?"

Louis Garretty. A name I was well acquainted with, and not for the reasons I was fearful of. I raised my head and looked at Arthur, who was looking at his brother. The expression on his face told me that Charles had hit the core of the problem. "Louis Garretty?" I repeated, the anger replaced by bewilderment. "You don't like me because of the man I work for?"

When I'd graduated from Cambridge, I had the option to apprentice under a few different London lawyers, and Louis Garretty had been the one I had eventually chosen. A man with a solid reputation and a large firm, he had been the best choice I could have made, the cases that I handled running the gamut from property disputes to wills to minor criminal trials. It had been a well-rounded education, if not the most exciting one, and I could think of nothing that Louis had done to warrant such a strong reaction from Arthur Ashford.

"Charles," Arthur said, almost an admonition in just one word. "There's no need for you to get involved. I was more than happy for you to bring a friend for the summer. I just don't see why I need to be his friend as well."

"You don't need to be his friend, but I was expecting you to be polite," Charles said, chastising in return. "I don't see how Louis Garretty has any bearing on what kind of man Tom is."

"If you apprentice for a swindler, then I think it isn't out of the realm of possibility that you may be a swindler too," Arthur said, as simple as could be, and while I knew that Charles was doing his best to head my infamous temper off before I could say anything, his attempt unfortunately failed.

"A swindler?" I asked, looking up from my chicken, which I had begun to cut into smaller and smaller pieces in an attempt to keep myself from speaking. "Please, elaborate. What gives you the right to say that?"

"This isn't very good dinner conversation," Charles said, but he seemed to have given up on trying to get Arthur and I to stop the inevitable fight we were careening towards. Instead, he picked up his glass of wine, swirling it around and taking a sip and watching me turn towards Arthur in the way I had a million times before with a million other people who had crossed that invisible line. When he spoke, it was with the resignation of a man who knew the situation was too far gone. "No, don't."

Arthur was looking at me now, and there was absolutely amusement in his eyes along with something else, an iciness that told me he was unbothered by whatever he thought I was about to say. "I have every right to say it, considering the man swindled me."

"I don't believe it," I said. "I simply don't believe it. Louis Garretty is a trustworthy man, and you're a lord. I don't see how he could have swindled you, how you could have even come into contact. What could you have possibly needed a lawyer for?"

"Yes, Arthur," Charles said, clearly giving up on whatever notion he had to stay out of the fight and instead adding fuel to the fire. "What could you possibly have needed a lawyer for?"

Arthur nearly tossed his head, turning his gaze on his brother before letting his eyes flit back to me. "That part isn't important in the slightest," he said, which told me that it was in fact very important. "What *is* important is that I hired Mr. Garretty to carry out a sensitive legal matter for me, and instead of conducting himself as a respectable businessman, he took my money and demanded even more as blackmail payments."

Despite how badly I didn't want to believe what Arthur was saying, one look at Charles told me that his brother was telling the truth. Charles was looking straight at me, and I'd known him long enough to read his face better than I could read most books. "He blackmailed you," I repeated, looking back at Arthur, whose smugness was beginning to grate on me. It was as though everything about him had been manufactured to destroy my holiday. The pride that he clearly clung to, the holier than thou attitude, the dislike of me simply because he felt wounded by the man who had trained me. "Do you have proof of this?"

Arthur's face darkened. "Do I need proof? Is this a court of law, *Tom*?" He used my nickname as though it was a derogatory term, and not the affectionate moniker Charles had given me, and it only made me dislike him more. "The man has accrued his considerable wealth, not through the legitimate means one would expect of a lawyer, but instead by blackmailing people like myself who are in precarious positions. I'm certain that a social climber such as yourself can appreciate why I'm suspicious of one of his pupils."

Social climber stung, I had to admit, but I was less concerned about the insult than I was about the insinuation. "I live in a one-bedroom flat at the top of a house," I said. "I'm hardly raking in money. And I'm certainly not doing so through the means you're implying, Lord Ashford. Do you really think your brother would be friends with me if I was?"

"Your predecessor proved that blackmailing Ashford men is a lucrative prospect," Arthur said. "Who knows what you think is appropriate?"

"Arthur," Charles said, visibly disturbed. "Are you actually insinuating that Tom is blackmailing me? I'd hardly have invited him here if that was the case."

"Your friend asked why I disliked him," Arthur said. "I'm simply outlining the reasons." He looked at me and I was ashamed to find that even now, with his borderline repulsive argument, that he was still troublingly handsome. It made sense that someone so beautiful was so dreadful; it seemed the latest in the line of men who caught my eye only to prove that they had undeniable inner demons. I was—and still am—a man with poor taste. "An opening argument, to use his profession's terms."

"Your argument has a massive hole in it, though," I said, pleased with how level I could keep my voice in the face of what was clearly a man needling for a fight. Upon reflection, I half think that Arthur was looking for an excuse to send me back to London early, but this attempt on his part failed spectacularly. I had been known throughout my school years as a right-fighter, the sort of person who simply could not back down from an argument until the other person changed their viewpoint or gave up from sheer frustration, and I was sure that Arthur had no idea what Pandora's box he had just opened in me.

"And what is that?" Arthur asked.

"I'm not Louis Garretty," I said, finishing off my chicken and dragging my fork through a wonderfully thick preparation of potatoes. "And you're assuming, rather foolishly, that he trusted me enough to let me know about his ill deeds, if they in fact took place. But I'd like to remind you that Charles and I have been friends since we were in our early teens, long before I ever became an apprentice under Mr. Garretty. Do you really believe he would ask me to participate in the blackmail considering my relationship with Charles?"

For the first time since sitting down to dinner, I could see on Arthur's face that my words had not fallen on deaf ears. He seemed to consider this point for a few moments longer before the ghost of a smile curled at his lip and he turned back to his meal. I saw Charles relax across from me and realized that while I had undoubtedly not fully changed Arthur's mind, I had made him reconsider his position.

It was nice to know that my living making arguments had served me in another way—I had become persuasive in general conversation as well. For a man who had never been particularly quick to come up with a witty repartee, it provided a great comfort to know that I was now able to hold my own, even though I very much had Charles acting as a buffer. I had not believed, not truly, that Arthur could do anything more dreadful than dislike me, and it had kept me from panicking as I might have had I thought him capable of actually driving me out.

After our slight argument, dinner passed mostly in silence, with Charles and I making small talk and Arthur eating quietly, replying only when his brother addressed him directly and never when I did. As soon as the meal had finished and the pudding had been cleared away, Arthur excused himself and made his quick departure from the dining room with hardly even a good evening.

Charles looked across the table at me, sipping his wine; I wasn't sure how many glasses he'd had by this point, but I knew that I'd had just as many. I wasn't fuzzy, not really, but I was feeling much more gracious about what had just transpired than I would have if not helped along by the alcohol. "So," he said, and I smiled at him.

"So. Did you know your brother held such strong views about me?"

"I knew he held such strong views regarding Louis Garretty," Charles said, sounding genuinely apologetic. "But I thought he would hold his tongue."

"He was being honest about Garretty blackmailing him?" I asked, because while I had read it on Charles's face earlier, I wanted to hear it from him in so many words. "Because I don't know anything about that. I was one of a half-dozen apprentices he took on that year."

"He was being honest, but I don't know what Garretty blackmailed him for," Charles said, leaning forward and looking at me across the flickering candle that sat between us at the oak table. "It was while we were at Cambridge, and by the time I got wind of it, you had already accepted the apprenticeship. I couldn't stand in your way, Tom, not when I knew how hard you'd worked for it. I didn't think Arthur would think you were taking after Garretty in more than just law."

"But he did think that, didn't he? That I'm corrupt, despite having never met me before."

Charles sighed, and I could practically see him knocking the toes of his left foot against the floor of the dining room, a nervous habit he'd had since we'd been at Eton together. "I think… no. I know that Arthur believes you're a social climber, Tom. He believes that you saw me at Eton and decided that I would make a good ladder."

The thought that my best friend's family had taken me for a parasite was not as shocking as I think Charles had expected it to be. I had heard it before, heard it from boys at Eton and men at Cambridge, heard it even now from people who were upset over legal dealings or who were jealous that I had done something nearly unthinkable by dragging myself out of middle class. I sighed, taking another sip of my wine and trying to think of a way to respond that would explain my position without making Charles feel poorly. He had always been a sensitive soul, and the idea that I had gone through any sort of trouble merely because of our friendship would upset him greatly.

My prolonged silence, however, was enough to tip Charles off. He looked at me, setting his glass of wine back down on the table. "You're joking."

"Charles, I'm a middle-class man whose best friend is sixteenth in line for the monarchy," I said. "Nearly everyone who has ever met you and I thinks that our friendship is solely because I am trying to gain something from it. Something more than just friendship, that is. Unfortunately, being connected to you means that most people doubt me as a result."

"But it's not true," Charles said, and there was the indignation I thought that the realization would evoke. "Never once have you tried to use me, Tom."

"And I never would, but that doesn't stop people from speculating. Do you really think that I enjoy being seen as a leech? I've worked extremely hard for what I have, but I'm sure most people believe that I have it only because of who you are."

"Including my brother," Charles said, breathing out with clear irritation. "I never realized people thought of you that way. You should have told me."

"I never wanted you to feel regret because of your friendship with me," I said, and his face softened.

"So you just felt poorly for the both of us," Charles said, rubbing his forehead. "I have never deserved you less and needed you as my friend more."

"Now, now," I said, laughing and getting to my feet. "You are far too drunk to get yourself upset this way. Ideally, your brother would have liked me, but since he doesn't… I won't let this ruin my vacation, Charles. And you shouldn't allow it to disrupt yours, either." I looked at the clock on the wall, an expensive piece that looked as though it had been brought straight from Switzerland. "We should sleep, Charles. If I'm to put up with your brother at breakfast, I need at least eight hours."

"So responsible," Charles said, but he got to his feet anyway, leaving his wineglass behind. He stepped around the table, setting a broad hand on the side of my neck and squeezing affectionately, his fingers warm. "I hope you know that I have only ever seen you as a positive in my life, Tom. No matter what anyone else thinks."

He left the room before me, and I hung behind, not wanting to walk up to my room with him, knowing we were going in the same direction. Despite everything I had told Charles, I was upset by his brother's reception of me. The late Lord Ashford had welcomed me, had told me upon our singular meeting that he trusted me to look after his son, who had a reputation for being more flighty than what was perhaps expected for the son of the lord even if there was little chance Charles would ever inherit the title. For Arthur to dismiss me outright despite the trust of his father and brother was disheartening.

I made it my mission, standing in the dining room and waiting until I was sure Charles had returned to his room so I could return to mine in silence, to have Arthur Ashford like me by the time summer ended.

4

THE FIRST week of my vacation passed without much to comment on. I spent my days alternating between going through the paperwork I had brought with me and spending time with Charles, who had always proved himself an easy source of entertainment. Wandering the massive gardens, exploring the woods, rambling around the lawn or reading books near the pond—all of it was enjoyable in those early days. Even work was made more tolerable, Charles often napping on the chaise longue or helping me sort through papers, but I still could not crack Arthur.

I saw him often. At meals, of course, but he was also perpetually within sight of my balcony. There was a bench in the garden, a good twenty feet from my balcony, and in the evenings Arthur would sit there and smoke, watch the stars, his pale hair gleaming in the moonlight. It almost felt like a taunt, as though he expected me to come down and join him, to perhaps even get the nerve up to speak to him, but I refused to make the first move.

In all honesty, I was still wounded. It may have been immature, even foolish, but I had expected Arthur to at least pretend to accept me, even if he secretly disliked me. The thought that I was going to spend the summer staying at an awkward distance from Arthur was a decided distraction from the pleasant vacation I had foreseen for myself.

Six days after I arrived, however, a storm blew in from the sea and brought with it a change both in weather and fortune. It was Saturday afternoon and the rain was relentless, thunder rumbling every so often seemingly as a reminder that we were housebound, and Charles and I had just settled into a game of cards in the sitting room when Arthur appeared, looking quite serious. "What are you two doing tonight?" he asked, and there was something in his voice that told me he expected us to be doing nothing.

Charles and I looked at each other, a silent conversation taking place before Charles twisted in his seat to look at his brother. "Why? I suppose we can find a three-man card game if you would like to join us."

"It will need to be a four-man game," Arthur said, stepping into the room further; I realized as soon as he was out of the doorway that he was holding a letter in one hand. "James Wright is going to be here by suppertime. He conveniently forgot to write until he was already in the county."

I looked at Charles, and he frowned. "James Wright is… is he a colonel now, Arthur?"

"Yes," Arthur said, looking down at the letter. "Colonel James Wright is the youngest son of the Lord of Westshire. He is our cousin on our mother's side." This last explanation was for me, more than he'd said to me in a week, and I was surprised to be included in the conversation at all.

"James was a playmate of ours as children," Charles said, continuing his brother's explanation. "He stops in every summer even if our welcome is… tepid.… He's dreadfully boring and terribly full of himself, which I suppose is why you'd like us to distract him with a game of cards, Arthur."

"All I would like is to not be alone with him," Arthur said, and I realized for the first time that he was actually asking a favor, and not just trying to be a good host. "Dinner, card games, a quiet night. He's on his way to Plymouth for military business, so I understand this is merely a stopover."

"An inconvenient stopover," Charles said. "And let me guess, he only informed you when he arrived in Taunton."

"That's less than an hour from here," I said, surprised. "He really didn't give you any prior notice?"

"No, that's precisely what James does," Arthur said. "He likes to surprise us with his visits so we can't say no to him." This time he looked at me and I could read on his face that as little as he appreciated my presence, I at least had not been a last-minute addition to the estate. He had been given time to anticipate my arrival and prepare, something James had clearly robbed him of. With a man like Arthur Ashford, it was clear to anyone who took the time to notice that an unexpected guest was the last thing he wanted on his estate. "You don't know him in the slightest, do you?"

"The name sounds familiar, but I can't say I would know him if I saw him," I admitted. "I'm not particularly good with recalling the faces of the nobility. After all, I've spent most of my life in deference to them."

"Point taken," Arthur said, and once again I was struck by the sensation that he was amused by me, a revelation that was both a relief and infuriating. If Arthur could just allow himself to like me—as I knew I was exceedingly likable by nearly all accounts—this summer would be so much more pleasant. It was my own charisma against whatever terrible thing my mentor had done to him, and at times it seemed my personality was winning him over before he reminded himself of my dreadful profession and the man who had trained me. "So, are you two going to join the dinner party, or are you going to leave me to the wolves?"

Another brief look between myself and Charles before Charles sighed, clearly pretending that he had no desire to help his brother despite the visible twinkle in his eye. "I suppose we could put aside our thrilling plans to help you keep James distracted until he sleeps."

"Thank you," Arthur said, taking his pocket watch out and studying it briefly. "I need to inform Felix and the kitchen that we have another guest. You know James will take any shortcomings back to his mother and say that the estate is in disrepair since our parents passed."

"Shortcomings?" I asked, and Arthur nodded.

"The wrong food, the wrong cutlery, even giving him a room on the wrong side of the house could create unwanted attention. James is… shallow, and those things matter to him. I have no desire to be the grist for some rumor mill among the Wright clan." He looked at the two of us for a moment, thoughtful, before giving an awkward half-bow and backing out of the room.

"He's very strange," I said, and Charles laughed, looking at his hand of cards as we resumed our game. "Am I incorrect?"

"No, but I think you're overlooking how nervous you make him," Charles said. "Your very existence is challenging his preconceived notions about lawyers. He enjoys your company, even if he's still pretending as though he doesn't."

"He makes *me* nervous," I said, although I doubted that Arthur was nervous for the same reasons I was. My nerves were born entirely out of attraction, the fact that Arthur was one of the most beautiful men I'd ever seen, and that merely acknowledging that was enough to put me in serious danger if anyone discovered those feelings. I had always been smart, careful, determined not to be caught, and I would not allow Arthur Ashford to undo my hard work in that arena. As nervous as he made me, though, I could not imagine that he would fathom where my nerves came from in comparison to his own. "I suppose we should dress for dinner after this game?"

JAMES WRIGHT proved to be quite the punctual guest despite his lack of communication beforehand. I had barely finished doing up the buttons on my shirt when Felix was at my door, rapping on it insistently. "Mr. Whitmore, I'm sorry, but Colonel Wright has arrived and I'm to fetch you and Charles immediately."

"You may open the door, Felix," I said, having rapidly discovered that I was exceptionally fond of the manservant. He was bright, funny, and good at his job, but above all else, he wasn't hesitant in the slightest to speak up when he felt Arthur was being unreasonable. At my invitation, he opened the door and stepped into the room, lifting my waistcoat from where I had it hung over the back of my desk chair. "Is Arthur down with the colonel at the moment?"

"Yes. Alone. And I'm afraid that Arthur isn't the most patient with Colonel Wright at the best of times. That's why he's begun this trick of letting him know when he's already in the neighborhood." He held the coat up and helped me into it, and when I turned to face him, he was looking at me with a slightly grave expression. "It will be an unpleasant evening. I'm terribly sorry."

"He's truly that bad?"

"He's… very obnoxious," Felix said, with the most diplomacy I'd heard him use until this point. After doing up the last button on my waistcoat, he patted me lightly on the chest. "Good luck, Tom."

"Don't say good luck," I groaned, already dreading what was going to take place. Felix and I left my room, Felix turning left to head to Charles's suite and I making my way to the stairs. I could hear Colonel Wright before I was even near the dining room, the man's voice damn near a shout. At first, I assumed he was actually yelling, only to find that it was just the natural volume of his voice, the first clue I had that Felix had been dead serious in his condemnation of the man.

When I entered the dining room, Arthur was in his usual seat at the head of the table, but Colonel Wright was in the seat I usually sat in, clutching a glass of brandy and still speaking. I was expecting a man who matched the voice I was hearing, but Colonel Wright was relatively handsome, perhaps a few years older than myself, with the blond hair that was clearly a family trait and piercing blue eyes that immediately flicked to me upon my entrance. "Oh, is this your guest?" he asked, and he must have read something in my face because he gestured to where he was sitting. "Sorry, but I never sit with my back to the door. Dangerous, you know. Even if I'm eating at a restaurant, I never let them put me anywhere where someone could sneak up on me. It's the lowest of the low who would stab a man in the back, but it's been known to happen, especially to military men like me. You understand. Besides, you can sit with your back to the door for one night. Won't kill you."

I looked at Arthur, who was sipping from his own brandy glass, and found that he was looking at me in return. As always, the expression on his face was unreadable, but there was a pinched quality to his eyes that told me I'd come to the dining room in the nick of time. "Oh, I wasn't married to that seat," I said, taking the seat directly across from Arthur. "It's a pleasure to meet you, Colonel. I'm—"

"Thomas Whitmore, attorney at law," he said, cutting me off before I could finish my introduction. I kept the smile plastered on my face, annoyed, but was pleased as could be when the serving girl poured me a glass of brandy as well. "Law's a funny profession for a man to take these days, isn't it? Now, military, that's something to be truly proud of. A man can do no wrong when he's in the military. Court has so much peril in it, so many people who are lying to you or trying to do you wrong. It's dreadful, truly. I don't understand how you can possibly do it. I've never had that sort of trouble. Knew I wanted to be military just as soon as I knew what the military was, you know. A selfless sort of thing."

The message of luck from Felix made sense now. James Wright was possibly the most grating man I had ever met, his need to self-aggrandize so obvious and so overwrought that simply listening to him made my skin prickle with annoyance. I was accustomed to men who enjoyed hearing themselves speak, but the sheer volume of nonsense coming from the colonel was hard to deflect. I took a sip of my brandy to consider my response and found that Arthur was still looking at me. To my surprise, I could read his expression as easily as I could read Charles's. A sudden surge of camaraderie swept through me despite the last week of being given nothing but ice; Arthur was as little a fan of the colonel as I was. "Have we met before? You seem to know quite a bit about me."

"London is a small city, Mr. Whitmore, and your relationship with my dear friend Charles is well known. I've kept abreast of your work out of a common interest. After all, I'm sure you've benefited from your friendship with Charles in terms of your legal career. It seemed prudent for me to make sure that you were conducting yourself well." He smiled at me like he hadn't just said one of the most obnoxious things I'd ever heard, the idea that I had been unwitting gossip material for a man I'd never met flooding me with irritation. "It really is something incredible, you know. A man of your standing, no title, no land, to graduate from both Eton and Cambridge. Among the more refined ranks, you're seen as quite the enigma."

"An enigma because I was capable of pulling myself out of the middle class?" I asked, as patient as could be—which, to be entirely clear, was not all that patient at the moment. "I don't see what's particularly enigmatic about it."

"Oh, don't get all offended, Mr. Whitmore," James said, rolling his eyes in the most exaggerated fashion and looking at Arthur for support. "You would think a lawyer would have thicker skin. In the military, you know, they teach you not to allow yourself to be upset by words. If every lawyer had to go through military training, I think our justice system would work a lot more smoothly, don't you, Arthur?"

"I believe the justice system already works quite well," Arthur said, and it stunned me to hear him say that before I realized that he would say anything as long as it was the opposite of what James was saying. "In fact, Charles tells me that our lawyer friend here is a shining example of the modern legal system."

"I do say that," Charles said, entering the room with Felix hot on his heels. Unshaken by the clear tension in the air, he took his seat at Arthur's right side; the moment he sat down, the maid returned with dinner, serving us each quickly. It was clear that she had no desire to stay in the room any longer than she needed to as she served the meal faster than she'd served any since I'd been at the estate. Once she was gone, though, Charles busied himself with cutting the meat off his quail, looking across the table at James. "Were you complaining about the quality of Tom's legal services?"

"Oh-ho, seems both Ashford men are your ardent defenders, Mr. Whitmore. Makes a man wonder if you had a hand in assisting with that nasty legal trouble a few years ago." Both Arthur and Charles stiffened at this, Arthur's eyes darkening as he glanced first at his brother and then at myself. James, however, looked pleased, as though he had been waiting for an opportunity to reveal this bit of information. It seemed separate from the blackmail case that had caused the ruckus on the first night I was here, but I soon had my answer. "Unless I misjudged. Did you not help with that case? I would have thought that a man who was so close with Charles would have been the first one to come to his aid."

"What year was this?" I asked, looking at Charles and offering him a direct way out of the situation. "I remember you reaching out during that big murder trial, but I was too busy at the time."

Charles, thankfully, realized what I was doing and latched on. "I did reach out to you about it," he said, nodding. "But we had to hire someone else, you're right." He smiled at James, looking as easy as could be. "Of course, Tom is our preferred lawyer in these situations, but in the poaching case, we didn't have a choice."

I made a mental note to have Charles fill me in on the poaching case later, although it didn't surprise me. There had been an uptick in poaching convictions on these large estates, and while I found the entire idea of prosecuting people for hunting on ground that was often disputed between estates a hopefully dying practice, it didn't particularly shock me that the Ashfords had been caught up in something like that. The wind out of his sails, having clearly been spoiling for a fight, James looked over at Arthur, who had been keeping quiet since Charles had appeared. "A lawyer from the middle class, though. Seems like a poor way to protect your assets. In the military, at least, men can prove themselves useful, work their way up, really climb without—"

"Enough," Arthur said, voice low, and it was so startling that the table fell quiet at the sound, even James getting the hint. "You are both guests here, which means that you are on the same footing while under this roof. I have no way of knowing why you dislike Mr. Whitmore so much, James, when you've made it clear that you don't know the man. Perhaps you should give him a chance." He looked at me, and the weight of his gaze caused my stomach to twist up in knots, an electric desire flooding through me. Before I gave myself away, I took a bite of my dinner just so I had an excuse to no longer look at him, no longer subject myself to that gaze that filled me with hunger.

"Of course," James said, but I could see on his face how irritated he was about this redirection from my flawed upbringing. A man like James Wright thrived in gossip-mongering, in bringing people down to make himself look better, and it was clear that he had arranged this entire visit as a way to size me up. It made me wonder what exactly he was looking for among the Ashford brothers, but the dinner lapsed into a terrible silence broken only by the scraping of forks on plates and the truly dreadful sound of James drinking from his glass.

After the longest dinner I had ever been subjected to in my life, pudding was brought and we thankfully dispersed. It seemed that Arthur's grand plan to rope James into a game of cards was abandoned, because after a bit of inane chatter in the great hall, James went off to bed, followed closely by Charles, who paused only to promise me he would fill me in on the details of the poaching case in the morning.

Left alone with Arthur, I had turned to go up the stairs when Arthur spoke. "Wait," he said, using that same tone he'd used at the dinner table to shut James down.

I looked back at him, heart twisting up at the sight in the dim light of the great hall. The shadows cast by the candles were doing nothing to mar his beauty, and for a moment I was seized by the utterly irrational desire to close the distance between us, run my hands through that feather-soft hair, kiss those lips that undoubtedly tasted of brandy at the moment. I attributed this momentary madness to my own drinking and forced it down, unwilling to expose myself even in the slightest. "What?"

"I'm sorry," Arthur said, and for the second time that night I was stunned by the other man. "For the way he spoke to you. I know how James is, and I knew he would target you over myself or Charles, but I still asked you to entertain him knowing you would bear the brunt of it."

"I don't doubt that you're sorry," I said. "Do you not think that the conversation tonight was an echo of the one my first night here, though?"

It was Arthur's turn to be surprised, the vaguest flicker of realization in those green eyes of his. "Did I sound like that?"

"More or less," I said. "Although James was slightly more… long-winded."

"Well, then, I'm sorry for that as well," Arthur said. "My brother enjoys your presence." He paused, and for the briefest of moments he looked as though his confidence was wavering before he regained it. "That's all," he finally said. "You can go to bed now."

I nodded, unable to say anything else in response. It had seemed like he wanted to say more but had stopped himself, a process I understood all too well. It was a strange walk up to my room, wrestling with the idea that Arthur might have left something unsaid, but I feel now that I know what had caused his turmoil that night and can understand it all too well, as it was the same feeling I'd been struggling with since first seeing him in the gardens.

5

I STAYED up too late after the unpleasant dinner with James, poring over one of the cases in my pile mostly just to keep my mind off the barbs that had been sent in my direction. Arthur's words, too, had left me ruffled. I hadn't expected Arthur Ashford to be my undoing, but the man was so handsome it was hard not to allow myself to give in to fantasies. The summer was proving to be less relaxing than first blush had indicated, and it was well into the small hours of the morning when I finally snuffed my candle and went to bed.

When I woke, it was to one of the maids pulling back the curtains in my room. It was one of those rare beautiful days in England, the sky already blue and vast despite the early hour, and I was beginning to daydream about spending my Sunday outside when the maid turned to me, an apologetic look on her face. "Colonel Wright has asked if you'd have breakfast with him in the sunroom," she said, wringing her hands. "I told him you usually ate with the young Mr. Ashford, but he was insistent."

I pushed myself into a sitting position, looking at her blankly for a few moments before I truly realized what I was being told. "Breakfast alone?"

"So I understand," she said, still apologetic, and I saw that James Wright had no doubt used his particular brand of discourtesy on her at some point. "I had Felix set some clothes out for you already. He seems to know your taste best."

"Thank you, Anna," I said, and she left after ensuring that all the windows were thrown open and the curtains pulled back. I washed my face and shaved quickly, avoiding nicking myself despite my speed, and by the time I was dressed and caught sight of myself in the looking glass I looked halfway presentable. Dread churned in my chest as I made my way downstairs, the thought of spending time with James nowhere near the pleasant day I had envisioned.

The sunroom, a large glass addition that had been put in place by the late Lord Ashford as a show of affection for his wife, was one of my favorite places in the house. It led directly into the greenhouse but served as an area more for entertaining, and Charles and I were fond of having our afternoon tea there. For it to be sullied by a man like James was genuinely annoying. Still, there was nothing I could do at this point; avoiding breakfast with the man was out of the question, and I was curious as to what he had to say to me. An apology seemed unlikely, so I had to assume that whatever James wanted was a continuation of the night before. I wasn't going to turn tail and run when I'd done nothing wrong.

James was sitting at one of the small tea tables when I arrived, breakfast already spread out before him, and as soon as I approached, he offered me a smile. "Good morning, Mr. Whitmore. Have a seat."

I settled into the chair across from him, surprised as he poured me a cup of tea. I dropped in a sugar cube, keeping quiet as I waited for him to say more. Once I had doctored my tea and helped myself to a scone, I raised my eyebrows at him in the most courteous way I knew how. "I must say, Colonel, I'm confused as to why you invited me to breakfast. I got the distinct impression last night that you weren't a fan of mine."

"Is that how it seemed?" James asked, looking at me. "I was merely trying my best to figure out what you were trying to accomplish by coming to Ashford Hall. I know you've been friends with Charles for most of your lives, but you've never been invited to the estate before. It seems strange that you would have been invited this summer, all things considered."

"Why would this summer be any different?" I asked. "Charles and I frequently spend time together during the warmer months. This year he just didn't feel like coming to London, so he invited me here. I'm not sure that necessarily points to anything strange."

James studied me, and there was something there that I had missed during our unpleasant conversation the night prior: shrewdness. As loud and abrasive as the man was, he was also planning something, and it was clear that I had come in between him and his plans. I realized that James had engineered his visit to Ashford Hall not as a last-minute drop-in but specifically to find out more about myself and immediately decided to abandon any attempts to dismiss his rudeness on my end. I settled back in my chair, taking a sip of my tea as I began to look at James from a lawyer's point of view.

"Do you think it was Charles's idea to invite you?" James asked. "If he's never invited you before, why now?"

"If you think it wasn't Charles, do you think Arthur decided that he wanted to invite me here?" I asked in return. The look in James's eyes told me that he thought that I had hit upon the truth, but I could think of nothing further from the mark. "Arthur and I had never met each other before last week, nor do we particularly get along. What possible reason could he have to invite me here?"

"There was a portrait of you published in the paper recently, wasn't there? You successfully defended a murder suspect. Quite the flattering sketch."

"I don't see what a sketch has to do with my presence at Ashford Hall," I said, concern creeping up the nape of my neck. What James was implying—that Arthur had only allowed Charles to invite me here after seeing my picture in the papers—was impossible. "Charles invited me."

"You really don't realize, do you?" James said, setting his teacup down. "How much you look like—"

"I thought I'd find you two in here." Charles walked over to the tea table, leaning over and plucking a biscuit from the tray. I looked up at him, startled by his sudden appearance, and found that he wasn't looking at me but was instead looking at James. "Felix mentioned something about breakfast in the sunroom. I'm hurt that I wasn't invited."

"I thought it would be nice if I had the opportunity to speak with Mr. Whitmore, just the two of us. Clear the air, you know."

Charles hummed softly, but I could tell he was bothered, still looking at James. "Your horses are ready. I think you should leave now, James. You won't be welcome back for the rest of the summer."

James looked up at Charles, and there was that shrewd look in his eyes once again before it disappeared and he got to his feet. "I see," he said. "Thank you for confirming my suspicions, Charles."

"I confirmed nothing," Charles said, and it was the iciest I'd ever heard him. "Please leave." He watched James walk out of the sunroom, clearly making sure that he didn't try to turn back around and rejoin me, and then he looked at me, his expression softening. He settled into James's abandoned seat and sighed softly. "I'm really sorry," he said finally. "Arthur and I should have told you from the beginning that James is…. Well, we aren't sure what his plan is, but it has something to do with Ashford Hall. He's the one who was responsible for the poaching incident in the first place."

"What do you mean?" I leaned forward, looking at Charles intently. I couldn't figure out what was going on between the Ashford men and James, but I had a feeling that both James's last-minute appearance at the estate and Arthur and Charles's discomfort at his presence were symptoms of a much larger problem. "Charles, if something is happening, you know you can tell me. I can help."

"I know," Charles said, pouring himself a cup of tea. "Two years ago, we had James here for the summer. He's always been annoying, but he's never been an outright problem, and we were having a host of childhood friends over, so we thought the polite thing to do would be to invite him to stay as well. His cousins were here, Ida and Rudolph Nelson, and with his older brother having recently taken up his father's lordship, Arthur and I thought James might like the chance to spend time with people with less responsibility."

I listened, the mention of the Nelson siblings not a surprise; I'd heard their names before in conjunction with the Ashford family and understood they had been raised essentially alongside one another. From where I was standing, the intermingling of the families was clear but convoluted: James Wright was the son of the late Lord Ashford's sister, who had married Lord Wright ages ago, and the Nelson siblings were the offspring of Lord Wright's sister in turn. "What does that have to do with the poaching incident?"

"We've always had a standing agreement with surrounding households that they're permitted to hunt in our woods," Charles said. "It's been in place longer than Arthur or myself has been alive, and we've never had trouble with it. There's game enough in those woods for us and anyone who'd like to help themselves to it. But there is a man who lives nearby who had served with James during the trouble in India. James never told us what his issue with the fellow was, but they were in a verbal confrontation not long after James arrived here. A few days later, the man was hunting in the woods, which I understand was a usual habit of his. He'd kill a deer and use that meat for his wife and children. This time...."

His expression grew grim, and he tilted his head back, looking at the ornate glass roof of the sunroom. "James must have seen him, and he was the one who went to the local constabulary before either Arthur or myself could intervene. It was terrible. The magistrate recommended death by hanging, but Arthur and I hired Louis Garretty to defend the man. It was a successful defense, but it caused a considerable amount of damage to our reputation among the local families, and it opened us up to the blackmail Garretty then carried out against my brother."

I stared at him, stunned into silence momentarily before I got my wits about me. "And you still let him return?"

"James is our cousin," Charles said. "We've tried to keep our relationship with him as normal as possible, but between what he did then and how he's treating you now, I have a feeling Arthur will agree with my decision to have him leave for the summer. I've no idea what his goal is. His mother was raised here, so perhaps there's some element of that in what's taking place, but he's become more hostile since his brother was named lord."

I considered this, a darker picture of the situation emerging than what I'd been anticipating. "Arthur thinks that James is trying to take Ashford Hall?"

"Well, he's a military officer with no title to come home to now that his brother has become lord. Ashford Hall would certainly be a prize, and the rules of succession make it clear that if Arthur or I were unable to perform our duties, the title would pass to the oldest eligible male of the next family line. That would be James."

"So James did all this to undermine you both," I said, frowning. "And Garretty is involved? But you don't know what the blackmail consisted of."

"No." Charles shook his head, looking at me again. "Arthur wouldn't tell me. All I know is that it happened after the poaching situation was resolved. I have no idea what he has against Arthur, but I know that it could have destroyed him if it had gotten out. That's most likely why he hasn't allowed me to find out the details."

I sighed, setting my empty teacup down on the table and trying to figure out exactly what was going on with the limited information I had at hand. "Do you know if Arthur still has the legal documents from the poaching case? I'd like to take a look."

"He should," Charles said. "I wanted this to be a quiet summer for you, Tom. I didn't want any of these issues to be something you had to deal with."

I reached out instinctively, gripping his hand with the most affection I could muster. "You and I have been brothers since we first met, Charles. Any issue affecting you is something I would be happy to help with. I'll talk to Arthur about getting the papers, and we can go from there."

He turned his hand over in order to squeeze mine in return, smiling at me. "Okay," he agreed, and while I had no way of knowing yet what it was I was agreeing to, at the moment all I wanted was to help Arthur and Charles, and damn the consequences. "Arthur's in the library. He took breakfast there this morning. Our routine has been disrupted by James, unfortunately."

"Understandable," I said, getting to my feet after forcing myself to let go of his hand. "I'll go see him now, see what he can tell me."

I left the sunroom, heading towards the great hall and mulling over the conversation that had just played out between myself and Charles. He'd revealed a great deal of information, but he had avoided my gaze at a few key moments, and I knew him well enough to know that he was still hiding something from me, some small detail. Even if he didn't know for sure what the blackmail had consisted of, brothers knew things, and I was sure that Charles had an inkling when it came to what had happened. Why he refused to tell me, I couldn't begin to fathom, only that it must have been something that even I could not be trusted with.

I found Arthur in the library as indicated, dressed plainly in a white linen shirt that draped him nicely and a pair of leather trousers that had clearly been tailored perfectly for him. I was reminded briefly of James's apparent feeling that I had been invited by Arthur and not by Charles and had to tell myself not to read too much into it. Clearing my throat, I waited until Arthur looked up before I spoke. "Good morning, Arthur."

He fixed his gaze on me, appraising, his mouth set in a thin line that told me I had interrupted his solitude. "Hello," he said in return, setting down his fountain pen. There was a letter on the desk in front of him, penned beautifully, and I thought briefly about trying to see who it was addressed to before composing myself. "Did Charles find you?"

"Yes," I said. "And he told me what James did to you in the poaching incident."

Arthur sighed, leaning back in his chair and eyeing me for a few moments before he gestured to the chair across from him. "Sit down." I did as I was told, settling into the lavishly upholstered chair, and watched him closely. Arthur was quiet for a while longer, lifting his pen and continuing his letter before he finally set it aside and looked at me again. "Why did you come to talk to me? Charles told you everything, didn't he?"

"I want to look at the documents from the poaching case," I said. "You still have them, don't you?"

"I do," Arthur said slowly, as though he wasn't entirely convinced. "You're welcome to look through them, but I'm not sure what you think you're going to find."

"James implied heavily that you invited me here, and he seems to think you had an ulterior motive for doing so. He was quite bothered by my presence," I said, and was pleased to see that Arthur shifted in his chair, somewhat uncomfortable. "He's planning something, if I'm not mistaken, and I think if we can pinpoint when it began, we can be better prepared for when it comes to fruition."

Arthur considered this, and as he thought, I considered him in return. He was more relaxed in this environment than normal, a softness about him that made me want to reach across the desk and run my fingers through his hair, and when he finally looked at me again it was clear that he was trusting this to me. "All right," he said. "I'll have Felix gather up the information and deliver it to your room." He paused, and his next words sent heat through me, fire in my veins. "I did ask Charles to invite you here. I thought it would be good for him."

"Even though you didn't trust me?"

"I knew he trusted you, and that was enough," Arthur said. "James no doubt came here to size you up, and he must have gotten what he was looking for when he saw you. But he is right. I wanted you here for Charles, and he wouldn't have asked you if I hadn't given my blessing. He knows how I feel about lawyers."

"Well, I intend to prove you wrong," I said, getting up again. "I'll begin reviewing the case as soon as I have the paperwork. By the time I'm finished, you'll trust me as much as Charles does."

Something like a smile flickered in Arthur's eyes, the corner of his mouth briefly turning upward before he caught himself and waved his hand in dismissal. "I'll have Felix bring them by afternoon. Now go. I have letters to finish."

"See you at dinner, Lord Ashford," I said, purposefully teasing, and the look he gave me buoyed my heart as I left the library, unable to ignore the sense I had that I had finally, however slightly, begun to worm my way into the good graces of the man.

6

FELIX WAS quick to bring me the documents from the poaching trial, and I spent the next few days with my regular cases set aside in favor of poring over the long-closed one. It seemed fairly cut and dry, nothing in it to suggest that anything untoward had happened, but the circumstances were certainly strange. There was a sworn statement from the local magistrate saying that he had been called to Ashford Hall by Colonel James Wright, who had sent for him after a local father of three had killed a deer in the woods. It was straightforward—James had accused the man of poaching, Arthur had said that there was a verbal agreement for hunting on the land, but the accused was ill-liked in the area and it seemed the magistrate was bent on taking him to trial one way or another.

Despite Arthur's refusal to push through with the poaching accusation, the man had been charged with the act of transporting the dead deer from Arthur's property to his own, the magistrate arguing that this was a blatant act of theft. Garretty had defended the man successfully, and Arthur had stepped in to make amends, but the damage was done. Despite the flimsiness of the charge and the legal wrangling that had to be done to even bring it to trial, the accused had been branded a thief and a poacher by virtue of public opinion, and Arthur had been branded a lord petty enough to persecute a man for killing a single deer.

After copious note-taking, reading and re-reading witness statements, the only glimmer of something interesting was in a statement taken from Rudolph Nelson, who said he had been with Arthur in the library at the time of the poaching. Neither man had realized the magistrate had been called until he arrived at the estate, nearly an hour and a half after James had first sent for him. What had they been doing in the library for ninety minutes? Obviously, my mind went to the first thing that I could see myself doing with another man for that length of time in an isolated area, and from there the path from the poaching case to the blackmail seemed clear. Approaching Arthur with my suspicions, however, would only serve to entrench him in his belief that lawyers were up to no good, and accusing a man—a lord, in fact—of loving another man was just as bad if not worse.

There were my own emotions to contend with as well. While the nature of the blackmail had not been revealed to me yet, those missing ninety minutes were distraction enough, a tempest churning in my chest as I continued to return to them. Where blackmail had been on Garrety's mind—a fact of which I was convinced now that I could see the accusation, even if it wasn't true—something decidedly different was on mine. Was Rudolph Nelson handsome? Had they sat in the same library where Arthur answered letters and engaged in a debauchery that I myself would have enjoyed? As I continued to work through the papers, I still found myself obsessing over the possibility that Arthur shared my inclinations, embarrassed by my desire for a man who disliked me but indulging in those fantasies all the same.

Despite my renewed suspicions, both of Garrety's actions and my own growing determination to find out if Arthur and I shared a proclivity, I decided to sit on that information until I could find a way to broach the subject delicately. Tired of being cooped up and needing a breath of fresh air, I took the tea Felix had delivered to me and stepped out on the balcony, taking a sip and scanning the garden. I was surprised to find that Charles and Arthur were walking together, having a clearly animated conversation, and I was considering calling out to them when the choice was taken away from me, Charles happening to glance up towards my balcony. "Tom!" he called, waving. "We were just discussing you!"

"Oh, is that so?" I asked, leaning over the railing and peering down at the brothers. Arthur, always perfectly coiffed, was watching me as well, and the sunlight caught his green eyes in a way that made them look like gems. "What could the Ashford brothers possibly be talking about?"

"We're going for a horseback ride," Charles said. "And we were discussing whether it would be rude to ask if you'd like to come since you're working on reviewing the poaching case, and we don't want to make you feel pressured into spending time with us when you're already doing so much."

"I haven't been on horseback for some time," I admitted. "I may not be the best companion."

"We'd still like you to come," Arthur said, and it was his earnestness that caught me off guard. It sounded as though he genuinely wanted me to join them, and if he hadn't said it in that exact tone of voice, I'm not sure I would have been so easily convinced. "Do you have the time? Felix has packed us lunch, and we have a horse that would suit you quite well."

"Give me fifteen minutes to find my riding clothes," I said, as I knew I had packed them, just wasn't sure where they could be at the moment. "Are you sure I won't be a disruption?"

"You've never been a disruption," Charles said. "We'll meet you at the front of the house. Bring a book, if you'd please. We're riding to the pond, and Arthur almost always falls asleep after we've had lunch."

"Can a man have no secrets?" Arthur asked, and it was the first time I'd heard such a clear joke pass his lips; as I retreated to my room, I realized with dread that the surface level attraction I had been struggling with since first laying eyes on the man was crystallizing into something else, a strange and potent hunger. I had the wherewithal to be ashamed of this attraction, not because it was towards another man, an appetite I had always recognized within myself, but because it was for the brother of my dearest friend.

The betrayal of Charles's trust felt like the most grievous damage I could do, and I had to find a way to either control myself or rid myself of that attraction forever. Already I could imagine that Charles would blame me for the seduction of his brother, a dual attack on Arthur's character due to the fact that I was a man and a man of a lower class. The rumors that would fly and the damage to his character would far outstrip anything done by the poaching case, and I could not fathom putting Charles in that position.

I found my riding clothes, almost brand-new, unpacked in a far corner of my wardrobe. After changing into them, I met the brothers on the front steps, a rather lengthy legal tome I was annotating held under one arm. Charles looked at it and shook his head. "I meant a novel, Tom."

"I know what you meant," I said in return, as teasing as could be. "I'm afraid I have little time for leisure reading. Would you trust a lawyer who spent his days reading *Emma* instead of Hegel?"

"I would find it an excellent marker of his taste," Charles said, clapping me on the shoulder. "But there is no accounting for you, man. Come along. Your horse is named Apple, and he is a wonderful little creature with a superb temperament. Lady Ida rides him when she visits."

"Are the Nelson siblings coming this summer?" I asked, following Charles towards the stables, Arthur tailing close behind. I imagined I could feel his eyes upon me and thrilled at the thought that he was gazing at me as I had gazed at him before reminding myself it was foolish to hope for something so far outside of the realm of possibility.

"They'll be here within the next week," Arthur offered. "Ida has been spending some time in France to help with an unfortunate illness, and Rudolph was with her, but their doctor seems to think it's appropriate for Ida to return. Certainly the fresh air here can only help."

"Their home is quite northern, isn't it?" We reached the stables, one of the boys clearly on lookout for us as he raced back inside as soon as he saw we were drawing close. "It's quite kind of you to allow them to stay here."

"Both Ida and Rudy are old friends," Charles said, watching as the horses were brought out, each ready to be ridden and the largest, undoubtedly Charles's, laden with a blanket and saddlebags of food. "We were practically raised together. Our mothers were great friends, and we are similar enough in age that it was only right we would spend our summers together. We never wanted to break with tradition."

Conversation was momentarily paused due to the necessity of mounting our horses, and I found quickly that Apple was as docile as promised. I had been a decent rider when I was younger, but the convenience of London hansom cabs had robbed me of some of this skill, although I knew that once we were on our way the memory would return and I'd have no trouble keeping up with the brothers. The pace of our horses was too disparate to allow us to resume chatting as we rode, making our way eastward towards the great pond that lay at the edge of the wood.

Arthur rode at the head of our little party, leading Charles and I onto a road that would take us through the wood, and the sight and smell of the trees was a comfort to a man who had spent far too much time in the oppressive air of London instead of this greenery. The trees met in an arch over the path we took, green light dappling the dirt as the sun fell through the leaves, and while my entire stay at Ashford Hall so far had been categorized by beauty, this was far greater than even I had come to expect.

I must have lagged behind, distracted by a desire to peer into every gap between the trees in the hopes of spotting some further beauty, because before I knew it, both Charles and Arthur had stopped their horses in the path and were looking at me, Charles grinning and Arthur with that slight glint in his eyes I had come to recognize as his most ardent expression of amusement. "Has the city warped you so much that you're in awe of the trees?" Charles called, and I laughed.

"I think being immersed in this sort of beauty every day has warped you, my friend. This is truly spectacular."

"We used to play Robin Hood in these woods," Charles said. "I would cry terribly every time Arthur tried to have me play the sheriff, though, and to have me stop he would allow me to be Robin Hood. Every last time."

"I feel for you, Lord Ashford," I said, bowing my head in mock sorrow towards Arthur. "Having been subjected to all too many crying fits before, I understand your pain."

"You poor man," Arthur said, and I thought I saw the hint of a smile before he turned his horse and continued down the path. The ride couldn't have been more than fifteen minutes, but it was exceedingly pleasant, and when we finally emerged from the wood onto the far edge of the Ashford pond, I welcomed the prospect of the sun on my face and a good meal on the banks of the water.

Charles dismounted first, tying his horse close enough to the water to allow it to drink if it pleased before removing the blanket and the food. He soon had a picnic set up, and the three of us settled in for the meal, our conversation light and cheery. Arthur proved himself a commendable conversationalist, his topics both varied and timely, and I was surprised to find that despite all the unpleasantness that had characterized my first day at Ashford Hall, I enjoyed his company.

After our meal, Charles convinced me to go for a swim, Arthur declining the invitation. The water was cool and clear, and we swam for a good while until, tired and beginning to grow cold, we emerged into the fresh sunlight. Charles promptly fell asleep in the grass with the instructions that we were to wake him if it looked as though he was beginning to burn, and Arthur and I were left alone.

I lay on my back against the cool fabric of the picnic blanket, eyes closed as I luxuriated in the sun on my body. I knew that it was quite out of the ordinary for me to be lying here half-nude with a lord of all things, but my comfort level with Arthur by this point was enough that I could be quite relaxed despite the unusual circumstances. My hair, curly when damp, was plastered against my forehead, my riding clothes discarded to the side and only my undergarments still in place and soaked through from our impromptu swimming session, and for a few moments I thought that Charles and my carefree swim had offended Arthur—a good reason to keep my eyes closed—when the other man spoke in a soft, contemplative voice. "I can't tell you how pleased I am that my brother has you," he said, and I opened my eyes to look up at him.

He was sitting with his left leg extended, his right leg almost to his chest, and was resting his chin on his knee as he watched me. There was a thoughtfulness in his green eyes that was not customary, a lovely softness about the corners that made me want to study him more. I watched him in return, the sun highlighting the parts of his hair that had grown lighter during the summer, and thought he could have easily played some grand Shakespearean hero, his beauty unparalleled. "I thought you were concerned I would be a poor influence," I said in return, lacing my hands together over my stomach in an attempt to look less caught off guard by the confession. That Arthur had thought it important to say this to me, that he thought I should know the thoughts that were inhabiting his mind at the moment…. It spoke to how well I had penetrated his defenses despite my profession, despite the man who had brought me into the legal fold to begin with.

"I was," he said. "I was concerned that my father had misjudged you, blinded by his love for Charles. He spoke highly of you, but I had always assumed that he was doing so because he knew how much Charles relied on you, and not because he was using his own common sense. But I see now that he was telling me the truth when he spoke of your unwavering loyalty. Since you've been here, it's become abundantly clear that you care for him as much as I care for him. You are as much a brother as I can be."

"Is that so surprising?" I asked. I could not mediate my own tone, could not make myself sound less sarcastic. I was touched by Arthur's candid confession, but I could not forget his clear concern about who I was and his disparaging comments against me upon my first arrival at Ashford Hall. "I have always presented myself as Charles's friend. I've never asked him for anything except for that friendship."

Arthur tilted his head to one side, pressing his cheek against his knee, and I had to swallow to force down the lump in my throat, considering him in a new and lovely light. He had always had the physical beauty to attract me, but there was a confluence of factors that were now contributing to my deepening affection. His ability to say what he meant despite how it might make others feel was no longer an annoyance but an intriguing quirk of his nature; his apparent capability to mask his emotions no longer meant that I was unable to read him but instead meant I just had to look closer, just had to peer into his eyes to understand what he was feeling in the absence of outward emotion. He was, in short, a mystery that was slowly unraveling before me, and I knew that he was allowing me to pull the string that was revealing more of his inner self each and every day.

"When our father died, he told me that Charles would need two things: my strength and your compassion. I have never been very good at showing empathy, and therefore I knew he would need it from someone else. I just… I think I hated the thought that he would find it from a man who was of a lower class than us, as terrible as that may sound. I know you never did anything to deserve that sort of condemnation from me, but it didn't matter at the time. I was certain that you would show your true colors, and yet…."

"I never betrayed him the way you thought I would," I finished, looking up at him as he gazed down at me in return. Half naked, I knew that I was, in theory, the more vulnerable of us two at the moment, but his words had served to crack the ice that seemed to form a shell around him and had rendered him momentarily defenseless. "The first night I was here, the first night we met… you were frightened, weren't you? That I would show you a face that Charles couldn't see."

"Yes," Arthur agreed. "I was afraid that I would meet you and I would see the sort of man you were and my fears would be confirmed. But you stood up to me and, honestly, proved yourself the opposite of everything I'd dreaded. I would be lying if I said that you haven't grown on me during your tenure here, as unwilling as I might have been to allow you to do so."

I looked at him, trying to solve the riddle that made up the man before me. His glances at times seemed nearly coquettish, a soft and tentative look that he seemed loath for me to catch as he almost always looked away upon realizing I had seen him. I had assumed that he was looking at me in this way to try and catch some terrible look in my own eyes, but now I wondered whether he was doing the same as I had been and sizing me up. The expression on his handsome face wasn't unlike the look I sometimes saw from men in pubs, and I was brought once again to wonder if my conclusion regarding him and Rudolph had been correct.

"Lord Ashford," I said, propping myself up on my elbows and looking at him. His face was remarkably close; in my half-prone position and with his bowed head, we were within a few inches of one another. I took a moment to study his face at this distance, making a mental note of the brown that speckled his green eyes and the length of his dark eyelashes before I continued to speak. "I think I may know what the blackmail consisted of. Did James—"

But I had waited too long, had reveled in the meaningful silences and soaked in the sweetness of his eyes on me to my own detriment, because just as the question was about to leave my lips, Charles gave an exaggerated yawn to my left and stretched to his full length, pressing his toes into my back to gain my attention. "I'm done with the sun," he said, sitting up rather gracelessly and looking around for his clothes. "I'll freckle if I'm not careful."

As though burned, Arthur had righted himself once his brother had stirred, sitting up straight and putting several inches more between us. I inwardly cursed my lost opportunity to find out more about the lord but outwardly offered Charles a fond smile. "You've already freckled."

"It's terribly unfashionable to be freckled," Charles said, clambering to his feet and lifting his clothes from the grass where he'd left them. He pulled them on, shielding his eyes from the sun and peering across the pond to the vast gardens beyond and the estate even further than that. I could see the very top of Ashford Hall from where we were sat, the roof a beautiful shade of red, and wondered at the circumstances that had brought me here to begin with. I had never anticipated spending any time on an estate, much less one as grand as Ashford Hall had proven to be. "It's beautiful here, isn't it, Tom?"

"Quite," I agreed, turning to lift my own clothes from where I'd folded them and set them aside. I dressed quickly and got to my feet, dusting off the knees of my trousers and looking at the two Ashford brothers. "Thank you for taking the time to invite me. I really was concerned I was intruding on your time together."

"We've had our entire lives together," Arthur said, already folding the picnic blanket up to leave. "It's quite nice to have an excuse to not see so much of one another for the time being."

"Rude," Charles said, but his tone was light as he helped his brother tie the blanket and the saddlebags back onto his horse. "Are we ready to return?"

"I believe so," Arthur said, looking at me. "Are you, Mr. Whitmore?"

"I hope you know that Tom is just fine," I said, and Arthur's gaze flicked over me briefly before he nodded and turned to his own horse.

The ride back towards the estate was just as pleasant as the one we had taken to reach the pond, only Arthur's mood seemed much less guarded than it had been before. His tone was the same, that slight flatness that made him seem disinterested in conversation, but there were actual jokes now, a softness underneath each word that I recognized as a genuine inroad. The thought of having won over both the Ashford brothers was a buoy, and I was occupying myself with fantasies of future such days when we emerged from the wood and espied a carriage sitting at the front steps of the estate.

For a moment, I considered the possibility that James had returned, but then Charles exclaimed in sheer delight, "It's Ida and Rudy!"

The Nelson siblings had arrived, and with their appearance a pit opened in my stomach and threatened to drag me down into it.

7

CHARLES HAD ridden well ahead of us to meet the carriage, and it seemed as though our timing was fortuitous. As we approached, it became clear that the Nelson siblings had just arrived themselves, and Charles met them just in time to help Ida out of the carriage, dismounting from his horse so smoothly it was hard to believe he was the same man I'd grown up with. As Arthur and I rode up and dismounted, passing our horses off to the stable boys that had come to meet us, Rudolph Nelson clambered out of the carriage after his sister.

It was as though I was looking in a taller, more handsome mirror. Rudolph Nelson could have been my brother, albeit with lighter skin than my own, a resemblance that made me immediately understand James's suspicions upon first meeting me. This is not to say I am not handsome—I had never before found cause to be upset about my appearance—but Rudolph…. Rudolph was handsome like Arthur was handsome, *storybook* handsome. Curly hair that was nearly black in the depth of its color, sharp, intelligent eyes the color of coal, full and pleasant lips.

James's words the day he had left came to the forefront of my mind again, and I realized he had been trying to tell me that I looked like Rudolph. I hung back a little as Arthur approached the siblings, turning my attention to Ida. She was as beautiful as her brother, her dark hair piled high on her head and her clothes the height of fashion, and I could see just from the briefest observation of the pair that they were perfectly at ease at the estate. "Arthur," Ida said as soon as he was within arm's reach, pulling him into a brief hug. "You look excellent."

"As do you!" Arthur said, and there was such force of emotion in his voice that for a moment, I thought I had misunderstood everything and it was, in fact, Ida that Arthur loved. Before that thought could linger too long, however, Rudolph had stepped forward and laid a hand on Arthur's shoulder, and I could see the way Arthur immediately moved to meet the touch. A jolt of recognition went through me and I quickly looked away, realizing that I was face-to-face with men who, if not lovers now, had been lovers in the past.

"What are you two doing here?" Charles asked, looking at the pair with clear delight. "Your last letter said you didn't think you would be back in England until the end of the month. You're two full weeks early."

"I do hope we haven't disrupted any plans," Ida said, her voice as pleasant as could be, lilting and kind. I immediately liked her, this feeling compounded as she looked at me and offered a smile. "You must be the infamous Mr. Whitmore," she said, offering her hand, and I immediately took it, her skin soft against my own. "Charles is quite the fan of yours."

"I'm a fan of his too," I said, smiling at her in return. I couldn't help but notice that Rudolph had dropped his hand from Arthur's shoulder the moment I had approached, and I wondered if he was having the same thoughts as I was except in reverse. Did he think that I was his replacement, a less handsome version of himself? As soon as I had that thought, I was ashamed of myself. Arthur had shown no romantic interest whatsoever. I was being delusional, pasting emotions onto him when there were none, and I needed to put the fantasy I had concocted aside.

Faced with Rudolph, I realized just how foolish my crush had been. The only thing to do was tamp it down and move along, distance myself from Arthur without ruining my summer. The first step was to look at Rudolph as a friend, not as anything else, and I stuck my hand out to him in greeting. "It's nice to meet you as well. Rudolph, isn't it?"

"You can call me Rudy, if you'd like," he said, shaking my hand, and his grip was firm and tight.

"Should we go inside?" Arthur suggested, and I had to avoid looking at him for fear that my expression would give everything away. I wanted nothing more than to return to those few hours by the pond, be the center of Arthur's attention once more, but that was gone now. "I'm not sure your rooms are ready, but I'll have Felix make sure they're aired out and ready by the time dinner is finished."

"How was the trip from France?" Charles asked as he began up the steps of the estate, Ida Nelson close behind. I noticed with trepidation that Arthur and Rudolph exchanged a glance before they started after them, and became even more convinced that my suspicions about the nature of the blackmail were correct. The ninety minutes the pair had spent in the library on the day of the poaching incident was at the core of all this, and I needed to find a way to bring it up without frightening Arthur.

"Long," Ida said. "Rudy was seasick crossing the channel, as always. I fear neither of us were very good traveling companions. I was longing for home, and he was as green as the grass."

"And you're well now?" Arthur asked, and I recalled that the brothers had mentioned that Ida had been sick and that they had been in France for that exact reason. The Riviera was known for being good for recovery, a place where the most elite in England could go to rest and heal, and if Ida had spent time there, then it meant she had been well and truly ill.

"Much better," Ida said, smiling at him. "Thank you for asking, Arthur. That's very kind of you."

I followed the four of them inside, hanging back despite how I usually thrived in these social situations, a lead weight in my chest. I had convinced myself, however briefly, that Arthur was looking at me with some… well, attraction. I was sure it had been attraction. But I had deluded myself, a mixture of my assumptions about those missing ninety minutes and my own desire when it came to his good looks and his thawing attitude towards me. As foolish as I knew it to be, I was smarting from the realization that I was merely a shade of Rudolph Nelson.

"I wish you had written ahead," Felix said, emerging from a side room looking harried, although he didn't check his tone with the Nelson siblings. He was clearly as comfortable with them as he was with the Ashford boys, and that was another sprinkle of salt in my wounds. I liked Felix, and he never pulled his words with me, but to know that it wasn't special…. I was feeling more ordinary than I had since I first arrived at Ashford Hall, a middle-class man amidst people well and truly out of my league. "Your rooms are terribly dusty. I don't think they've been touched since the spring clean."

"I'm afraid I wanted to surprise you all," Rudolph said, sounding genuinely apologetic. "I didn't think of the repercussions."

"Well, we've had a bit of excitement with unexpected guests this week," Arthur said, his tone flat. "James dropped in without notice a few days ago. It was… unpleasant."

"Oh dear," Ida said, and I could tell by her voice that she was bothered by the idea that James had been at the estate. "Are you all okay? Did he try anything this time?"

"He gave Tom a few vague threats, and then I made him leave," Charles said, crossing his arms over his chest and looking at the Nelsons. "I think he believed that we brought Thomas here to look at the poaching case and find out what had gone wrong and was hoping he could scare him away if he said the right things."

"And are you?" Rudolph looked at me, brow knit. "You're a lawyer, aren't you? Charles speaks quite highly of your skills."

"I wasn't looking into it before," I said, caught off guard by the plaintive look in his eyes. I was anticipating a man as unemotional as Arthur, as prone to hiding his feelings, and instead I found myself watching someone who plainly exhibited what they were feeling. It surprised me, humanized him, and made me feel altogether worse about my own fantasies. "But after James tried to warn me off of it, I decided that it was important. That the poaching had led to something else."

For a second, Rudolph's dark eyes flickered with realization, and I knew he fully recognized who I was in that moment. It was almost laughable, how easily men like us could find one another when the situation was just right, and I held his gaze for a few moments before he nodded and looked at Arthur. "You have quite the trustworthy lawyer in your hands now, Arthur."

"I think so too," Arthur said, and it was a stunning admission for a man who not two weeks prior had denounced me as the worst of the worst. It touched me, if I was being honest, and only heightened my feelings that I was being a fool in all of this. How dreadful would I be if I turned around and told this man who trusted me that I suspected him not only of being an invert but having an affair with Rudolph Nelson. "Now, as your rooms aren't ready, can I distract you both with tea?"

"We can bring it to the greenhouse," Felix said, looking at Ida. "You like taking tea there, if I recall."

"No need for formalities, Felix," Ida said, smiling at him. "That would be lovely. I'd like the chance to catch up, if I'm being honest."

"We'll be with you in a moment," Rudolph said, nodding to his sister. "I wanted to talk to Arthur for a few minutes alone."

Ida looked between the two of them and then nodded, turning her attention to Charles. "Shall we?"

"We shall," Charles said, offering her his arm. I followed them towards the greenhouse, far at the western side of the house where it would get the most sun; it was a massive, sprawling glass structure, larger than the sunroom where I had taken tea with James before. It was a beautiful place, another gift to the Ashford's mother from their father, but today beauty wasn't enough to replace the sickening feeling that was growing inside me.

Envy was not something I dealt with often, but I was working through it now. I knew that I was being a fool, but like a boy with affection for a girl who hardly noticed him, it was difficult to shake the desire for Arthur to notice me and not Rudolph. I wondered desperately what they were talking about, and as we reached the greenhouse and Charles pulled a chair out for Ida, I did my best to put it out of my mind.

I sat across from her and she smiled at me, as pretty as could be. "I'm glad I finally got to meet you. Charles has been talking about you coming here for years now. I never really thought you'd actually come."

"Oh, my understanding is Arthur wasn't ready for me to come," I said, shrugging one shoulder. "We've put that behind us now. Although I have to say my first few weeks at Ashford have proven more exciting than I anticipated."

"That was like last summer for Rudy and myself," Ida said, glancing at Charles as he settled into a seat before turning back to look at me. "What with the engagement being called off and everything."

"The engagement?" I asked, my eyes going a little wider. "I'm afraid I hadn't heard anything about that."

"Arthur and I have been engaged since we were young," Ida said. "We were always intending to carry out that marriage, but he called off the engagement last summer. It was quite the surprise."

"He called off the engagement?"

"Yes." Ida shrugged, and I got the feeling she wasn't really all that torn up about losing the opportunity to marry Arthur. I had to remind myself that marriages in this stratosphere of class weren't made for love but rather for politics, and aside from the social hit Ida undoubtedly took, I can't imagine she was truly upset. "I suppose he realized he wasn't interested in marriage at that point and didn't want to lead me on further."

I considered that, slotting it into the known timeline that I had when it came to Arthur. Really, I wasn't meaning to plot out his entire life before I had come to Ashford Hall, but there was something deeper going on that I wanted to uncover. I had always been overly curious, and I needed to know what had changed in Arthur to make him so guarded when Charles had previously described him as open, sociable, easy to read. Or, well, I *wanted* to know. I wanted to know everything there was to know about him, and putting together the events leading up to this summer was the best way for me to do that. "Did you take that personally?"

Ida looked surprised by my question, tilting her head back for a moment. "No," she finally said. "Although we had been engaged for so long, I don't think I ever really believed we would get married. I always had romantic notions about marrying for love and I never loved Arthur, not the way I wanted to. But I couldn't call the engagement off, it wouldn't have been proper. I was… well, I was relieved when he finally called it off. I knew he didn't love me, either."

"If our mothers wanted us to love you as a wife, they shouldn't have allowed us to play with you as children," Charles said. "I've seen you eat far too much dirt to take you as a bride."

Ida laughed, her face turning the barest pink as she looked at Charles again. "You believe your brother didn't want to marry me because I ate too much dirt as a child? Because I distinctly remember a boy who—"

"No, don't," Charles said, laughing as well and leaning across the table as though to grab her hand, Ida leaning back to avoid him. "Don't say it, you'll make Tom think less of me!"

"A boy who used to eat grass because he said it tasted sweet in the summer!" Ida finished, and I couldn't help but laugh, looking at Charles.

"You ate grass?" I asked, and Charles looked at me, shaking his head. "Ida says you ate grass."

"I ate a little bit of grass," he admitted, and at that moment Arthur and Rudolph entered the greenhouse, Rudolph hanging behind a little as they approached the table.

"Are we talking about when Charles ate grass because we ran out of cake?" Arthur asked, stepping out of the way as one of the maids appeared and set the table. "I still don't understand why he did that."

"I was five. I think it's perfectly acceptable," Charles said. "That was the same winter you nearly died from illness, Arthur, and I think it was the grass that saved me from suffering the same fate."

"I highly doubt that," Arthur said. "I don't believe grass has any medicinal properties."

I glanced at Rudolph, who had settled into a seat alongside his sister, and noticed that he was watching Arthur closely, as though unable to tear his eyes off the man. I understood all too well the allure, but it made me wonder even more what they had talked about, Arthur seeming unaffected and Rudolph seeming more morose than he had been when we left them in the great hall. Clearly they'd had some private conversation, and I was more convinced than ever that there was some hidden history there.

I highly doubted that anyone at the table had the suspicions I currently did, but I wanted to confirm what I thought I knew. I couldn't ask Ida or Charles, and asking Rudolph or Arthur straight out was impossible, but there was someone I could ask, someone who most likely knew the answer to the question and would tell me without making a fuss. Felix had to know. It was unlikely for a manservant to not know every detail of his employer's life, and I knew Felix well enough by this point to recognize that he would tell me if I asked him with the utmost sincerity.

In the back of my mind, I knew that it was an invasion of privacy, but I had to know. That summer laid bare a deficit in my character that I had been unaware of before, a desire to uncover the truth even if it would harm another, and in the weeks to come I would begin to understand that when it came to Arthur Ashford, I could only give into my basest nature.

8

THE REST of the day passed pleasantly, the Nelson siblings both far more fun than James had been. Once he seemed to shake himself out of the sorrow that had seemingly consumed him since the conversation he'd had with Arthur upon arrival, Rudolph proved himself a quick wit and a much better chess player than either of the Ashford men could claim to be. Ida was a delight, conversational and sillier than I was accustomed to the women I knew being, her clear comfort with the setting allowing me to gain a friendship I had not anticipated. It was quite nice to while away the afternoon and evening in the parlor, Rudolph and I discussing a formidable trial that had taken place the month prior, Arthur, Ida, and Charles playing whist, and by the time we needed to retire it seemed quite certain to me that the arrival of the Nelsons was a welcome addition to our summer festivities.

It was well after eleven when I finally made my way upstairs, having said good night to our small and pleasant party before taking my leave. It was pure coincidence that resulted in Felix and myself crossing paths in the hallway at the top of stairs, Felix holding a jug of water for Charles's room. I caught up to him in no time, touched him on the elbow, and smiled when he started slightly. "Oh, Tom," he said, grinning at me, the formality of my last name long replaced with the comfort of my first. "Goodness, you're light on your feet."

"Sorry I frightened you," I said. "When you've taken that water to Charles's room, can you meet me in my suite? I'd like to ask you about something."

Felix searched my face, his eyes crinkling slightly. "Of course," he said. "Is everything okay?"

"I just have some questions," I said, patting him lightly on the shoulder. "Don't worry."

I made my way to my suite, finding, as always, a freshly brewed pot of tea. The servants had clearly picked up on my habit of staying up far too late and drinking my weight in tea, and I was thankful for the refreshment as I settled on my small sofa and waited for Felix. He wasn't long, knocking lightly on the door before letting himself in, and I waited for him to take a seat before pouring him a cup of tea and pushing the sugar bowl towards him. He doctored his drink and then looked at me, blue eyes glinting slightly in the low light of my room. "Well? I can hazard a guess at what you'd like to know, but perhaps I'm wrong."

I took a deep breath, looking at him to see if he was showing any sign of being disingenuous but seeing nothing whatsoever to suggest as much. "Why don't you tell me what you believe I want to know?"

"You want to ask me if Rudolph and Arthur were lovers," he said, and my surprise and relief must have shown on my face because he laughed, leaning back in his seat with his teacup in hand. "Did you think you were being terribly mysterious?"

"No, but I didn't think I was being that obvious, either."

"Not obvious," Felix said. "But it's easy enough for someone who's been in service all their life to intuit what people want. And you do spend an awful lot of time gazing at Arthur when you think he isn't looking."

"Is that so?" I asked, because to be quite honest I thought I'd been doing an excellent job of keeping my eyes to myself. "How did you know I would ask about him and Rudolph?"

"Because they are even more obvious than you are," Felix said, and my heart dropped into my stomach. The way Felix said it made me think immediately that I had been incorrect in my assumption that the love between Arthur and Rudolph was a thing of the past. "You noticed as soon as Rudolph arrived today, didn't you?"

"Yes," I said. "I could see it immediately. The change in Arthur."

Felix sighed, taking a sip of his tea and looking at me with some intensity. "It started when he and Arthur were teenagers. They had always been close, but they began to find time to be alone together. I'm not a fool, and my position necessitates my proximity to Arthur. We were inseparable in most things, and he began to confide in me that his feelings for Rudolph were beyond friendship. I was stunned, but Arthur has always been my purpose in life, so I quickly convinced myself I would support him no matter what. It turned romantic before Arthur departed for university."

"So they're lovers," I said, and Felix shook his head. "They're not?"

"I'm sure this won't come as any great surprise, but Arthur is not the easiest man to love. He barely allows Charles and I to show him affection. I understand this particular defect, despite existing his entire life, was a strain on Rudolph. The man is like his sister and laughs easily and often. I believe he hoped that Arthur would eventually reach that point with him, but he never did."

I remembered Arthur, the way he looked at me at the pond, the grace in his movements and the softness in his eyes. He was a serious man, but there was still a tenderness there if you knew what to look for, and I knew that if given time and opportunity it could be uncovered fully. "That isn't in Arthur's nature."

"No," Felix said. "When Rudolph realized that it wasn't going to change, he called an end to things. That would have been… four years ago now, I believe."

"Before the blackmail case?"

"Yes," Felix said, nodding and setting his teacup down on the table between us. He looked down at the dregs for a moment before turning his attention back to me. "I'm telling you all of this because I know what you are, Tom. Birds of a feather, after all."

"You…?"

"I've dabbled," Felix said, and I couldn't help but smile at that.

"Does Arthur know?"

"I think he suspects. We've never had a conversation, but when I was a teenager, I had a dalliance with one of the stable boys. I'm fairly sure Arthur caught us once, but he never said a word." He got to his feet, his brow furrowed. "This is all to say… I hope you use this information for good. I like you, Tom. I would like it even better if you had a positive change on Arthur. As much as he's loath to admit it, he's lonely. He loved Rudolph, even if it wasn't the same sort of love that Rudolph had for him. He's opening up to you."

"Thank you, Felix," I said, getting up as well and walking over to the suite door with him. "I'm glad you told me about this. It helps me put the pieces together in all this. I only have one last question, though."

"What is it?"

"Does James Wright know about Arthur and Rudolph?" I asked, and Felix scrunched his face up, clearly considering the possibility.

"He might," he finally admitted. "They used to walk in the garden together. It's possible James saw something he shouldn't have. Why do you ask?"

"Before he was sent away, he made a comment that I looked like Rudolph, and he thought perhaps Arthur had invited me here for that purpose. He seemed to think it was strange that Charles and I have been friends for so long and I've just now been allowed to visit."

Felix looked up at me, a thoughtful look in his blue eyes. He studied me for a moment before shaking his head. "No, I don't think that's it at all. You bear a passing resemblance to Rudolph, but I doubt that's why Arthur finally allowed you to visit. It seems much more likely to me that Arthur said yes because he realized that you had proven yourself unlikely to have a friendship with Charles solely to social climb. Your exploits in court have made a name all their own, and your presence here has only cemented that. I have no doubt you'll find yourself a frequent guest to Ashford Hall for as long as you please." He yawned, failing to stifle it before looking at me. "Now, I implore you, no more questions. I'm so tired."

"Dreadfully sorry," I said, patting him on the shoulder. "You've been a great help. I promise, I won't impose on you quite so late again."

"Good night, Tom," Felix said, patting me on the arm in return and leaving the room. I settled in for another few hours of poring over the legal documents I'd been provided, my candle flickering in the cool summer breeze coming in from the cracked balcony door. I had hardly made it through five pages when I heard what sounded like heavy rain falling abruptly on my balcony, and I turned my head to peer towards the darkness. Seeing only my watery reflection in the thick glass, I stood and walked to the balcony in time to see another handful of pebbles land on the stone.

The moon was full and bright and I stepped out onto the balcony without my candle, leaning over the railing to find that Rudolph was standing below, dressed only in trousers and a thin sleep shirt. It seemed he had begun to undress for bed before some other business had struck him, and I had a suspicion it was the same sort of questioning that had brought me into conversation with Felix that night. "In the future, I believe one or two rocks thrown at the glass should suffice," I said, kicking the loose pebbles from the balcony. "Are you looking to continue our chess game?"

"Care to take a stroll?" Rudolph asked, spreading his arms to either side of him. "I was told you suffer from insomnia, and I simply cannot pass up the company of another night owl."

"I'll be down momentarily," I said, my curiosity as to what Rudolph wanted outweighing my desire to continue with my legal review. "Wait there."

Charles had shown me a secondary staircase at the end of our hallway, ostensibly for the servants but ill-used because it ended in a dusty sitting area. I slipped on my shoes and headed down these steps, making my way through the sitting room and out to a small hallway that took me directly to the garden. Rudolph clearly knew the path I would take, because as I emerged into the night, he was already waiting for me. I noted, with some surprise, that he was barefoot, and wondered if he and Arthur had done this same thing countless times before. "So," Rudolph said as I fell into step beside him, following him towards the entrance to the gardens. "Did Felix sate your curiosity?"

I had always heard the dangers of estate gossip, but to bear witness to it taking place so quickly was a genuine surprise, my gaze flitting to Rudolph briefly before I looked away once again. "I suppose I shouldn't be surprised that you found out so quickly."

"I'm quite good friends with one of the maids," Rudolph said, and there was a note of apology in his voice that was quite foreign to me. "When she mentioned he'd visited you so late, I could think only that you had asked him."

"How did you know?"

"I am in the public eye far more than I can stand," Rudolph said. "There have been times where I've worn a new hat or spoken a little too loudly in a pub and it has ended up in the newspaper. It has made me all too aware of eyes upon me and excellent at reading the thoughts of those who are looking. And you… I'm afraid to say that your eyes are quite expressive for a man in such a precarious position."

It was what Felix had said too. I was obvious in my gaze, but I didn't know how to stop it. I couldn't understand why I was so different from other men, why I could be so easily caught. "Has Arthur noticed?" I asked, the words sticking in my throat, and Rudolph breathed out through his nose, a single, stifled laugh.

"You could have your lips on Arthur's and he would still doubt your intentions," Rudolph said, and his blunt acknowledgment of the sexuality that I had long tried to keep to myself sent a small, thrilling jolt through my body. "No, he has not noticed. And I hope Felix's words haven't made it so you want to bring it to Arthur's attention, either."

I looked at him, searching his face, but as he was sidelong to me it was difficult to read what was written there. "I wasn't planning on saying anything," I said.

"No, but as easy as it was for you to figure out myself and Arthur's relationship, I figured out yours and his. At dinner tonight, and in the hours after, he could not take his eyes off you, regardless of who was speaking to him. He is already fascinated. You need not say a word, and yet his feelings will only grow, and it is not safe for him to allow himself to have that sort of relationship again."

Something twisted in my chest, a simultaneous pang at the thought that he may already feel the way I felt and a realization that Rudolph was telling me this for some greater purpose. "You think he would be in trouble?"

"You're looking into the case," Rudolph said, looking at me. "Tell me, Thomas. You know he was blackmailed. Do you have any idea why?"

"I thought it was because of you," I said. "There's ninety minutes unaccounted for on the day of the poaching accident where you and Arthur were in the library together. I thought that may have led to the blackmail, but Felix told me tonight that you and Arthur were no longer lovers when the blackmail began."

"We weren't, but the evidence of our relationship remained, and James had his suspicions. The legal proceedings allowed the lawyer access to Arthur's library, and I understand he found letters that Arthur had kept." I felt sick, but Rudolph continued, his head tilted back slightly to face the moon. "We had not signed them with our names, but they were… explicit enough that anyone could make an educated guess."

"How did the blackmail end?" I asked, and Rudolph laughed again softly. "What?"

"It was Ida," he said. "She got it out of me, found out the truth, and she took responsibility for the letters. She claimed that Arthur was the intermediary between her and another man, and that he had held on to the letters so no one would suspect her of no longer honoring their betrothal. As a result, they had to publicly renounce their engagement."

Horror twisted up inside me at the revelation and I stopped in my tracks. For a woman in Ida's position, a marriage was the most important thing she could hope for, and to have to rescind her engagement to save her brother was terrible. Rudolph came to a stop as well, turning to look at me with his hands in the pockets of his trousers. I looked at him, a knot of emotion in my chest. "Louis Garretty did all this? Just to blackmail Arthur?"

"Arthur is extremely wealthy, with a huge amount of influence," Rudolph said. He took a step towards me and for the first time, I realized that the way he was looking at me was familiar, a hunger that I recognized all too well. "Eyes are always on him and he's unable to avoid that sort of scrutiny. It makes him a poor choice for a lover."

I looked up at him, searching his face, and realized exactly what was happening. "You're not jealous of any feelings I might have for Arthur."

"No," Rudolph said. "I don't have any illusions that Arthur and I will ever become lovers again. The blackmail was the final nail in the coffin."

"But there's a reason you're warning me about this," I said, and stayed stock-still as Rudolph closed the distance between us, resting his slim fingers on the side of my throat. "You're jealous of Arthur."

"I can easily see why he would be smitten with you," he said, and that same damned thrill went through me. Despite the heat of Rudolph's fingertips on my skin, I could think only of Arthur, of the idea of him being attracted to me, although I didn't see it that way myself. He was opening up to me, of course, becoming more comfortable, but smitten seemed far from the truth. "You are terribly handsome, and your unwillingness to speak with deference is refreshing for men like Arthur and myself."

"You've known me for less than a day," I whispered, his thumb pressing against the soft underside of my chin, pushing my head back. "How could you possibly know?"

"Arthur will never be able to love a man without inhibition," Rudolph murmured. "He will do his duty and he will marry a woman and you will be left behind. All I ask is that you give me the summer. Do not be so hasty in your choice. I've told you everything I know, so there is nothing you can leave out of your decision. I may be two weeks behind in terms of courting, but I would be a fool to give up."

Any rebuttal died in my throat as he kissed me, his fingers still on my chin as he pressed his lips to mine. His mouth tasted of tea and the brandy we had been indulging in after supper, but there was an undercurrent of his own taste running beneath it all, especially as his tongue slipped over my lower lip, attempting to coerce me into opening my mouth. The kiss was far from chaste, and I am ashamed to admit I leaned into it, a distinct lack of sex in the preceding months opening me up to the sudden affection.

He pulled back slowly, chasing my mouth for a few more lingering kisses before he let go of me, his dark hair wreathed by the moon behind him. "We have the summer, Thomas," he said, and my name on his lips tugged at my stomach as though an invisible string had just been tied to the both of us. "I hope you consider it. I've laid everything out for you." He took a step back, looking up at the estate. "All I want is a chance."

With that, he began to walk back towards the manor, leaving me alone in the night air to contemplate what had just taken place. I had not anticipated Rudolph's actions in the slightest and, unexpectedly, they had left me feeling far more curious than I had thought possible.

9

AFTER A night of little sleep, my thoughts occupied by the sensation of Rudolph's lips against my own, I was in a dreadful mood. I took tea before I went down to breakfast, hoping it would give me a much-needed boost, but by the time I reached the dining room and took my seat all I had accomplished was achieving the clarity that I had kissed a future lord in the garden of Ashford Hall the night before. When I had met Rudolph in the garden, I hadn't anticipated that his words would be in the pursuit of convincing me to see him as a viable romantic partner.

For two weeks now, my eyes had been firmly on Arthur in terms of interest, and now I had a man I'd known for less than a day telling me to pay him attention instead. Rudolph Nelson was handsome, and I had done more with men I'd known for less time, but the thought of turning away from Arthur, particularly after the way he'd looked at me by the lake yesterday, was almost impossible to consider. The fact was I found Arthur Ashford a far more intriguing possibility, a damaged man who nevertheless deserved love, and if I could unlock that part of his heart, I knew it would pay off.

That didn't make the morning any easier, nor did it make me feel particularly good about facing the two men I was feeling so conflicted about. When I entered the dining room, though, I found that Rudolph and Charles were in animated conversation. I caught Arthur's eye, the man sitting listening to them at the head of the table, and when he looked at me, I could see the faintest hint of amusement in his eyes and knew that Rudolph's question of my interest in him over Arthur was not one I could answer easily.

I sat down alongside Ida, who was looking similarly amused, and spoke to her in a stage whisper. "What is the argument this early in the morning?"

"I'm not sure even they know," Ida said, shaking her head. "This is a bad habit our fathers instilled in the two of them, ostensibly to keep them occupied at parties, but they never outgrew it. One of them picks a topic, and the other debates them on it until… well, I suppose until they decide they're finished."

"That… explains a lot about Charles," I said. Charles had always been a hearty debater, the sort of man who never backed down from an argument, and I had seen firsthand during the course of our friendship that he would defend a position until the end. Usually, the position was that I shouldn't be the victim of whatever vitriol I was currently enduring, but there had been a few times where I had been on the other end of the argument and had seen his persuasiveness for myself. It made us a formidable pair, considering how neither of us would let an argument end naturally. "Your fathers instilled this in him?"

"Believe it or not, but Charles was quite shy when he was a child, and Rudy was damned near mute," Arthur said, and I was surprised to find that he had leaned across to me and begun to pour tea into my cup. The simple gesture touched me deeply, my heart twisting up in my chest, and I wondered what it meant that the head of the household was deigning to do this for me when I could see a servant already in the room. "This was an exercise in opening them both up, and it clearly worked."

Abruptly, the debate stopped, Charles laughing in that way he had that spoke to his complete lack of self-consciousness. "You win, Rudy," he said, grinning across at the man before turning his attention to me. "You'll have to join our debate tomorrow, Tom. We should see if your debate skills have been honed by your law practice."

"I should hope so," I said, touching Arthur's wrist lightly as he finished pouring the tea, a small bit of gratitude, and he looked at me with surprise, his green eyes bright in a way that I hadn't seen before. Rudolph's warning the night before had not fallen on deaf ears but rather had heightened my feelings, had made me realize that if Rudolph had recognized my attraction so quickly, it meant that I had been ignoring it for longer than I had known. I had confirmation of who Arthur was at his core now. He liked men, and from there it was easy to convince myself that he had an interest in me.

There were signs of it, of course. His apathy towards me had turned to friendship quickly, and I knew that I looked like Rudolph, although I was still convinced at the time that I was a pale imitation of Rudolph— even though that idea had been somewhat challenged by the events of the night before. I will not pretend I was some blushing virgin, that I had not had my share of men who I knew no more about than that they had looked at me across a dark room with *those* eyes, but having a brief one-night tryst was far different than whatever was happening at Ashford Hall this summer.

However badly the romantic side of my mind was excited by the idea of having two noblemen interested in me, however, the logical side was unmoved. To Rudolph Nelson, I was an exciting new toy, an interloper in a close family relationship he'd had since birth and an easy man to take as a summer lover. To Arthur Ashford, I was his brother's best friend, a nuisance turned something else, and I highly doubted that he viewed me with romantic intentions as much as he had just grown comfortable with me. Misinterpreting these feelings could very well lead to a downfall of the worst kind, and I had to be cognizant of my position in this house. That Arthur had not pulled away when I had touched his wrist boded well, but I could not pretend to know what a man of his standing thought when he looked upon someone like me.

That breakfast was the first of a long string of pleasant days spent at Ashford Hall. June faded into July, the heat grew, and despite my growing comfort with the Nelson siblings and both Ashford men, nothing came to pass between myself and Arthur nor between myself and Rudolph after that first night. I threw myself into my work in the mornings, spent my afternoons and evenings lazing about with Charles or swimming with Rudolph or reading with Ida and thought that if nothing else, it would be a pleasant summer spent among pleasant people. My conviction that I was unlocking something in Arthur was put aside and I was, for a time, happy merely to be among such company.

On August 17th, nearly two months after the Nelsons had arrived, I was sitting in the garden with Ida, Charles, and Rudolph, sprawled out on a picnic blanket and reading through a file of notes that had been delivered to the estate when Felix appeared, his cheeks flushed pink as though he had been running. We all looked at him, Rudolph's brow knit in concern. "Is everything all right?"

"I'm dreadfully sorry," Felix said, and his eyes were on me. My stomach plummeted and I sat up, looking at him. "There's been a messenger just now, Tom. From London."

"Oh no," I said, pushing to my feet. "I told them only to send a messenger if it was truly important."

"He's brought a carriage to take you back."

My eyes went wide, but before I could speak, Charles had done so for me. "To take him back? To London? Whatever for?"

"It seems there's been a development in one of your cases that requires your presence," Felix said, wringing his hands. "He mentioned something about a trial being moved up."

"He's out front of the house?" I asked, giving the rest of the group a hasty apology before following Felix out of the garden. "Thank you for getting me so quickly."

"I got the impression he wanted to leave right away to return you to London on time," Felix said. "I'll let you speak with him, but would you like me to pack you a bag?"

"I think that will be necessary, unfortunately," I said, sickened at the thought of leaving Ashford Hall so quickly but knowing that I could not ignore a summons from the city, particularly if a trial was at hand. "Pack just enough for a month, Felix. I have no intentions of leaving for the summer yet."

"I speak for all of us when I say that if you don't return, our summer will be immeasurably worse," Felix said, pausing as we reached the front drive, a carriage sitting in front of the steps and a young man hovering near the front of it. "I'll put your bag together for no more than a week."

He turned to leave and I reached out, grabbing his sleeve. Felix looked at me, surprised, and I was surprised by my action as well before I realized exactly why I had done it. "Where's Arthur?"

"In the library," Felix said. "Good point. You cannot leave him without saying goodbye."

"Thank you," I said, and with that he hurried off again, leaving me to approach the carriage driver. "Good afternoon," I said, and the man, who couldn't have been more than twenty and who I vaguely recognized as a clerk at the firm, looked momentarily startled before he realized I was no doubt the man he sought. "What's happening?"

"Oh, Mr. Whitmore," the clerk said, half bowing in an entirely unnecessary way. "I'm so, so sorry to interrupt your holiday in this way. The trial for Mr. Landry has been moved up to Wednesday and we desperately need you in London to act as his defense. I'm here to take you back."

"I see," I said, furrowing my brow as I considered this. "He was supposed to be tried in October."

"There was a change in judge, so they moved the date," the clerk said. "We need to leave within the hour, sir. I'm so sorry."

"All right. Give me some time to tie up loose ends here, and I'll be ready to leave," I said, already heading up the steps. "Get one of the stable boys to change your horse for you, and get lunch for yourself, yes?"

With that said, I hurried into the house, my heart pounding in my throat. I was frightened, genuinely frightened, that if I returned to London I would not have the opportunity to leave again. The fact that Landry's trial had been moved was almost unheard of, and it spoke to something greater, something strange; not for the first time I was concerned that Louis Garretty had discovered that it was Ashford Hall where I was spending my summer and was doing his best to put an end to it before I could find out what he had done. If that was the case, I doubted very much that he would just allow me to return once the trial was finished, and the idea of being separated from people who I had genuinely begun to think of as dear friends was a terrible one.

Even so, my feet were not carrying me back to the garden where I had left the Nelsons and Charles. I was moving, almost of my own accord, up the grand staircase and to the left, towards the great library where I knew Arthur was. I reached it, out of breath and flustered, and took a few moments in front of the door to smooth down my hair and settle myself. I don't know why my impulse was so strong, but I had to be the one to tell him I was leaving, had to see his face when he heard the words come from my lips.

I knocked and heard him answer from inside. "Come in."

The door swung open readily at the touch of my hand, and I stepped inside, closing the door behind me. Arthur was seated at his desk, letters scattered around in front of him. Since I had been here, I had begun to realize how many people wrote to him, asking for money or time or help or anything he was willing to give, and with Felix now running the day-to-day operations of the hall, it had fallen to Arthur to reply lest he inadvertently cause offense.

Arthur looked up, and I was touched to see that there was that slightest of smiles on his face, the gesture almost impossible to see unless you were, as I was becoming, familiar with his usual expression. Almost immediately, however, his expression grew sober, and he rose from his chair. "What's happened? Weren't you at lunch? Why do you look so winded?"

"It's okay," I said, but my tone apparently did little to convince him of this and he came around the desk to stand in front of me. A shudder passed through me as I saw the concern in his eyes, the news I had to give him dying in my throat. I didn't want to leave, but to allow a man I knew to be innocent to face trial alone or, even worse, with Louis Garretty at his defense, was antithetical to why I had become a lawyer. "There's a clerk from my office come to take me back to London."

"Back to London," Arthur repeated, his brow furrowing as he took in those words and seemed to realize what I was telling him. "You're leaving? Tom, I—Is there no way you can continue your work here?"

"I have a trial. I had no intention of leaving, but the date was moved and I have no choice. Believe me, no part of me wants to leave behind Ashford Hall so quickly. These few months seem like not enough time in the slightest."

Arthur had begun to pace back and forth, fiddling with the ivory cufflink on his left wrist. "I see," he said after what felt like an eternity. "How long will the trial last?"

"I've no idea. A week, perhaps more. It's a complex case with a huge log of evidence, and the prosecutor is… a dogged man, who is sure of my client's guilt. I'm sure he'll attempt to drag out the proceedings."

"But you'll return?" Arthur asked. "The ball is at the beginning of September."

Of course. The words were ice thrown in my face, a needle driven into my heart, and I immediately saw that Arthur's concern about my sudden business in London was not because he truly wanted me to stay at the hall but rather because my departure would undoubtedly put a damper on the ball. An annual tradition for the Ashford family, the ball was something I had heard plenty about from Charles over the years and had hoped to attend during this summer stay. Since it was usually held on the second Saturday of September, I had a mere three weeks to wrap up my business in the city and make it back in time.

I wondered how many people Arthur had already told of my attendance. I'm sure my presence would cause some stir, a lower-class man and a lawyer at that. While at any other time I would have felt guilt, I was so stung by the realization that he was more concerned about the possibility of me missing the ball than he was about our time together being cut short that I found it exceedingly difficult to feel anything beyond irritation. I had practically run here in order to say goodbye and was yet again reminded of Rudolph's warning that the man I was so attracted to was incapable of feeling the same in return.

"I'll do my best," I said, and my tone must have been so icy that even Arthur noticed, his gaze turning to me with some surprise. It was laughable, how easy he had become to read in the last two months and yet how far out of my reach he still remained, how I could interpret a flick of his eyes or a twitch of his lips and yet could not figure out what lay underneath it all. "I have a feeling that this sudden trial update has less to do with the judge's availability and more to do with Louis Garretty discovering where my summer is being spent."

"And so he schemes to take you away from us," Arthur muttered, a note of disdain in his voice. "I see," he repeated, and he stopped his pacing, turning to face me. He stepped in my direction, clutching his hands together behind his back and looking at me with knitted brow. For a brief moment I wished desperately that his face, those eyes, could be captured in paint so I could gaze upon it for all eternity, grow old a man driven to madness simply because of a hunger he could not sate. "If you must go, you must go, but I will come to London to fetch you myself if you are not back in a fortnight, Thomas."

"Yes, forbid I do not return in time for your ball," I said, and he searched my face briefly before a pink flush came into his cheeks. When he next spoke, it was with such vehemence that I was very nearly taken aback.

"Damn the ball! Having you back here has nothing to do with the ball, and I would not care tomorrow if every last invitation returned with a refusal! You are a fool if you believe that my reasons for wanting you here have anything to do with a silly gathering, and not for something far more—" He stopped himself, dragging his hand over his mouth and looking at me with an intensity that I had not seen before, not even during that first argumentative night. "Never mind. Go to London if you must, but for God's sake come back."

I couldn't understand what had caused the sudden flare of emotion, unable to tear my eyes from him, his face now a lively shade of pink, even the tips of his ears flushed with color. A memory of Charles from university surfaced, a confession he had made regarding a girl he had met and he was enthralled with. His ears had gone that same pink at the tips, his embarrassment of emotion so overflowing that it had burned hot through all of him, and the longer I looked at Arthur the more I became convinced that the emotion I had awoken was of the same vein.

"Finish what you were going to say," I said, bolder than I thought I was capable of being. "Something far more what, Arthur?"

"I won't say," Arthur said, and whatever had been on his lips was gone now, lost to his own stubborn pride. For a moment it had been possible to convince myself, however stupid it was, that the lord had been on the cusp of some sort of confession. As he stood there looking at me, however, I realized just how fanciful that idea was. He had been no closer to admitting any sort of feelings for me than he had been before my announcement. Rudolph Nelson was correct in his assessment that Arthur Ashford would always do the right thing for his title, and not for the matters of his own heart.

"You don't want me to return to London because you worry what I'll tell Garretty," I said, and Arthur had such a violent reaction to that statement that I knew I'd hit the nail on the head, his head snapping towards me from where he'd been pointedly staring at the wall. "I have no desire to tell him a thing about you, Arthur. I am not a snake in the grass here."

Arthur continued to stare at me, and when he spoke it was now his turn for ice-cold words, his tone more dismissive than I had heard it until now. "If that is what you want to believe of me, then fine," he said. "I think you a rat who would go crawling back to your mentor and expose whatever family secrets you've dredged up, Thomas. Is that what you would like to hear? That I still think of you the way I thought when you first arrived? If it pleases you, I can be that man."

I was momentarily stunned, speech failing me as I looked at him. This was not a man who was speaking out of genuine dislike or a desire to wound; I had seen it in clients before. This was a man who was putting a wall back up, a wall that I had painstakingly dismantled over the last month. "Arthur, no—"

"You've made it quite clear what you think of me, *Mr. Whitmore*," he said, my formal name dripping from his tongue like venom. "That despite my best efforts you still think that I have no use for you. Then don't allow me to disabuse you of that notion." A knock came at the library door, and he turned away from me, his shoulders a tense, cold line. "Have a safe journey."

"Tom, the carriage is ready," Felix said, poking his head in the library; if I had been able to take my eyes off Arthur, I know I would have seen Felix recoil from the tension in the air. "Said your goodbyes?"

I stared at Arthur's back, watching as he returned to his desk. Instead of sitting, he leaned his hands against the wood, head bowed as though in thought, and I had to physically force myself to stop looking, turning to hurry towards the escape Felix had provided from the situation of my own making. The disgusting, creeping guilt worming its way through every single inch of my body would not dissipate, and as I hurried down the stairs towards the carriage that would take me back to London, I found myself wondering if I would ever lay eyes on Ashford Hall—and its beautiful, enigmatic master—again.

# PART TWO—LETTERS

# 10

*Sunday, August 17th, 1851*

*Dear Thomas,*

*Were you friends with Charles the winter our mother died? It was the November I turned eighteen, so you must have been. When she passed, there were dozens, hundreds, millions of things that I desperately wanted to tell her still. The truth about me, who I was and who I have always been. The fear of this title, the anxiety of being responsible for an entire estate, my brother, and all the people in it. It was Felix's idea that I write her letters filled with these unsaid things, and now I suppose I am doing the same for you.*

*I will never send these, of course. As you saw today, I am a coward where it counts. I was, perhaps, on the cusp of admitting that in the last two months you have opened walls that I had long built around myself. I find you intriguing, not only because you refuse to be a sycophant because of my title but also because of you. Just you.*

*For years, I could not understand why Charles was so insistent on your friendship. His other school friends always spoke of you in slightly disdainful tones, as though you were a stray kitten he had found in the rain and insisted on bringing in to warm in his light. When my father met you, he saw what Charles saw and it only made me more certain that they were both being taken in.*

*Imagine my surprise when I saw you, Thomas. You were far different than what I had anticipated, truthfully. I had expected you to be using my brother for his money or his position, and I could not believe that they were unable to see it. But as soon as I met you, I knew that they had been right, and it angered me. I suppose that's why I was so awful to you that first night, why I struggled to change my perspective, but you changed it for me.*

*I wanted to tell you today that I would have you stay at Ashford Hall long after your summer has ended, the thought of losing you to London a terror that I cannot face. In the last few months you have thoroughly worked your way past the wall I so carefully constructed, and yet the words died before I could admit what I felt. I am glad, in the end, that I said nothing, because your accusation that I wanted you to stay solely to prevent you from seeing Louis Garretty cut me so sharply that had you stayed a minute longer, I would have lost my temper completely.*

*I thought I was showing you that my feelings had changed. Yet you made it all too clear that you still see me as the suspicious man I was upon first meeting, and perhaps that is all my own fault. It's clear to me now that I was a fool to have hardened you against me from the start and an even bigger fool to believe that I could have changed that impression in a mere summer. There were moments where I was sure I saw a softness in your eyes that I liked, that I coveted, and yet it seems clear now upon your departure that this was nothing more than the idle fantasies of a man who no longer understands what love looks like.*

*One fortnight and you will come back, even if I have to go to London and beg for you to return.*

# 11

*Tuesday, August 19th, 1851*

*Dear Thomas,*

*I have spent every summer of my life with the same core group of people, and yet after your departure it no longer feels as though they are enough. Charles has been positively miserable, and even the Nelsons are suffering, despite their short acquaintance with you. I am supposed to be working on the last of the invitations for the ball, but I find my thoughts wandering to you against my better judgment, hence this letter so shortly after the last. You must be sad, too, to have been pulled from us so quickly this summer, and I have to admit that the idea of you thinking of me has sparked an imaginative fire in my heart that I long thought I had quelled.*

*I know that Rudolph told you about us, and I cannot fault him for doing so. I was dishonest with you from the onset of your time at Ashford Hall, dishonest through omission, because I saw in your gaze from that very first moment that you thought me attractive. It is a dangerous thing for men like you and I to recognize one another so quickly, and yet I felt the weight of your eyes on me and I knew. It was not the same with Rudolph; my attraction to him and our subsequent affair were a result of years of dancing around one another, and yet with you I knew right away that to capture your attention was no small feat.*

*I do wonder if Rudolph told you as an attempt to warn you away from loving me, which would be prudent. There is a clearcut path that my life must take, the trajectory of who I am meant to be something that simply cannot change, and since I realized what sort of man I am, I have known that my desires are at odds with what is most needed for my title. My father's expectations for me were always high, a necessity of the lordship, and if he knew that I was risking it all for love, the disappointment would kill him all over again.*

*These letters must work both as a documentation of my feelings and a way for me to convince myself that it is not worth it. When you were leaving, I could think of nothing more than keeping you; now that you are gone, I can think of nothing except your absence. Both of these things are a weakness during a time I should be focusing on the diplomacy that comes with hosting a ball, and all I can hope is that my affection for you is a temporary disadvantage, that it will fade as you're gone and as I write.*

*Do you know what effect you had on me? I doubt it, or you would not have left. A man like you strikes me as someone who recognizes the attraction he awakens in people. Or perhaps you've made it as far as you have without knowing your own charisma, but that seems impossible.*

*I have spent long enough today musing on your character, and while it is not out of my system, duty calls. I wonder if confiding in Felix would take away some of this dreadful emotion, but I have little hope. This hunger seems ever present.*

# 12

*Wednesday, August 20th, 1851*

*Dear Charles,*

*My farewell to you was too short and for that I am sorry. I reached London with ease, but before I could properly settle into my house after travel, I was brought to the law offices. As I suspected, it was due to Louis Garretty's influence that the trial was moved up, and I believe that it was because someone told him where I was spending my summer. For now, I am pretending that you and Arthur told me nothing about the blackmail and focusing on the case at hand, although I am concerned that I am unable to hide my expression when Garretty speaks to me. You know as well as anyone that I am hardly a master of emotions.*

*I already miss you and your brother, and I hope that you are not too despondent without me. Two weeks is not that long, and I swore I would be back before the ball. I promised Ida my first two dances and to let her down would be horribly impolite. I fear that this may be my last letter until I return, as the volume of work is quite overwhelming, but it will make our reunion all the better.*

*Please tell Arthur that I didn't mean what I said, and I will talk to him further when I return.*

*Yours fondly,*

*Tom*

13

*Thursday, August 21st, 1851*

*Dear Thomas,*

*How many times can I re-read that sentence?*
*Charles came to me after the mail had arrived yesterday afternoon, and along with the usual notes about business and about the ball there was the envelope from you. I have to give him credit, honestly, as he was more perceptive about how your absence was affecting me than I thought he would be. He opened it in the library with me and we read it together, and that last sentence... it struck me in the heart as true as any arrow.*

*You did not mean what? To accuse me of thinking you a rat? That is already forgiven. I know the sort of man I am, and I know that despite thinking I was doing well, I had not shown you even a glimpse of my true feelings. I believed that day at the pond sufficient, that perhaps you had looked at me and seen the truth then, but I see now that my subtlety was too great. Or did you mean that you should not have bristled when I asked you if you would return in time for the ball? I saw your face in that moment and knew that you had taken it not as I meant it but instead as a slight, as though I expected you to attend only as a show pony and not as a guest I deeply desired to be there.*

*Let me say now that I wanted you there out of an abundance of hunger. I wanted to see you dressed in clothes that I chose for you, wanted to watch you mingle with my guests and astound them with your mere presence. I wanted to take you to the rose garden, slip my hand in yours, admit to you that I was consumed by the idea of kissing you the moment you gazed up at me from the grass in the noon sun.*

*It has been four days since you left and despite my resolve to erase my feelings for you from my heart, it seems that I am unable to be so pragmatic. There, too, is the worry that Charles knows more than he's letting on. Once or twice he has made offhand remarks regarding romantic relationships between men, as though gauging my reaction, and I am afraid of what he would say if he knew that I had coveted you from the first moment.*

*All I can hope is that this madness passes. I keep these letters in my desk drawer to re-read them in the hopes they will prove an effective balm against the sting of this attraction, but so far they have done nothing except make me miss you more. I have never thought myself so weak as I do now.*

# 14

*Sunday, August 24th, 1851*

*Dearest Tom,*

*Something strange has happened, and I wonder if you knew. It seems a recent development, and one that I could not have seen coming, as I would have thought them ill-suited had I not seen it for myself.*

*On Sunday evening, I was out for a walk with Rudolph. I hope you know that nothing happened between us, and he was, in fact, utterly annoying. I'm not even sure what he was speaking of, except that it was nonsensical and hard to follow, and I was getting ready to tell him that I was done with walking and ready to head back to the estate when we heard voices from deeper in the roses. I recognized one immediately as Charles's, but we could not make out who he was talking to until we got a little closer and Ida's became clear as well, albeit much softer than his.*

*My brother was speaking loudly, which is not unusual, but there was a note of passion in his words that caught both Rudolph and myself off guard. Before we could reach the alcove where they were speaking, I pulled Rudolph aside and we stopped for a while and merely listened. The conversation was clearly one that had happened before, but that itself was genuinely startling. A hasty, whispered conversation between myself and Rudolph confirmed what I had already suspected: that neither of us were aware how our siblings felt.*

*Charles was asking Ida to marry him, and while it was obvious that neither of them were truly opposed to the idea, Ida had refused. As we listened, though, her reasoning became clear. She had once been promised to me, as you well know, and with that marriage would come an elevation of her position. Charles could not promise a lordship, and while I believe both of them knew I would provide for them in any way I could, her father had made it clear that she must make up for the loss of me by finding someone of similar status.*

*Rudolph and I slipped away unnoticed, but I am consumed with worry for my brother. Charles is a good man but he has never, to my knowledge, been in love to the point of considering marriage, and from the way he spoke in the garden it seems like he has been pursuing Ida since she called our engagement off.*

*I wonder if he has told you. As a man unconcerned with these silly affairs of class, would you advise him to pursue Ida? Or would you do what I would do, and tell him to forget about it because class is more important than anything else in this echelon of society? I cannot even comfort my own brother, and all I can do is think of what you would say.*

*I desperately miss you and sink more and more into these feelings the longer you are away.*

# 15


*Monday, August 25th, 1851*

*Dear Thomas,*

*We are over halfway through our separation, and I have to admit that I thought by this point I would be cured of this foolish crush. Yet every time I close my eyes, I see your face. I know that you must see the resemblance you have to Rudolph, and you must think that I like you solely because you remind me of him, but the truth is you are so much more beautiful because you lack the arrogance that has defined Rudolph since childhood.*

*I suppose that itself must sound like a lie, but for a man who's been surrounded by the upper class since birth, it has become dreadfully easy to grow exhausted amidst inflated egos and obvious pandering. Do you think that I have heard the truth from anyone in my life beyond my brother? Even Felix tends to hide the truth from me, and yet he is my closest friend. I'm sure this comes across as foolish to you, my problems as a lord nothing compared to a man of your upbringing, and yet I feel so dreadfully certain that you could commiserate with my loneliness that I am comfortable expressing it. How silly is it that I can only tell you of my situation here in these letters, when I know I have no intention of sending them?*

*Nearly every invitation to the ball has been replied to, and at this point we will have dozens of guests in attendance. The idea of handling that sort of pressure is making me quite sick, but Charles swears he will help me to the best of his ability, and Ida promises that she will play lady of the house. And yet....*

*I'm scared.*

*After my father died, I was put in charge of the day-to-day operations of the estate. I have always had a head for this sort of work, and with my upbringing only training me further, I thought it would be a simple enough task. I was not, however, adequately prepared for the reality of the situation: this title requires me to be social, and as I'm sure you've realized, I do not have what it takes. I despise what is asked of me when it comes to engagements like the yearly ball and even what is needed when dealing with the locals.*

*You are bright and smart and quickly able to gain the trust of those around you, while I struggle to show the barest of emotion. It is why Rudolph and I failed so spectacularly, why the idea of making my feelings known to you is so impossible that I have to confine those emotions to these notes. I cannot let myself love you any more than I could have ever let myself love Rudolph.*

*Oh, to be born in a different time where perhaps this would not weigh on me as heavily, but for now I have duties I must attend to and cannot allow myself to be ruined by the man I wish I was.*

*Perhaps I should put an end to these letters, Thomas, because all they are doing is making me mad with things I can't have.*

# 16

*Thomas,*

*You know by now that you are dear to me, or
at least the version of you in my imagination who is
reading these letters as they pile up in my desk drawer
knows it. How pathetic that a man of my standing, a
man of my upbringing, could not make it even three days
without writing one of these missives to someone I am
too cowardly to say all this to in real life. And yet I still
write, and I do so because there is something I've grown
to suspect over the last week or so outside of the obvious
interest in the relationship between Charles and Ida.*

*I told you that at the end of a fortnight, I would
come to London to get you no matter what. I meant it,
and as I was making preparations to leave tomorrow,
Rudolph joined me. Thinking nothing of it, I assumed he
was merely bored when he let me know that he thought
it prudent if I stayed at Ashford Hall, considering how
much remains to be done for the ball. At first, I thought
he was saying it out of concern for how busy I am bound
to be. Taking four days out of my schedule to come and
get you from London is four days less I have to devote
to planning, and yet the idea of spending that time alone
with you seemed a worthy distraction.*

*I was prepared to let Rudolph down easily, inform
him that I wanted nothing more than to take a break
from the estate and be the first person to get to see you,
and yet he told me that he was asking if he could go get
you because you had asked him to do so. I was struck
by a sudden misery, so severe and so overwhelming that*

*I thought I might be sick, and realized for the first time since beginning these letters that perhaps you had never had any interest in me, that I had misinterpreted our last meeting.*

*That perhaps you liked Rudolph better.*

*As a man who had loved Rudolph terribly before, I knew how easy it was to fall for him. I had offered to get you, and in turn, you had turned to Rudolph to save you from that fate. I agreed to let him and hoped against hope that I had concealed my disappointment, but as I write this I am finding myself more distressed than I thought I would be. I deserve it, I think, for not recognizing until the last moment that I liked you as much as I did, but it still stings.*

*However, it's for the best. Rudolph is a good man and will no doubt make an exceptional lover, something I could not promise myself. I have put on hold my designs for the ball and any thought of confession to you; my feelings will have to be kept in these letters, hidden away. I cannot justify to myself the cost of letting you love me when you have someone who would be better.*

*I'm sorry for the wall I will have erected by the time you return. Just know that I've done so because the idea of allowing you to love me when there is someone far more suited to endeavors of the heart is far more selfish than I can ever be. Perhaps that itself is selfish, but I trust Rudolph with your heart more than I trust myself.*

# Part Three—The Autumn Ball

## 17

TWO WEEKS in London at the height of summer had never been the most pleasant time of year for me, and when coupled with the difficult trial I was undertaking at the Old Bailey and the ever-present eye of Louis Garretty, it was truly hellish. Cooped up in my small flat by night, days spent sweltering in court and listening to testimony I knew to be false… it all added up to an itch to return to Ashford Hall and remove myself from the heat and stench of the city and the pressures of the courtroom.

I had thought, however foolishly, that distance from Arthur and Rudolph would make my feelings come into clarity, but with nothing but my client's bid for innocence to keep my mind occupied, I was finding myself increasingly thinking about the two of them. Clarity was coming, but it was veering away from the logical conclusion that Rudolph was a safe choice and instead focusing on Arthur. The fight we'd had before I'd left was sticking in my mind, an impossible situation to undo, and all I could hope was that the sentence I had tacked on to the end of my letter to Charles would open the opportunity for me to make it up to Arthur when I saw him next.

A knock came at the door of my flat, my landlady's voice drifting through the door. "Thomas, love, your carriage has arrived."

A jolt went through me as I finished packing my bag, the memory of the last time I'd spoken to Arthur returning. He had sworn to come and get me after a fortnight himself if that's what it took, and while I hadn't thought him capable at the time, I was now exceptionally concerned that I had Lord Ashford downstairs in a carriage waiting for me. I had just begun to pick up my bags when the door to my room opened and, anticipating my landlady, I spun to meet her.

"Rudolph?" I could barely manage the man's name, my surprise so great. I am ashamed to admit it, but I was struck by a sense of serious disappointment at the sight of him, my desire to see Arthur having outweighed any idea that he might not actually come and get me. Had he not wanted to? Had he sent Rudolph in his stead as some sort of consolation prize? To be honest, I stared at him for far too long before composing myself and managing a pleased smile. "I was sure that Lord Ashford was just going to send one of the footmen to gather me. It's a two-day ride. How could they spare you at the manor?"

"I couldn't wait two days longer to see you," Rudolph said. "Arthur will manage just fine with Ida and Charles there to assist. Did Arthur not send you a letter to let you know?"

"Arthur's sent me no letters," I said. "I've heard from Charles and Felix, although I did receive this." I looked over my desk, finding the ornate invitation I'd received a week ago inviting me to the ball; having verbally confirmed my intent to go, the invitation was unnecessary but touching nonetheless, a souvenir of the first ball I had ever been asked to attend. I held the invitation out to Rudolph and he smiled, reading it over before setting it down back on my desk. "Did he say he was going to write?"

"He mentioned to me the other day that he was writing you a letter to let you know that I'd be picking you up instead but may have decided it was unnecessary since you would, of course, figure it out on your own as soon as I'd arrived." Rudolph leaned towards me, and I braced myself to be kissed again, but instead he took hold of the handle of my bag, lifting it easily and looking me in the eyes. "Make sure you have everything. I doubt you'll be allowed to leave Ashford Hall for the remainder of the summer if Charles has his way. I don't know if I've ever seen a more miserable creature than him these last two weeks."

"Oh, believe me, the volume of letters he's sent me is a study in sorrow," I said, taking one last look around the room before turning my attention back to Rudolph. This time I was caught quite unawares; as I turned my head back to face him, he kissed me on the cheek and rested his forehead against my temple. "Rudolph," I managed, surprised despite knowing full well what he wanted from me. "I never gave you an answer."

"I know," Rudolph said, and when he pulled away, I could read the amusement on his face. "Do you think that would serve to stop me? I have been patient, Tom. Two months of no answer followed by two weeks of separation has left me wanting in more than one way. Have you really paid it no further mind?"

It wasn't that I'd paid it no further mind. If I was being wholly honest, the two months I'd spent at Ashford Hall with the Nelsons prior to my departure had been so pleasant that I hadn't wanted to inadvertently ruin it by swaying one way or another. I knew, however, that I was just as twisted up as I'd been when Rudolph had first admitted his attraction to me. My feelings for Arthur, complicated as they were, seemed to outshine anything I felt for Rudolph, and yet… my stomach had done a flip as soon as his lips had met my cheek, and I was reminded yet again that I had known no companionship since the winter before.

He seemed to read something in my silence and grinned. "You are a fascinating creature," he said, taking a step back with my bag still in his hand. "Come along, Tom. We have a long ride ahead of us. I won't kiss you so suddenly again without your permission."

I followed him after shrugging into my traveling coat, locking my door behind me, and pausing briefly downstairs to thank my landlady and let her know that I would be returning by the end of the month. A carriage was sitting in the street waiting for us, and I was pleased to find that the driver was one of Arthur's footmen I recognized. "Good morning, Harry," I said brightly, and the man's wrinkled face lit up when he saw me.

"Mr. Whitmore!" he said, climbing down from his bench and taking my bag from Rudolph. "What a pleasant surprise. Felix told me that I was picking up an old friend, but I had no idea it was you."

"I'm so glad to see you," I said, shaking his hand. At the time, I wholeheartedly believed that his presence would discourage Rudolph from being so openly flirtatious with me, but I had underestimated how little Rudolph was bothered by the idea of being caught. "I'm sorry you had to make this journey on my account."

"No trouble at all, sir," Harry said, smiling. "I'd much rather fetch you than some of the other ball attendees. You're always pleasant." He set my bag into the cubby underneath the rear seat and patted me on the arm before looking between myself and Rudolph. "We'll be stopping in Marlborough for the night, but we should reach the estate by tomorrow afternoon with good horses."

"No rush," Rudolph said, and the way he said it made me momentarily look at him askance. I had never been faced so blatantly with a man who wanted me as much as Rudolph clearly did, and as little as I thought I was romantically interested in him, his sheer determination was making me reconsider it. Perhaps those feelings were being helped along by the idea of returning to Ashford Hall and seeing Arthur again, the memory of our parting not exactly a pleasant one. I had wounded him deeply, I knew it from the way he had turned his back on me before I left, and I did not think myself capable of repairing what I had so terribly broken. "Come along," he said to me, giving me a hand into the carriage, and once we were safely inside, one of us on each bench, he yawned and lay back on his seat.

We were soon on our way, the carriage rumbling over the cobblestone streets, and I had busied myself with reading through the papers on a case I was going to bring to trial when I returned at the beginning of October when Rudolph spoke. "Did you win?"

"Sorry?" I said, looking up from the papers and looking at him; he was still in repose, his dark eyes closed, but a few brief moments of thinking through the question was enough to tell me how to respond. "My client was found innocent, yes."

"And Garretty?"

"He asked me nothing of note about the Ashford men or about you," I said. "I spoke to him as little as I could and never once hinted that I knew about the blackmail, so whatever suspicions he had must have seemed entirely unfounded." He opened one eye to look at me and I frowned. "What?"

"You must know that Garretty was working alongside James Wright," he said, and I nodded; I'd been told as much when everything had first come to my attention. "So how do you think Garretty heard that you were spending the summer with Arthur to begin with?"

The thought hadn't even occurred to me, but as soon as Rudolph brought it up, I was immediately sure that he was right. "Of course," I said, sitting bolt upright. "He was upset with me when I refused to listen to him, and I'm sure he thinks I'm the reason he was forced to leave to begin with. It makes sense he'd go to Garretty, especially since it's public record that I work for his firm."

Rudolph smiled, dark eyes fixed on mine. "You have to understand the lengths James will go to in order to get a foothold in the Ashford fortune. When Lord Ashford was still alive, he was far more tolerant of James and would pass him money whenever he required it, but Arthur doesn't treat him with the same level of deference, and I think that's what motivated James to carry out the blackmail in the first place."

"Why is he so hellbent on Arthur's fortune?" I asked. "I thought he came from means himself."

"He does, but his older brother has always been sickly, and there was quite a bit of speculation that he wouldn't survive to take their father's title. His health has improved quite drastically over the past five years and as a result, James has been shut out from the title, first by his brother's ascension and again by the birth of his nephew. He's a man obsessed with living beyond his means, and his family allowance and his payment from the military is meager compared to what he thinks he deserves. When Arthur's father was alive, that money helped to support his lifestyle, but with his death he's had to rein in his spending." He paused, crossing his arms across his chest and leaning his head back against the small window behind him. "There are rumors he's accumulated a lot of debt and is unwilling, or unable, to begin paying that debt off."

I considered this, although my view of the situation was understandably biased. I had never come from means the way that Rudolph was speaking of; everything I had was something I had worked impossibly hard to gain, and the idea of spending so above my income that I was willing to blackmail to make up for the difference was absolutely antithetical to the way I approached my own finances. My view was colored, too, by a sincere dislike of James, everything that had come to light since his visit to Ashford Hall having left me entirely prejudiced against him. "So he concocts this poaching case, which I will assume was a ploy to get a lawyer into Ashford Hall to find—or manufacture—a scandal to use for blackmail. Garretty finds the letters you and Arthur sent one another, and the blackmail begins… with Garretty the intermediary, not the actual instigator. Did Arthur pay anything?"

"No, Ida intervened before Arthur could capitulate," Rudolph said. "I don't think James, or Garretty for that matter, was anticipating an outsider being the one to intervene and undo their work, but I wouldn't be surprised if the failure of their blackmail plot has left their relationship more tenuous than it already was. They have no personal loyalty, only financial, and without money to tie them together, well…. It seems to me like they would become more desperate."

It made sense, the idea that a pair of men who had already agreed to engage in blackmail together would find themselves at odds once their scheme fell apart, and yet it also left a door open that I had not previously considered. "If their blackmail failed the first time, then they must be looking for a chance to try it again."

"Exactly," Rudolph said, stretching his legs out on the seat and tilting his head to look at me. I had already noticed his good looks, unable to ignore them when comparing his face to my own, but in the soft light seeping through the carriage windows, it was impossible to ignore how handsome he was. I wondered if his interest in me was genuine or, as I had suspected since that night he had kissed me, if it was predicated more on the thrill of the chase than an actual romantic interest. "I know I've warned you off of Arthur for selfish purposes, but I believe wholeheartedly that James will want nothing more than to use your presence at Ashford Hall for another attempt at blackmail. If Arthur allows himself to fall into that trap—"

"I'm not a trap," I said, incensed at the idea that I had stumbled into this blackmail plot with nothing but innocence. "And I told you before that Arthur has no interest in me beyond the most basic curiosity. The man has never spent any significant time with someone of my upbringing, and he enjoys asking me questions, that's all."

Rudolph closed his eyes again, clearly intending to take a nap as soon as this conversation with me was finished. "Is that truly what you believe?" he asked. "That his curiosity is merely professional? Would you say, also, that I like you only because you are of a lower class?"

"No, you've made it clear to me that you find me attractive, for whatever reason, although I doubt your intentions quite seriously."

He laughed softly through his nose. "Is that so? Well, then, you may assume that Arthur has made it clear to me that he finds you attractive, although he would never in his life admit as much without being pressed to do so. Now, I've brought this all up not to alarm you, but to ensure that you understand what you are returning into. And, I suppose, to warn you that James will be at the ball."

"What?" I asked, thoroughly alarmed despite his caveat. "Why?"

"The amount of trouble it would cause to remove him from the guest list outweighs the annoyance of him being there." He shrugged, turning his head towards the back of his seat. "Now, we have quite the journey ahead of us. I'd suggest you get some sleep and think this over, but I'll be happy to talk it over once I've had a nap."

With that, he fell asleep quite rapidly, and I returned to my papers, chewing absently on my thumbnail as I considered everything he had told me. To be caught up in a blackmail plot was exceedingly unpleasant, but I had become aware of something even more unpleasant: I was more pleased by Rudolph's insistence that Arthur was attracted to me than I was upset by the idea of inadvertently contributing to the troubles with James Wright. There were a hundred different emotions swirling unchecked in my chest, from anger at what James was putting the Ashford men through to joy that Arthur was apparently interested enough in me to make it obvious to Rudolph, but as I sat with those feelings another one arose, a guilt that burned at the back of my throat.

I looked across the carriage at Rudolph, who was snoring softly and clearly fast asleep, and recognized that he had been nothing but honest with me from the beginning. His attraction to me was clear, and yet here I was fixated entirely on another man, and I could not even claim that it was because my own attraction was negligible. I found Rudolph handsome, felt those small yet undeniable sparks of interest that, in a different setting, would have been all I needed to act upon my attraction. I had done more with other men for less, and I was left to wonder if it was my loyalty to the idea of Arthur that had kept me from acting upon my attraction to Rudolph or if I was genuinely uninterested.

# 18

"WHAT MISERABLE weather," Rudolph said, standing at the window of our shared inn room as he stared out at the ink-black night. The rain had started about halfway to Marlborough, a downpour that had left the roads muddy and treacherous and had cast a decidedly unpalatable light over our journey. At Ashford Hall, the rain made things cozy and calm, the drum of water on the ancient roof a balm for any insomnia a man could be struggling with, but at an unfamiliar inn with company that I had spent all day deep in thought about, I was finding my inability to go for a quick, head-clearing walk an annoyance. "I hope it clears up by the morning."

"That would be ideal," I said, sitting on the edge of my bed as I unlaced my boots. We had left Harry with the horses, and I was looking forward at least to a good dinner and the decent night's sleep I was sure to get despite… well, despite my continued uncertainty regarding Rudolph. What had happened in the morning had left me with more questions than I thought possible, not only because of my role in James's ongoing attempts to infiltrate the Ashford fortune but because I was finding it more and more difficult to deny the physical attraction I had to Rudolph despite my lack of romantic feelings.

I was, contrary to how this memoir may make it seem, not much of a romantic at this time in my life. To that point, I had engaged in a string of dalliances with men who were of like mind, who recognized that the pursuit of true romance was far riskier than one-night love affairs in inns that catered specifically to a clientele like myself. Before Arthur, I had made peace with a life of acting only on this attraction, and despite my feelings for the lord it was a difficult habit to shake, particularly when faced with Rudolph. If I had met him in one of those smoky gentleman's clubs inhabited by my kind, it would have been easy to take him as he was, but in this situation…. I had the rest of the summer to spend with this man, and if he was interested in me above and beyond mere sex, using him for just that would only complicate a matter that already felt so complex.

Blackmail, too, was weighing on my mind as I finished taking my boots off, setting them beside my bed and looking at Rudolph's back. He was standing with his hands in the pockets of his trousers, his coat draped over a nearby chair, and in only a light traveling shirt I could see the muscles of his shoulder through the fabric. I could see his reflection in the window, his dark eyes gazing outside before he abruptly looked at me, a smile twitching on his lips. "Mr. Whitmore, please," he said, turning away from the window and taking a step towards me. "What could you possibly be staring at me for?"

"I'm thinking," I said, looking up at him, my fingers digging into the edge of the bed where I sat. "You know, don't you?"

"Know what?" He was right in front of me now, and I was all too aware that I was moments away from opening a door that I couldn't close, a Pandora's box that would color the rest of my summer. There were two reasons why I was considering this: first, to get it out of my system, and second, because I wanted to prove to myself that even considering this in the first place was a result of physical attraction and nothing more. "We've already deduced that I know you're a sodomite."

"That's not what I mean," I said, even though I knew full well that he was trying to bait me into admitting my attraction. I didn't care anymore, not really, because I felt deeply that Rudolph was not the sort of man to hold it against me. Everything he had done to this point had been mostly teasing, not malicious, and as irritating as it tended to be, I doubted that if I told him the truth he would do much worse than make fun of me for the rest of the summer. "You know that I find you handsome."

"Everyone finds me handsome," Rudolph said, and he was abruptly kneeling on the edge of my bed, a hand resting on the side of my throat as his thumb pushed my chin up so I was looking at him. "But do you find me handsome in a way that makes you want to act on it?"

"If we had met under different circumstances, yes," I said, my eyes meeting his dark gaze, a thrill going down my spine. "But you... well, *this*, feels like a betrayal. I can't change how I feel about Arthur the same way you can't change how you feel about me."

"And how do I feel about you?" he murmured, a dangerous note in his voice.

"Stop asking me questions," I said, my own tone dropping to match his. "You need to understand how seriously I'm taking this. I have no desire to hurt you, nor do I have any desire to prevent what could be a perfectly good friendship between us by saying the wrong thing."

"Friendship," Rudolph echoed, a thoughtfulness in his voice that I was unaccustomed to in a man who was constantly treating everything with a great degree of flippancy. "Why is it when you look at me you see friendship and not more?"

I looked at him, took in his dark features that mirrored my own, considered what he was asking. "I think it's Arthur," I said finally. "I think that has colored everything else around me, if I'm being honest with you."

He sighed and let go of my jaw, twisting a little so he could sit down on the edge of my bed alongside me. The tension had gone out of the room now, and I realized that I had successfully defused the situation; the decision I had just made was the one that Rudolph was prepared to accept. I realized a few moments too late that I had genuinely thought about kissing him and was glad that the madness had passed. "I thought you would be more logical than this."

"Normally I am," I admitted. I had never encountered a situation before where I was acting on pure emotion, and it was unsettling that it was happening now. After all, I was in a position now where I had no idea whether Arthur shared even a tenth of my emotions, and yet I was willing to throw away a perfectly good chance at an affair just for the opportunity to show Arthur that I was serious about him. "You said before that you thought Arthur was fond of me, but when I left… I said some things that I can see now would have only hurt him. Did he confide in you?"

"He won't confide in me, not about this," Rudolph said, leaning back on his hands. I wondered if this was part of being in my thirties, passing up a perfectly beautiful man for the mere possibility of another, and tamped down that feeling; I was beyond the point of being able to doubt myself. "When our relationship ended, we made a promise to one another that we would keep our romantic lives private, both to guard against future blackmail attempts and to spare each other any sort of pain. Everything I've said to you until now has been based solely on intuition, but…."

"But?"

"He's been writing you letters," Rudolph said, confusion rocketing through me at the words. I hadn't received a single letter from Arthur, unless I counted the invitation, and yet Rudolph made it sound like he'd written more than one. "He claims he wasn't, but I caught sight of one when I took lunch with him one day. It absolutely had your name at the top." He looked at me, brow furrowed. "What has he been writing you?"

"I wasn't lying to you in London," I said, shaking my head. "I didn't receive a single letter from him while I was away. Whatever he's been writing, he hasn't been sending me."

"Interesting," Rudolph said, but for me it was far more than interesting. If Arthur had been writing me letters and not sending them, what could possibly be his motivation? The thought of unsent letters sitting in his library, some sort of testament to the state I had left him in, filled me with an anticipatory fear, an anxiety that he was aware of my feelings and was so upset by them that he found himself needing to journal them away. As though figuring out where my thoughts had led me, Rudolph turned to face me. "Did you know Charles when their mother died?"

"Yes," I said. We had known one another for a year at that time, awkward youths of fourteen when his mother had passed away, and I remembered being in our dormitory when the messenger had come to deliver the news. She had been sick, we had known that much, but death had not seemed possible. He was changed after her death; Charles had never been a man I would accuse of being mature, but there was a seriousness in his nature that had not existed before that winter. I would catch him in these fits at times, staring out a window or focusing on some spot in the wall, and would know that it was because the thoughts of his mother were too strong to allow him to exist entirely in the present at the time. "I remember it better than I thought I would."

"If Charles was affected, think of Arthur, too. He was a misery, honestly, and he was having trouble coping. We were fresh to university at the time, and it was hard to see him, but it was Felix who came up with a remedy. He was to write letters to his mother as though he were just telling her how university was going, and it did seem to help. I think being able to pretend she was alive, even if it was just for the amount of time it took him to write a letter, was a balm to his soul. If he's taken up the habit again… well, that tells me that your departure was weighing on him quite heavily."

I sighed, tilting my head back to look at the water-stained ceiling of the inn. "Before I left, he accused me of returning to Garretty with news of more blackmail," I said. "Or, rather, I put those words in his mouth. I told him I was sure that he was angry with me for leaving only because he thought of the detriment to his reputation that could come from my confidence in Garretty, and I could see that I had hurt him so badly with my words, but I didn't try to fix it. I just fled."

"You and Arthur are far more alike than I think you know," Rudolph said. "All I'll say to you on the subject further is that you need to talk to him when you return, because the thought of having you dance around one another like this during the damned autumn ball is terribly annoying." Before he could speak further, a brief knock came at the door of our room and Rudolph got to his feet, answering it to find the wife of the inn's owner.

"Dinner is ready, if you gentlemen are prepared," she said, smiling. "It'll be downstairs when you'd like it."

The evening that followed was more pleasant than I had anticipated. Dinner was surprisingly good, if a little rich, and I found that now that Rudolph and I had cleared the air with one another we had quite a bit in common. A solid friendship was at the very beginning stages now that the initial attraction had been dealt with, and he proved himself a witty conversationalist and well-versed on a variety of topics. After dinner, we retired back to our room, chatted for a while longer, and when time came to sleep, I was well-satisfied with both food and conversation.

My relationship with Rudolph now on substantially better footing, the night passed without incident, the morning spent with a good breakfast while the horses were prepared. By nine, we were underway again, and I spent the better part of the journey absorbed in my work while Rudolph alternated between naps and reading a novel that he was keen to tell me the plot of. On the whole, I reached Ashford Hall with a sense of belonging that had not existed the last time I'd made the journey.

As soon as we'd crossed the threshold into the estate lands, I became aware of the sound of another set of hoofbeats alongside the carriage. I leaned forward in my seat and pulled back the curtain that hid the window on the door, having pulled it across to give Rudolph a darker environment for his sleep, and was greeted by the sight of Charles on the other side, keeping easy pace with our carriage on his own mare. Startled, I let out a small cry of surprise and Rudolph opened his eyes, sitting up in his seat. "What's wrong?"

"Charles," I said, unlatching the window and pushing it open, the warmth of the late summer air entering the carriage as I did. "What are you doing?"

"I came to greet you!" he called back, and I could tell by his grin that he was pleased with himself for having managed to catch us so quickly into the Ashford forest. "Rudy said before he left when he thought he'd be back, and I decided I would wait for you. You have no idea what sort of melancholy we've all been in since you left, Tom!"

"Melancholy?" I echoed, laughing. "I hardly think it was as serious as you make it sound."

"Quite the opposite! Take the misery you're imagining and multiply by ten—no, a hundred!"

"He's exaggerating," Rudolph said from where he had returned to leaning against his seat, stifling a yawn. "We missed you, of course, but none of us were lying about in terrible sorrow because you weren't there. Besides, we had quite the nice visit from some of Ida's friends. That was a good distraction."

"Just because there were beautiful women to distract me from Tom's absence does not mean I didn't spend every day in abject despair," Charles said, keeping his leisurely pace alongside the carriage, Harry having slowed down to make sure Charles's horse was not at a full-out trot. "You were quite spot-on about your timing, Rudy."

"Harry's an excellent footman," Rudolph called back. "Always quite prompt. Are you going to follow us the entire way to the manor?"

"I was planning on it," Charles said. "Am I disturbing you?"

"Always," Rudolph said. "I was sleeping before you appeared."

Charles rolled his eyes before looking at me. "Did you get your invitation?" he asked. "For the ball. It's quite soon."

"I did get it. Will I not be let in if I don't have it with me?"

"Hm, I don't actually know," Charles said thoughtfully. "By the way, I took the liberty of ordering you a suit for the ball using one of the outfits you left behind for measurements."

My eyes went wide, and I leaned towards him, touched in a way that surprised me. When Charles and I had first become friends, he had made an overly grand display of buying me a new sweater, the price of which left me frankly stunned, and it had very nearly put an end to our budding relationship. Over the years, he had learned to keep his shows of affection to the more modestly priced, but I was touched by the fact that he had undoubtedly noticed that I had nothing nice enough for a ball. "You ordered me an entire suit, Charles?" I asked, unable to hide my surprise and delight at the news. "I was going to do that as soon as I'd determined what the theme was."

"Oh, I told Arthur not to tell you so I could ensure that I was able to order it instead," Charles said, sounding pleased with himself. "It should be delivered next week. I hope you're not offended, but I had noticed that you didn't have anything appropriate and thought I would do you a favor since you've been working on the poaching case for Arthur."

"I appreciate it," I said, struck again by how things that would have been impossible for me to accept at the beginning of the summer were now effectively run of the mill experiences. I was ingratiating myself into a class that I had very little experience with, and in doing so I was setting myself up, unintentionally, for the greatest fall I would take in my life. As we approached the estate, I reminded myself of what Rudolph had advised—to try and make things up to Arthur—and I hoped that he would be as thrilled by my reappearance as Charles clearly was.

We pulled up to the front steps and, unsurprisingly, Ida was waiting to meet us. She hurried down the steps and caught Rudolph in a hug almost as soon as he'd stepped out of the carriage, squeezing him briefly before turning to me. She hugged me as well, her slim arms squishing me around the middle, and when she pulled back, she was beaming at me. "Has Charles been regaling you with his misery on your ride in, Thomas?"

"He has indeed," I said, rolling my eyes. "According to him, he's been confined to his chambers weeping since I was away. He looks remarkably hale, however."

"Strange how that happened," Ida said, laughing as she let go of my waist and looked towards the manor. "Arthur has been cooped up in his library preparing for the ball, but he told me to let you know to come and say hello once you'd arrived. To be perfectly honest, I think he's pleased that you've returned."

So, Arthur had manufactured a reason for me to meet him one-on-one, without any of the others around to disrupt our reunion. I knew that this was either a way for us to fight or make up, and I was determined to have it be the latter, determined not to allow my foolishness to get in the way of the rest of my summer and the beginning of my autumn. I would not give up on this, would make things right if it killed me, and did not want to waste another moment without letting Arthur know that I had not betrayed his trust nor did I think him suspicious of me. "Thank you, Ida," I said, smiling at her. "If you see Felix, can you let him know I'm happy to be back? I have to clear something up with Arthur straight away."

With that, I hurried up the front steps and into the estate, unaware—at least consciously—that the entire course of my life was about to change.

19

THE LIBRARY was, as always, a few degrees cooler than the rest of the house, due in part to Arthur's insistence that no fires be lit in order to keep the books safe from any soot. I let myself in quietly and was unsurprised to find that Arthur was sitting at his desk, although when he looked up there was something in his eyes that I couldn't begin to recognize. "You're back," he said, and my joy at seeing him was quickly replaced by a chill as I realized he had erected those walls around him once again in my absence. "I hope your time with Rudolph was elucidating."

"With Rudolph?" I echoed, and the pieces began to fall slowly into place, a realization that I had been terribly delayed in making. "You knew?"

"Knew what?" Arthur said, with a slightly smug tone in his voice that sounded as though he thought he'd lured me into a trap.

"I think you and I should be honest with one another," I said, approaching his desk and resting my fingertips on the wood lightly. "We left with some enmity, didn't we? And you've clearly had time to ruminate on it. I don't like that, not one bit."

He looked at me coolly before getting to his feet, leaning his own hands on the desk. He wasn't that much taller than me, but as he tilted his head towards me, I could see why people found him intimidating. "What did I know, Thomas?"

"That Rudolph is attracted to me," I said, unflinching. "That's why you sent him to pick me up instead of coming yourself."

"I did not send him," Arthur said. "He offered to come and get you, and I allowed him to do so. I thought it was in the best interest of everyone. After all, the way we parted didn't make me believe you'd have wanted to see me there instead."

"Is that what you think?" I asked, digging my fingertips into the desk in a failing attempt to keep myself placid. "Did you not consider that I was waiting two weeks in the hope that you would be the one who fetched me from London? So you know that Rudolph was attracted to me, and you assumed that I wanted him in return."

For the first time, his smugness faltered, his green eyes suddenly growing serious. "But you kissed him."

I furrowed my brow, frowning. "How do you know that?"

"Felix saw you," Arthur said, and another piece of the puzzle was solved as a result. "In the gardens."

"It never occurred to you that perhaps he kissed *me* with no action on my part?" I asked, although I was tiring quickly of having to ask question after question to lead Arthur to the truth. By the look in his eyes it was clear he hadn't considered this, and I studied him closely before sighing and pushing away from the desk. "If, perhaps, I'd met Rudolph under different circumstances, a case could be made for romance. But I did not meet him under different circumstances, and I'd already come to know you before I met him. If you're too dense to understand that, then—"

While making my case, I had turned my back to him and begun to make my way to the library doors, intent on leaving since he did not seem interested in seeing reason. Before I could make it more than a few steps, though, he had caught hold of my wrist and spun me around, and the look in his eyes sent a wave of lust through me that culminated in my stomach lurching as though tugged on by an invisible string. "You have no idea what you've just said," he finally murmured, every muscle coiled as tight as a snake, as though he was desperately attempting to keep his composure. "You aren't attracted to Rudy because you met me first? What sort of nonsense is that? Have you not seen enough of me to realize what a perfectly dreadful man I am?"

"Dreadful?" I grabbed the collar of his shirt, gripping the fabric tight in my fist and yanking him towards me, knowing full well I was standing on a precipice that I could not very easily avoid falling from if I continued down this path. "What are you talking about? You're the furthest thing from dreadful, and the fact of the matter is I have no more romantic attraction to Rudolph than I have to Charles. Frankly, I—"

But I was prevented from finishing that sentence when Arthur, who had been looking at me with a growing madness in his gaze, lurched forward and kissed me so hard on the mouth I was immediately surprised he hadn't drawn blood. Stunned by his impulsivity but otherwise suffering from similarly inflamed passions, I kept my grip in his shirt and kissed him back. His mouth tasted like tobacco and tea, and if I had been expecting some demure show of affection, I was certainly proven wrong. It seemed two weeks had been the catalyst he needed to realize his feelings for me, although I would be lying if I pretended I hadn't undergone a similar transformation, a fortnight of absence after months together just enough time to give me clarity.

I had closed my eyes as soon as his lips were on mine, and I kept them closed for a few seconds after he'd pulled away, afraid that I would open them to find that he had rapidly realized he did not enjoy what he'd just done. Instead, when I opened them I found that he had not pulled back, and was instead looking at me closely, the intensity in his eyes enough to take my breath away. We stared at each other for a moment before he spoke, his voice barely more than a whisper. "I swore to myself… I swore I would leave you be. I swore that once you returned, I would keep these feelings locked away. And yet you've been here for less than five minutes and…."

"Why do you feel like you need to keep these things locked away?" I asked, twisting my fingers further in his shirt to prevent him from trying to pull away. In response, he dropped his forehead against mine, gripping my wrist with one hand and the edge of the desk with the other. "Arthur."

"Rudy is the only person I've let myself love," he said. "And it ended in disaster. You are my brother's childhood friend from a class several steps below my own. Even if you weren't a man, the feelings I have for you can only end in things far worse than blackmail."

"You don't know that for sure, and if you don't allow yourself to take the very first steps, you don't allow yourself to know how things end," I said. "I'm only here for the summer, Arthur. This does not need to carry over beyond that if you don't want it to." Even as I said it, I knew that it wasn't something Arthur was capable of; while I may have indulged in casual dalliances, I could not imagine Arthur doing the same.

"You're saying we just… have sex," he said, and just hearing the word come from his lips made my mouth go dry. "Felix has suggested the same thing before. Not with you, mind, but to take my mind off of Rudy. The prospect of allowing a stranger in my bed is not something I could stomach." Disappointment flooded me until he continued, an undertone in his voice that told me everything I needed to know about his decision. "But you aren't a stranger."

At this point, I will freely admit that I was being selfish. After having kissed him, I did not want to scare him away, did not want to forget the feeling of his fingers on my bare skin or his mouth on my own. I was not thinking about his feelings or his position in life, was not considering what this would do to Charles if he found out what I was doing with his brother. Everything was self-serving, and I did not care if I could only have him for a few more weeks before I returned to London and fell out of his story.

To have him for any amount of time was enough.

"I'm not a stranger," I agreed. "Felix is undoubtedly right, Arthur. And when will you get this chance again? A man in your house, willingly offering this to you… and with a time limit."

Arthur looked at me, and I could see that he did not fully believe me, that he knew what I was trying to pull. But he didn't say anything, and his grip on my wrist tightened, his other hand moving to the top button of my shirt. "You've done this before? Had… temporary lovers?"

"Yes," I admitted, my breath hitching in my throat as he forced the button through the hole, smooth fingers slipping into my shirt and over my collarbone. "There are clubs in London for men like us. If you want something, you can get it there."

"I see," Arthur said, thumb pressing to the side of my throat, my blood thrumming in my veins. "And you didn't want that with Rudolph, just me."

"I explained it to Rudolph already. He knows why I chose you."

"Even if you have to give me up in a month?"

I did not tell him that I would do anything to have him for a night, much less a month. "Are you not attracted to me?"

He let out a soft huff, almost a laugh. "Can you not tell?" I did not respond and he sobered, searching my face. "Can you really not tell?"

"Arthur," I said, briefly overwhelmed by a moment of sheer amazement at his apparent inability to see how I might be unable to read his mind. "The only reason I had the slightest inkling that you may have any interest in me is because Rudolph insisted it was the case. Before that, I was merely… well, hoping, I suppose."

"No," Arthur said. "I find you horribly attractive and the conflict it awoke in me…." He swallowed, the warmth of his hand on my bare skin sending fire through my every nerve. "Thomas. I cannot give you what you want."

"I will take whatever I can get," I said, and I kissed him again, drawing him down towards me and dragging my tongue over his lower lip. He kissed back, his breath soft against my cheek as he sighed out through his nose, and I could have had him right then and there in the library had the sound of one of the heavy oak doors opening not torn us away from one another. Arthur moved with a rapidity I had not expected from him, flitting back around to the chair at his desk and sitting in it just as Felix came around the bookshelf that blocked where we were standing from sight. "Felix!" I said with the most delight I could muster despite how shaken I was at the moment. "I've missed you dreadfully."

"And I've missed you," Felix said, and he looked at me briefly, searching my face before apparently deciding that whatever he saw there was not worth pursuing at the moment. "Dinner is ready, if you're both hungry. It's just something cold and small to tide everyone over." He raised an eyebrow at me. "Your suite is ready as well. I'll stop by tonight to make sure everything has been set up to your liking."

I knew enough to realize that he was expecting to be told what had happened between myself and Arthur, and to be perfectly honest I wanted to tell him, finding the idea of hiding it from someone who knew me as well as Felix did quite miserable. "I look forward to it," I said, and he nodded, giving Arthur a look as well before leaving the library. The moment the door closed again, Arthur looked up from the letters he was pretending to read. I looked at him in return, my lips tingling as I remembered how it had felt to have his there, and managed a lopsided smile. "I suppose we should go to dinner."

He got to his feet, coming around the desk once again and taking my chin in his hand as though inspecting me. "When we leave this room, Thomas, I'm not sure if I can act as though I haven't kissed you."

"You have to," I said, and I leaned forward, resting my forehead briefly against his collarbone, breathing in the scent of him. "I'd like to take a walk with you this evening, if it's all the same to you."

"A walk," he murmured, his breath hot against the shell of my ear, a chill going down my spine. "I'd like that. I'd like that quite a bit. And…." He paused, and I felt his fingers toying with the tail of my traveling coat, plucking gently at the fabric. "If you'd like to tell Felix, you may."

"How—"

"I know he told you about me in the first place," Arthur said. "He trusts you, and I trust him. If you need a confidant, you could not ask for better. He won't tell another soul." He sighed, and I knew that there was tension coiled beneath his skin, knew that he was holding himself back. I recalled what Rudolph had told me—that Arthur would never allow himself to be wholly comfortable with me—and knew that I had made a Faustian bargain in agreeing to this time-limited relationship. He would never grow comfortable with me, and I would never have the time to show him that he could, but in return I at least got a chance. A man needed an outlet, and I was more than happy to provide it. "Let's go eat, then. I will do my best to contain myself around the others."

It turned out to be a non-issue. Arthur outside of the library was much the same as he had always been. Dinner passed with good company, both of the Nelsons seemingly pleased to have me back and Charles obviously as thrilled as could be. The only appreciable difference in Arthur's attitude now and his attitude prior was that at one point during dinner he took my hand under the table, squeezing it tightly as though gaining some sort of emotional strength from the act. The idea of Arthur—stoic, put-together, aloof—wanting to hold my hand left me dizzy, and it suddenly became difficult to hold my fork, but aside from that brief interlude there was little to worry about in terms of our companions discovering what had transpired since we'd arrived that afternoon.

It wasn't until after dinner when we were preparing to move to the parlor, Ida having received some new sheet music she was eager to show off, that Rudolph caught me by the arm and held me back from the others. "You kissed him," he said, an accusation and not a question, and though I looked at him in surprise, I know that he was not convinced. "*Thomas.*"

"It's more like he kissed me," I said quietly, cheeks flushing at the memory of his mouth on mine. "We were arguing, and then he just kissed me. Does he… do that?"

"I told you last night that you needed to talk to him," Rudolph said, still holding my arm gently. "As much as I hope the two of you can work things out, I have my concerns. I don't think Arthur can give you what you want, Tom."

If I had taken the time then to think about it, if I had truly stopped to soak in those words, I would have agreed in a moment. I knew that Arthur, as he was, could not let himself love me. But the idea of passing up the opportunity to have him pretend, even if it was just for a month… I could not bear it. "He said as much," I admitted. "That he would give me until I had to return to London."

He looked at me, and there was something almost pitying in his gaze. "Do you want this?"

"I've done this before," I said. "Had affairs that have not lasted long."

"With men like Arthur?"

I looked at him in return, baleful. "You know the answer is no."

"I'm happy for you, but I'm also just worried," Rudolph said, moving to pat me gently on the cheek. "If it comes down to it, don't let him break your heart, that's all."

"I won't," I said and moved to follow him up the hall towards the parlor, unaware that I had just made a promise I couldn't possibly keep.

# 20

We spent a pleasant evening in the parlor, alternating between playing games—Charles, unsurprisingly, was excellent at charades, but so was his brother—and taking turns at the piano. Ida had a lovely voice and a keen interest in playing, and I was a capable replacement when she wanted to give her fingers a rest. By midnight we had easily re-established the camaraderie that we had enjoyed before I'd left for London and slowly trickled off to our rooms, each of us a little further in our cups than we had meant to be at the beginning of the night.

Having exchanged a brief look with Arthur as we parted, I did not head for my suite but rather for the door that would take me out to the garden. I found him waiting at the archway that led into the hedges, the late-summer blooms of the flowers almost pearlescent in the moonlight, and when he saw me, something almost like a smile flicked at the corner of his lips. "I wasn't sure if the look I gave you would be enough," he said. "You're quite perceptive."

"I try my best," I said, and as I approached him, he turned and walked into the garden. We walked in relative silence for a while, and while I am no mind reader, I knew he was doing his best to ensure that we would not be caught if one of our companions decided they were also in need of some air. We stepped into an open area, a fountain in the middle surrounded by benches, and I followed him to one of them, settling myself on the cool marble. I could not help but wonder if this was a trick he did with Rudolph, if the two of them had sat on this very bench in this same sort of silence.

"Thomas—" he said.

At the same time, I turned to him and said, "Arthur, do—"

I laughed, unable to help it, and he took my hand tightly in his own as though not seizing it right then and there would be utter madness. "What were you going to ask?"

"If you wanted to continue where we left off," I said, searching his face and finding that he was looking at me with his usual intensity, albeit for a different reason. Now that I knew his true feelings, I was no longer intimidated by the fierceness in his eyes. Still, the warning Rudolph had given me was ringing in my ears, and as much as I wished I could forget it, I could not. I had agreed to let things run their course over the summer, but some silly, naive part of my brain was convinced that I could change his mind.

Having never had a long-term relationship before, much less any sort of real romance, I was still a fool when it came to expectations. I looked at Arthur in that moment and thought I could change him, and I wonder now if he was looking at me in return and wondering the same. Instead of speaking, however, he raised his free hand and took my chin in his grasp. Arthur closed the distance between us, his lips solid against my own, and in no time at all he was kissing me with a fervor I simply didn't know he was capable of.

I parted my lips to allow him better access, his tongue slick and hot against my own, and I soon found that his hand, which had been holding my own, was now gripping the outside of my right thigh. Instinctively I shifted to meet his touch, the cool night air sending goose bumps crawling over my skin even as he let go of my chin. He undid the top button of my shirt and I pulled back, recognizing that we were now at the same point where we had been interrupted earlier. He seemed unconcerned with being caught, and the madness that had clearly overtaken him was contagious, so that I only realized the danger of the situation in the aftermath; at the time, being found seemed secondary to having him before he changed his mind. He considered me briefly, searching, before he leaned back in. Mouth on the sensitive skin of my throat, he continued to undo my shirt, leaving my bare chest exposed to whatever ministrations he desired.

His slim fingers slid over my left nipple, a thrill going through me at the touch, the sensitive skin stiffening at the merest sensation. I gripped his shoulder with one hand, pressing my face against his blond hair and breathing in his scent. His hair was slightly perfumed, his curls soft against my skin, and I could think of no one I had ever taken to bed before who filled me with such a strong feeling of hunger. I was no saint, but Arthur Ashford made me desirous of things I had never lusted after before.

I let my free hand go to his waist, my breathing soft as his mouth moved lower, teeth scraping against my collarbone in a way I knew was meant to leave a bruise on my dark skin. He forced my shirt back over one shoulder, briefly raising his head to look at me. His mouth was pink, lips slightly swollen, and he pressed his thumb against my chest with a little more insistence. "Look at you," he said, and there was something in his voice that made every inch of my body thrill with desire. Under his touch, I felt almost virginal. "Do you know I dreamt about this the first night you were here?"

"Dreamt about undressing me in the garden?" I asked, pulling him into another kiss as he pushed my shirt over my shoulders. I helped him remove it, shrugging it off so I could lay it over one arm of the bench, and he quickly moved to unlace my trousers. I was half-anticipating him to stop at this point so when he hoisted my legs up into his arms in order to fully pull the linen down over my ass and ankles I let out a small yelp of surprise, grabbing his shoulder to keep myself steady.

"Did I frighten you?" he asked, pulling my pant leg down over my right boot but leaving them hanging from my left ankle; in this state of mostly undress I was at his mercy, and the thought was titillating. "I would not let anything happen, I swear it."

"I know, I just wasn't expecting it," I said, struck momentarily by the darkness of his green eyes in the full moonlight. Absently, I twisted my fingers in his hair and he tilted his head to meet the touch, briefly allowing his eyes to close. I swept my thumb under his eye and over his cheekbone, and he looked at me again, tightening his grip on my thighs and forcing my legs back so my knees were nearly touching my chest. The next moment, he had slid off the bench onto his knees before me, twisting me on the bench so I was exposed to him, only the thin layer of my underclothes separating me from the night air.

He made short work of my underthings as well, and soon I was posed naked before him, my entire being on full, unabashed display. My cock hung heavy and semi-erect between my legs, my dark bush of hair concealing the very base from him, and I was unbothered by his examination of my nude body. After all, if I was to believe what he and Rudolph had told me, I was the first naked man Arthur had seen other than Rudolph. Besides, I knew—without sounding overproud—that I was a handsome specimen of a man. My dark skin was unmarred by any blemishes or scars, and while I was perhaps a little stouter than my taller counterparts, I was well-proportioned and had never had any complaints about my looks. The longer Arthur gazed upon me, however, the more self-conscious I became, and when it felt as though an entire minute had passed without him making another move, I finally spoke.

"Do your knees not hurt upon the stone?" I asked, and he raised his head from where he had been gazing at my navel. I was briefly stunned by the look in his eyes, an expression of such intense consideration there that I hardly knew what to do with it.

"You're beautiful," he said as though he had really, truly realized it for the first time. "I am just taking it in. The sight of you."

My pulse quickened in my throat, and I was overcome again by that strange sinking feeling that by agreeing to this short-term romance, I was closing off a path that would have suited me exceptionally well; while I could say with confidence my attraction to Rudolph was solely physical, the avenue of having him as a lover would have been a path with perhaps less heartbreak than was coming my way. "You better take advantage of it before someone comes," I said, and he looked at me thoughtfully before grabbing my knees and forcing them apart.

Whatever I expected from Arthur was not what I got. Within moments of pressing my legs apart he was kissing my inner thigh, drawing up a deep bruise that would linger for days. With one hand he pushed my right leg up onto the bench and kept the left gripped tightly in his hand. I was struck with gratitude that I had bathed upon my arrival at the estate, and that Felix had the foresight to provide perfumed soap. I would have to ask him later if he had known this was going to happen, the thought that perhaps Arthur's intentions with me were so abundantly clear that they had made even his staff take notice.

He kissed along my thigh before nuzzling his face into the crux of my leg, his cheek hot against the side of my cock, which by now had begun to grow hard. Arthur sighed softly, breath sending a chill over my skin before he pulled back and, without hesitation, took the throbbing head of my member into his soft and skilled mouth. I let out a small whimper, fingers digging into his scalp as he slowly took me deeper, his tongue pressed flat against the underside of my cock. It was clear that he had perfected this, and my mind went, unbidden, to the image of Rudolph on this same garden bench, spread-eagled with a lord's face between his thighs.

It wasn't jealousy, not truly, although I know it may sound as much. We were both grown men with entire lifetimes behind us, and Arthur and Rudolph had assured me things were over, but the estate was nevertheless haunted—however inaccurately—by their relationship. I would just need to use the next month to overwrite those memories with ones of me instead.

He dug his fingers into my inner thighs and pressed down further, my cock hitting the back of his throat, and yet he did not try to pull away. He breathed out through his nose, looking up at me through his long eyelashes, and swallowed. The pressure it created sent shocks of pleasure through my body and I cried out again, this time a little louder, and there was some devilry in his eyes as he slid his tongue over the sensitive spot on the underside of my cock. When he pulled back, there was a thick rope of saliva connecting me to his lips, which glistened in the moonlight and made my stomach go tight with desire.

Lazily, as though his every move wasn't driving me near mad with desire, he moved his right hand to the base of my cock, stroking it slowly and with purpose. My back arched off the bench, and I grabbed the arm of the marble seat to brace myself, more because I was unable to breathe as I was seized by a paralyzing need for more. "Arthur," I managed, looking down at him, and he looked back at me, dragging the thumb of his free hand over his lower lip to collect his own spit. It was an image I would never forget, a perfect snapshot of how incomparably beautiful Arthur was: his blond hair, dark in the night with one lonely curl falling on his forehead, his lips plump and wanting, his entire being seemingly crafted solely to give and receive pleasure in that moment.

He did not answer me when I called his name softly, instead taking the opportunity to swallow down around me once again. Something near to a whimper tore from my throat, my inhibitions having gone out the window the moment he had begun to undo my shirt, and my toes curled in my boots, some long-dormant part of my brain remembering that we were doing this where we could easily be found but no longer caring. I did not last much longer under his skilled tongue, my climax coming upon me with only a lurching wave of pleasure to warn me of its arrival.

Arthur pulled back, my seed pearled on his lower lip, and without considering the depravity of the act I grabbed him by the collar and pulled him up into a bruising kiss. His mouth, salted as it was with my orgasm, was a familiar taste by now, and he allowed himself to be pulled essentially into my lap, returning the kiss with similar hunger. I was about to pin him against the bench and have my way with him when he moved away, cocking his head to one side to listen like a particularly well-bred dog. "Wait," he whispered, and the spectacular rasp in his voice caused by what we'd just done was a distraction I could ill afford at the moment. "Do you hear that?"

I was quiet for a moment, listening intently for what he may have heard, and for a few long moments I heard nothing but the usual sounds of night. I was preparing to go back to the activity that had rapidly become my favorite pastime—defiling the lips of the master of Ashford Hall—when I finally heard what had startled Arthur moments before: the distinct barking laugh of Charles. "Oh no," I hissed as soon as I realized what danger we were in.

Arthur quickly stood up, and I realized with some satisfaction that he was hard, his trousers bulging as though in invitation, but now was no time for me to take care of that problem for him. I was mostly nude aside from my clothes dangling from one ankle, and to be caught by Charles of all people in the garden would be a sure end to our friendship. Charles knew nothing of my proclivity and would not take it well if this was how he found out. Hurriedly, I yanked on my underclothes but found that my trousers were impossibly tangled and time was rapidly running out. We could now clearly hear Ida, and as she was not a loud woman, it was all too apparent that they could not have been more than ten or fifteen feet from where we now were.

I cast a desperate eye on Arthur and he, thinking rapidly, grabbed my shirt in one hand and my wrist in the other, barreling across the small courtyard we had suitably defiled and through a hedgerow just as Charles and Ida stepped into the space behind us. We tumbled against the cobblestone—my elbow still scarred to this day from the fall—and Arthur yanked on my loose trouser leg that had become entangled in the hedge. We sat there for a moment, listening, Arthur still holding my wrist.

"Did you hear that?" Charles was asking, and I could picture him craning his neck to see where we had disappeared to. I could only hope that the moonlight was not illuminating the part of the hedgerow we had tramped during our escape.

"It was a cat or a fox, most likely," Ida said, as sensible as ever; then again, to suspect the noise of hedges being pushed through as a result of two grown men fleeing the scene of a tryst was pure madness, even if it was the truth. "Come and sit and don't bother with the wildlife."

A long pause followed by Charles's familiar footsteps moving away from our direction, and Arthur and I exchanged a glance as we simultaneously realized he must have been directly across from us past the hedge. A few more feet of investigation and we surely would have been discovered. Murmuring voices reached our ears and I began to redress, this time successfully untangling my trousers and getting them on without further difficulty. I was in the process of doing up my blouse when the murmuring stopped and a silence fell, except....

"They're kissing," Arthur whispered, barely audible even with our close proximity. Indeed, I had thought the same thing, but a quick look through the hole I'd left in the hedge during my escape confirmed it. I was struck by a sudden sensation of pride; Charles had never wanted for female interest, but I liked Ida quite a lot, and they were well-matched. The pride was immediately replaced by concern, however, as I recalled Ida's betrothal to Arthur. She had once been engaged to a lord, and while Charles was rich and handsome, he was not titled.

Worst of all, I could not even comfort him without revealing that I'd been out in the gardens at that time of night.

"Let's go," I said, getting to my feet, and with a resolute nod Arthur rose after me, the pair of us returning to the estate in comfortable silence.

21

IT WAS well after two in the morning when I reached my suite, suitably dazed by the night's events. After escaping the garden with Arthur, we had lingered at the servant's entrance for far too long, neither of us quite willing to let the night end and seemingly unable to keep our hands or mouths off of one another. It was only upon the realization that we might encounter Charles and Ida returning from their own dalliance that we parted, but in doing so I was overcome by an overwhelming lightness.

I was under no delusions that Arthur Ashford would ever come to love me, but he certainly *wanted* me, and I was foolish enough at the time to believe that was enough to sate the growing intensity of my feelings. I wanted him, too, wanted to memorize the sensation of his mouth and his fingers and his teeth, and as I let myself into my rooms I fell face-first on my lounge, overcome with what had taken place. I was not a particularly sentimental man and had always been driven mostly by a desire to rise above my class and the occasional need for companionship, but that late night in the privacy of my chambers, I allowed myself a few brief moments of unabashed joy.

I rolled onto my side, a man overcome by emotions, and spotted a piece of paper on the low table before me, lying on top of one of my books. I pushed myself up on one arm, reaching over and picking up the letter, which consisted of only one page and a few scrawled sentences.

> *Tom,*
> *I stopped by your room for our chat and found*
> *you missing. Strangely, I found Arthur missing, too… I*
> *wonder if the two incidents are related. In any case, I*
> *will stop by before breakfast in the morning instead. Get*
> *a good night's sleep, if you are capable.*
> *Yours,*
> *Felix*

In the excitement of the evening, I had forgotten that I had asked Felix for a conversation after dinner. I groaned, setting the letter back down and making a mental note to do what I could to apologize in the morning, which now seemed terribly close. Despite my insomnia, it had been a long time since I had stayed up so late after such strenuous activity, and sleep came upon me with little warning. The next thing I knew, I was waking up to the sound of my drapes being drawn back before a shadow fell over me.

"My goodness," Felix said, sounding appropriately scandalized. "Look at you. Do you have any idea how late it is?"

I groaned, dragging a hand over my face before opening one eye and looking up at him. He was clearly amused, and I struggled to sit up so he could take a seat on the lounge next to me. He did so with relish, plucking at the collar of my shirt. "That is quite the bruise, Tom."

"Oh no," I said, raising my hand to touch where he had indicated. "Is it really that bad?"

"You have several," he said, touching them in turn and raising an eyebrow at me. "Did you really not know?"

"I fell asleep without looking in the mirror," I said. "Is it really very late?"

"It's well after ten," he said, and I must have looked utterly blown away because he quickly laughed and patted me on the arm. "Don't worry. You're in good company this morning. Charles still hasn't awoken, and both the Nelsons were up far after they usually rise as well."

"And Arthur?" I asked, not missing the amused smirk that flitted across Felix's face at the mention of the man's name.

"Oh, he was quite on time, but he looks like death warmed over. And strangely enough he is wearing a shirt with a high collar this morning despite having no occasion to do so."

"You are painfully obvious while fishing for information, my friend," I said, leaning my head against the back of the lounge and closing my eyes against the summer sun now streaming in the glass doors of my balcony. "Just ask what you'd like to ask so I can go down to breakfast."

"You and Arthur are in terrible moods for two men who spent the night doing what I think you were doing," Felix said. "I knew he was going to be unable to help himself as soon as you returned. He was spending the entirety of his time while you were gone scribbling in the library. I knew it wasn't all preparation for the ball."

"What was he scribbling?" I asked, my curiosity piqued, but when I opened my eyes to look at him, Felix merely shrugged.

"I don't know," he said, the words ringing true. "But he was damned miserable while you were gone. It doesn't take a genius to put it together, and last night… well, one of the maids told me that you had all indulged a little too much in celebration of your return. When I arrived here for our conversation and found you missing, the pieces fell into place. I'm just curious what you said to make him change his mind."

I considered him, brow furrowed. "Change his mind about what?"

"When things went so poorly with Rudolph, he swore off love," Felix said, and it was basically a modified version of what I had heard before, that because of what had transpired in terms of the end of their relationship and the subsequent blackmail Arthur had decided it was safer for everyone if he just kept his emotions to himself from then on. "I'm surprised but happy that he changed his mind."

"He didn't," I said, and in the sobering light of day it seemed like an albatross had just been placed around my neck, anchoring me back in reality. The day before I had been so excited to see Arthur again, so consumed with the simple sight of him, that agreeing to a temporary relationship just to have the chance to bask in his light seemed well worth it. Now that I had gotten a taste of it, though, a glimpse into what it would be like to have him love me, I had to admit to my own stupidity. "I told him I thought we should be lovers until I had to leave."

Felix was quiet for a moment, fidgeting with the end of his shirt sleeve, and when he spoke next there was an uncharacteristic gravity to his voice. "And he agreed?"

"Yes," I said. "It is no fault of his. He was explicit with what he wanted and I was not. I lied to him about the depth of my own attraction, and I'm the one who will have to live with that choice. I had hoped that I would be well away from here before the regret sank in, but I can see now that isn't the case."

I looked at my companion and found that he was looking at the balcony, observing a bird that had come to perch on the railing. At first I thought he may not have been listening, but he soon turned back to look at me. "He wasn't always like this," he said. "Closed off and afraid. We grew up side by side, and Arthur was always sensitive, always so aware of what everyone around him was feeling. His father saw it almost as a defect, but his mother understood that this softness would make a good lord one day. When she died, I saw the change in him. He became so unwilling to allow anyone in. I thought with Rudolph he had uncovered that softness that he'd lost, and perhaps he had for a time, but everything that happened reopened those old wounds and undid the work he'd put into healing. Truthfully, I don't think he knows how thick the walls he's erected are."

"So you think his capacity for love is truly gone?"

"No, I think it's just so tightly locked away that it will take time and patience to uncover it," Felix said, putting a hand on my knee and pushing himself to his feet. "You've put a time limit on this relationship, but I don't think you should count yourself a lost cause just yet. Arthur cares for you more than he realizes, and if you let him grow to meet you… I think you'll be okay."

He turned to leave, and I was struck by a sudden thought, lurching unsteadily to my feet. "Wait! Felix, hold on. Did you know about Charles and Ida?"

Felix grinned, taking the bait splendidly. "It's a lovely match, isn't it?"

"Honestly, yes," I said. Now that my shock from the night before had disappeared, I could easily see that Charles and Ida were well-suited for one another despite the difficult logistics surrounding the match. Ida was smarter than Charles, which he desperately needed in a partner, and Charles was capable of an unfailing amount of love, something I knew all too well from my own relationship with him. "How long have you known?"

"I caught them together a few weeks ago," Felix said. "They're doing a poor job of keeping it hidden from the rest of the house, but they haven't officially told anyone, at least not to my knowledge."

I considered this, wondering if perhaps it was a less serious endeavor than I had first supposed. I knew that Charles could be a Casanova, and far be it for me to damn either him or Ida for carrying on what amounted to a summer affair, but they made such a good couple that to think of them not caring a whit about one another was an impossibility. "Thank you," I said, considering everything that had transpired since I'd returned to Ashford Hall. "There's a late breakfast set up?"

"Yes, in the sunroom," Felix said. "I'll see you when you're more put-together, yes? And perhaps you should consider a high collar as well."

I did as I was told, freshening up and finding a suitably high-collared shirt. Once I no longer looked nor felt like death walking, I left my room and walked almost straight into Charles, who caught me by the arm as I nearly fell backwards. He studied me briefly before grinning. "Poor Tom. Looks like you overindulged just as much as I did. Fools, the both of us."

"I've been working for the past two weeks straight," I said, clutching at his wrist in return before I steadied myself. "I think a little drunkenness was well called for." I reached up, pressing my finger against the dark bags under his eyes. "And you look far worse for wear."

"I am," Charles said, as dramatic as anyone could sound. "Look how late I slept in. That's so unlike me."

"You are really going to stand there and lie to my face?" I teased, shaking my head. "Come along. Felix says there's breakfast waiting."

"Ah, he woke you up, too? I'm sure it has nothing to do with being tired of the food sitting untouched in the sunroom." He slung an arm around me, leading me downstairs, chattering the entire time, and I couldn't help but wonder if he would be as friendly with me had he realized that I had spent most of the night allowing his brother to defile me outside. I had never even dreamed of letting Charles know that side of me, afraid that the way he saw me would change, and if he knew that I had feelings for his brother? I couldn't imagine the fallout from that, the way my lifelong friendship would undoubtedly shatter into pieces in the face of such a monumental betrayal.

Despite my relative comfort with my sexuality, I knew that if I was suddenly to shout it from the rooftops, I would lose nearly everything. That Arthur had kept the truth behind his blackmail from Charles told me that his brother was not privy to the relationship he and Rudolph had shared, that he would not be privy to whatever was developing between myself and Arthur. Wrapped in these thoughts, I allowed Charles to lead me to the sunroom, only half listening before he shook me by the shoulder. "Are you still drunk?" he asked, and I laughed as I sat at one of the chairs at the breakfast table, beginning to help myself to the pastries that had been left for us.

"No," I said. "I was just thinking about continuing to work on the poaching case now that I'm back."

"You'll continue to work on that despite the ball being so soon?"

"It's not as though I have anything to do in terms of the ball," I said, shaking my head. "I'm merely a guest."

"Oh, Thomas, my naive friend," Charles said, stirring an inordinate amount of sugar into his tea and looking out the sunroom window to the lawn stretching away from the manor, the late-summer sun having already burned off the dew. "You have no idea how highly your taste is esteemed by the rest of us. You'll be in the thick of it, mark my words."

"Why would you hold my taste in high esteem?" I asked, genuinely amused at the idea of it. "You said yourself that you ordered a suit simply because you knew I couldn't be trusted to do so myself. I've never been to a ball, much less had any say in the planning of one."

"But you're from London," Charles said. "None of us have been there in ages. The Nelsons have been trapped in France, and Arthur never leaves the estate." He dropped his voice to an almost conspiratorial whisper. "Besides, I have an idea. Arthur is obviously in the market for a new lawyer, and if he sees how good you are at planning the ball, then he might feel like you're the obvious choice to hire."

"Or he could feel that way if I actually work on a case for him," I said, busying myself with preparing my own cup of tea and hoping he didn't see the way my neck turned red at the idea of Arthur hiring me. The idea of having a natural reason to spend more time with him was enough to foolishly get my hopes up, and for the briefest of moments I could picture it: a life out here in the country, covert meetings in the library, Arthur's lips on mine whenever I wanted them there. With the line we had crossed the night before, however, this dream was no longer viable. I had to tell myself not to pay heed to idle fancy. I had put a time limit on our relationship, and for good reason. I could not expect Arthur to put himself in danger just to remain with me. "The question of my taste in things is one that's easily answered, Charles. You know I'm not a man who pays attention to trends or fads. If I'm asked for my opinion on a ball, I'll be next to useless."

"Are you trying to convince him to help with the planning?" Rudolph's voice came from the far side of the sunroom and I looked up from my drink, watching as he slunk in, clearly as hungover as I felt. "Why are you so hellbent on not helping?"

"I'll still help," Charles said, sounding indignant. "I just think it would be a good idea for Thomas to be included."

"True," Rudolph said, and he looked at me like he had immediately figured out what had transpired the night before. I wondered if he had seen Arthur in his high-collared shirt and had now used my similar dress to put two and two together. "After all, he's part of the family now."

"Exactly," Charles said, tapping the table as though Rudolph had just said something profound. "That's exactly right."

"After all, we're all so fond of him," Rudolph said, and I shot him a look as if to say he needed to watch the knife's edge he was walking. He just grinned in return and poured himself his own cup of tea before gesturing towards the ceiling. "Arthur mentioned that he'd like to chat with you if you have time," he said, and I knew at that moment that was his real reason for coming down here, to send me upstairs to see Arthur. Had he been recruited as some co-conspirator in our affair? A go-between to divert attention from any clandestine meetings? "Something about legal documents."

"See?" I said to Charles, using his shoulder to get up from the table. "Arthur has no need for my input as a party planner. It's my legal mind he's after."

Charles patted my hand as though comforting me, an expression of mock sympathy on his face. "Of course, dear Tom. Your brilliant legal mind...."

I smacked him lightly on the arm before glancing at Rudolph, who was pointedly stirring sugar into his tea, and taking my leave of the sunroom. Had I known how great a mistake I was about to make, I would have lingered in the sunroom a little longer, as the meeting in the library would set in motion events I could not fathom at the time.

22

HE WAS on me the moment the library door closed, his fingers undoing the buttons of my collar as though to view his handiwork, and I gripped his shirt to pull him closer, unable to ignore my visceral attraction to Arthur now that the floodgates had opened. "This doesn't seem like a legal question," I murmured as his lips found my throat, my surprise at his absolute passion outweighed by a realization that it had no doubt been years since he had allowed himself this sort of outlet. He wasn't like me, able to go to some gentleman's club and find a man to sate his pressing desires, and at the moment… I was it.

"It's not," Arthur said, his breath hot against my neck, his mouth becoming more and more familiar by the moment. "Charles ordered you a suit, did he not?"

"He did," I said. "Although I have not seen it yet."

"I picked the color," he said, and a thrill went through me; Arthur raised his head to meet my eyes. "Does that please you?"

"Yes," I said, surprised that he had so quickly figured it out but realizing that I was an easy man to read when it came to Arthur. "I like that you had a hand in it." I raised a hand to drag my fingers through his hair, pulling him in for a slow, methodical kiss. Last night had been a fluke, fueled by nothing more than excitement and passion, but if I only had a short time left with Arthur, I wanted to learn all I could about the man I'd thrown my lot in with. "Charles mentioned wanting me to help with planning the last details of the ball."

"Did he now?" Arthur said, resting his forehead against mine. "That would be quite the nice excuse to keep you by my side, wouldn't it? But you have a case to work on."

"As I told him," I said. I left out the fact that Charles had me in mind for the new family lawyer to replace Garretty, the thought of telling Arthur that I might be a more permanent fixture heightening my nerves to a terrible extent. I knew that if Arthur thought I would be around more, he would undoubtedly put an end to our affair, and I was so desperate for the opportunity to have him in my arms that I could not fathom telling him the truth. "Besides, I have no ability to help with a ball."

"Don't sell yourself short," he said, tilting my chin back with two fingers and peering at me for a moment before stepping back. "Anyway, I just wanted to see you this morning, see that you weren't regretting how we had spent the night."

"No regrets," I said. "I would not regret a thing with you." I nodded towards his desk, which was covered in papers that were no doubt integral to the running of the estate. "It looks as though you have rather more pressing concerns," I said, and he turned to look at the desk, his expression thoughtful. "I want to collect some more paperwork about the estate," I said. "Did your father keep any documentation about possible agreements with the village?"

"If he did, it would be in the far shelves by the northern window," Arthur said. "Help yourself. I'll be at my desk if you have any questions." He stole a last kiss before returning to his desk and, reinvigorated about my task due to a few weeks of removal from the drudgery of it, I moved to the shelf he had indicated and began looking through what was there to find if the late Lord Ashford had set anything in stone regarding the use of the manor grounds for hunting.

Arthur and I worked like this until well after lunch hour, the silence of the library punctuated only by occasional questions floated back and forth between the two of us. I found that not only was any tension between Arthur and I gone thanks to the steps we'd taken the night before, but I was now able to look at him not as the older brother of my closest friend but a friend in his own right, the awe he had once inspired in me replaced by a comfortable respect. I was halfway through an account written by a lawyer for the family in the late 1780s when there was a sudden burst of noise in the doorway, Felix and Charles talking over one another.

"What's going on?" Arthur asked, and Felix and Charles began to answer him before Felix shushed Charles, gaining the brief opportunity to speak.

"The band has pulled out," he said. "They've just sent a messenger to inform us that they received an offer to perform in France the same night as the ball."

"Oh no," Arthur said, and I ceased my reading to eavesdrop, my curiosity piqued; without a band, the ball would be a true disaster. "Is the messenger still here?"

"I offered him a meal and a fresh horse," Felix said. "Truthfully, I was hoping that I could stall him long enough so you could make your argument. Charles has already made his, but—"

"Felix thinks I came on too strong," Charles said, and I could easily tell what face he was making despite being out of view; he was absolutely imploring his brother to believe his version of events. "But they have a contract with us to uphold. And to choose France over their native England? Foolish."

"Hold on, I'll come down to the kitchens with you," Arthur said, before footsteps rapidly drew closer and he paused at the end of the aisle I was standing in. "I'll be back in a bit," he said. "If you need anything at all, help yourself to it. There's ink and paper on my desk if you require it." He turned and left, and a moment later I heard the library door close behind him; for the first time, I was alone in Arthur's inner sanctum.

I busied myself with the journals I had been left to hunt through, but after only a few more minutes of reading I found an entry made by the Ashford's grandfather, a description of a civil ruling made by the local magister when a hunting friend of the Ashfords had accused a villager of poaching. The example was so strikingly similar to what had transpired the summer before that it was difficult not to see the parallels, and I wondered if perhaps James had read, or perhaps heard from his father, a similar account of what had happened.

I kept the page open to the account and made my way to Arthur's desk in search of a fountain pen, immediately finding paper, but not a pen. I searched for one on top of the desk before opening the drawers on the right side of the desk; in the bottom drawer, I finally found one. I lifted it out and was about to continue on my way when I caught sight of the paper that lay beneath the pen, my eyes growing wide at what I read.

*Dear Thomas.*

A letter addressed to me, unsent but still meant for me all the same. I lifted the page and found another beneath it, another, another, each letter clearly penned during my absence. I glanced towards the library door before lifting all six letters from the drawer, reading through them like a man possessed, each subsequent page revealing more and more of Arthur than he wanted me to know. It was a clear violation of his privacy, and yet I could not stop myself, phrases jumping out at me from the writing.

> *The thought of losing you to London a terror that I cannot face.*
> *The idea of you thinking of me has sparked an imaginative fire in my heart that I long thought I had quelled.*
> *This hunger seems ever present.*
> *I wanted to take you to the rose garden, slip my hand in yours, admit to you that I was consumed by the idea of kissing you the moment you gazed up at me from the grass in the noon sun.*

This last sentence made my stomach do a flip, made my heart thrum in my throat like nothing I had ever felt before. Without thinking, I folded the last letter into thirds and secreted it in my inside breast pocket, the idea of Arthur's words so close to my chest almost unbearable. I knew it was wrong even as I did it, knew that the man was entitled to keep these things secret. I had been told that these were the equivalent of a journal to Arthur, and I would never have even considered tearing a page from his diary had I stumbled upon it, and yet I still stole the letter.

I replaced the other letters in the drawer and jotted down the note I'd come over here to find—the name of the man who'd been involved in the poaching case in the 1700s. If his family was still in the area, I wanted to speak with them to see what had happened, if they had anything that might help me undo the damage that had been done three years prior during the most recent poaching case. There was no way to overturn what had happened, but I wanted to mitigate the reputational harm that had come to Arthur from James's actions.

After finishing my notes, I replaced the pen and closed the drawer, my fingers going to my vest where the letter lay, only thin fabric separating me from what was essentially a confession of love. My conviction the night before that he was repeating what he had done with Rudolph with me was gone, replaced by a clear knowledge that he had in fact only been living out the fantasy he'd written about in this letter. What I had read only made me more certain than ever that Arthur had true feelings for me, a crush that he was trying to bury, and if I could use our affair to spark that crush into adoration, even *love*?

It was a naive thought, my usual logic obscured by how badly I wanted him. How badly I desired a happy ending for the both of us, a way forward through a seemingly endless labyrinth intent on keeping us apart at the end of it all. I could not see—or perhaps just did not want to see—that it was dangerous for me to want more than what I had, and that I was teetering on the edge of a cliff that would ruin me if I fell.

I returned to the shelf I had been perusing before finding the letter, trying to focus on the accounts I was reading, and not on the letter burning a hole in my pocket. According to my pocket watch, it was nearly forty-five minutes before Arthur returned, his confident footsteps an indicator he was back long before he appeared at the end of the shelves, an exasperated look in his eyes that I don't know I would have recognized at the beginning of the summer, but which I could now read as clear as anything. "Did you convince him?"

"He's agreed to return to the band and make my argument for me, but I'll have to spend some time finding a backup in case they decide they'd like to go to France still," he said, running a hand back through his hair; a single curl fell over his forehead and sent a lance of longing through my chest, tempered only by the guilt I still felt at the theft of the letter. "But the band is the least pressing issue at the moment, unfortunately. More bad news came when I was downstairs."

"What could possibly have happened?" I asked, setting aside the book I was working my way through and stepping towards him; he caught my hand and raised it to his lips, kissing me on the knuckles gently. The gesture touched me, affectionate and soft, and goose bumps ran down my arms at his touch. "Arthur…."

"We received word from Lady Jane Wright," he said, and immediately I put two and two together. "I invited her to the ball because to snub her would cause more trouble than having James here would. She has informed us that she'll be coming with her youngest daughter and, unfortunately, James."

"I see," I said, considering this carefully. "Did you know that there was another poaching case here about fifty years ago?"

Arthur shook his head, his brow furrowing as he looked at me. "You're sure?"

"It's nearly the same circumstances," I said. "I'm going to take Charles to talk to some of the families involved in both cases tomorrow and see what they have to say. I think if I can collect enough evidence that there was an agreement between your family and the surrounding residents for hunting rights on the land, we can have the agreement formalized and restore relationships with the populace after the damage James did. I know we can't undo what happened, but we can fix your reputation. I'd like to see how they feel about you, too, and work with that."

Even as I was saying it, I wondered if I was doing too much, going too far. After the line I had crossed with Arthur yesterday, there was no way I could be the Ashford lawyer, and yet here I was, doing things that were within a family lawyer's purview, and not within the scope of a family friend. Arthur voiced my concerns before I was even truly aware of what I was thinking myself, a thoughtful tone to his voice. "You're committing yourself quite fully," he said. "Charles has no doubt mentioned to you that we're without a lawyer at the moment. Were you hoping to fill that position?"

"I don't think it's a good idea," I said, raising my gaze to meet his. "Had you asked me before yesterday, I would have considered it, but this… I can't go back to a professional relationship with you, Arthur. We should hold to our agreement that this ends when I leave."

Like a fool, I had hoped to see disappointment in his eyes at this, but instead he just nodded, an immediate agreement to my terms. "If you can think of anyone who would suit our purposes, send them my way," he said, still holding my hand in his. "And the help you give now is more than enough. You have a true knack for this."

"Thank you," I said, leaning in to kiss him before I could stop myself, and as soon as our lips met I was back where I'd started, overcome by such strong affection for him that it was hard to concentrate on anything else. I knew I was being a fool, that I had cost myself an opportunity that would lift me out of the class I'd been born into, and yet my desire to have Arthur, even for just these few weeks, was so overwhelming that I would have gladly given up anything just to have him close to me.

I had no idea yet what the true cost of our relationship would be, or the ripples it would have into the rest of my life, a pebble in a pond that caused waves to crash on the shore.

# 23

FOR THE next week, life at Ashford Hall continued without many visible changes. Arthur was distracted by preparations for the ball, a million little details needing his stamp of approval before they could be put into motion, and Charles and I were busy with our work on repairing the damage the poaching case had done. We spent many a day studying the map of the surrounding areas, finding our next home to visit, collecting details about both the historical poaching case and the newer one, using Charles's substantial charm to undo the ill effects of James's interference. It was hard but rewarding work, and the breadth of what we were undertaking meant that Arthur and I had little time together aside from stolen kisses in empty rooms and occasional moonlit walks.

The day before the ball finally came and I was sitting with Ida on the front lawn, the weather far too nice for me to be cooped up in my room as I transcribed my hurried notes from house visits to notebooks that would serve as the proper documentation for the case. Ida was reading a novel, lying on her stomach and leafing through the pages, and we were both quite content when the sound of hoofs reached us. I looked up from my papers, a carriage approaching, and Ida merely glanced at it before returning to her novel. "It's Lady Wright and her children," she said, and I started slightly, looking at her.

"How do you know?"

"I recognize the horses," she said. "And Charles said yesterday that they would be staying the night before the ball to avoid the congestion. She is their aunt, after all."

I considered this; Charles had mentioned to me before that James was their cousin—and that the Nelsons were James's cousins by way of his father—but it hadn't occurred to me that the families shared a close relationship after what James had pulled. "What is James hoping to accomplish with Arthur?" I asked, sounding genuinely confused. "Charles told me that his older brother is the lord now that their father died but that James was lacking a title as it's going to his nephew now. Is he truly that hard up?"

"Not at all," Ida said. "When our uncle died, he had provisions in place for all of us. He was the only man in the family, so my mother was well looked after, and trusts were set up for Rudy and I as well. He did the same for James as the military does not pay enough to keep up the lifestyle James has grown accustomed to. Whatever he's doing to Arthur, it's because he isn't content with what he has. He wants more, and it's not as if he wants Arthur's title or even his money. He just doesn't want Arthur to have it."

"And Arthur still allows him to visit? Still invited him to the ball?"

"He didn't invite *James*," she said, slipping her bookmark into place and closing her book over so she could sit up and face me. The carriage was rounding the drive now, approaching the steps, and already I could see Felix and one of the footmen coming down the stairs to meet them. "If he'd failed to invite Lady Wright and her daughter, then it would have caused trouble with Lord Wright, James's brother. He would have asked why his mother and sister weren't invited when he arrived tomorrow, and if Arthur had said it was because of James, it would turn into a political nightmare. It is better to have James here for a few nights than to risk offending someone who is not only a member of the family but a peer as well."

"But James is the reason you had to call off your engagement," I said, unsettled by the total lack of justice in what was transpiring. I was doing what I could to reverse the damage that James had done, but if he was a continued presence for the Ashford family, then I couldn't guarantee he wouldn't cause trouble in the future. "Does that not bother you?"

Ida tilted her head to one side, looking at me for the first time with true confusion furrowing her brow. "You are so strange," she said finally. "Arthur's position, and my position to a certain extent, is dictated by the political choices we make, not by a sense of justice. There are trusts, legalities, that are meant to keep us toeing a line that we cannot step over. I would call off our engagement a thousand times over if it would keep them safe, but it doesn't mean that James can be cut out of this family entirely. The strings connecting us are too tangled."

"So he just gets away with it?" I asked, and Ida shrugged one delicate shoulder, looking towards the carriage as it came to a stop. "That's not right, Ida."

"Some things are just meant to be swallowed," she said, looking back at me. "There's nothing to be done about someone like James."

I couldn't begin to believe that, but I gathered up my things nonetheless and followed her to the carriage. Felix glanced at me before opening the carriage door, helping out Lady Joanna Wright; she was tall and stately, her graying hair done in a flattering updo with minute curls around her handsome face, her dress made of finer fabric than I could easily identify. Next came her carbon copy, who I took to be the unmarried daughter, Hattie; she was really quite pretty, and I recalled a tidbit of gossip I'd heard earlier in the season that she was being courted by a young marquess of some repute. It made sense, and I hoped that the ball would prove the final piece of the puzzle to bring the two together.

Last out of the carriage was James, dressed in what I assumed was his finest suit, his hair perfectly coiffed. To be honest, he was handsome; he just had a dreadful personality. He met my gaze without flinching, almost taunting, and I did not look away until Felix spoke. "Lady Wright, Hattie, this is Thomas Whitmore, Charles's school friend and the acting family lawyer. He's been staying with us this summer."

I looked at Felix, surprised at the last modifier he'd placed on my name, but he showed no sign of having said anything strange, and I was soon pressing deferential kisses to the back of both women's hands in greeting. Lady Wright was looking at me closely, and once the introductions had passed and we began to make our way indoors, she took me by the arm and had me lead her inside. "Whitmore," she said, and I knew what was coming next. "That isn't a name I'm familiar with, I'm afraid. What title does your father hold?"

"Oh, he hasn't one," I said. "He's a retired military man."

"And yet you went to Eton?" she asked, her surprise all too clear. "That's quite unusual, isn't it?"

"I was quite lucky in receiving a scholarship," I said, glancing back as we reached the doors and finding that Ida and Hattie were arm in arm, heads bowed together and no doubt discussing something far more important than what was happening to me. "And my grades ensured that I was able to go to university as well to become a solicitor."

"And you've been staying here all summer?"

"Yes, Charles was gracious enough to invite me," I said, and she made a small noise of clear disapproval; I immediately knew where

James had gotten his unpleasantness from. "This is the first summer I've been free to visit. It's quite lovely."

"It's really very unusual for Arthur Ashford to allow guests in such a way," she said, like Charles had somehow bamboozled his brother into allowing me into the manor. "Will you be in attendance at the ball?"

"I will," I said. "Rudolph Nelson actually brought me back from London to ensure my presence." I added the last bit solely so she understood exactly how much I had ingratiated myself into the life at Ashford Hall since arriving, and by the way her lips pursed, I could see I had hit home. We had reached the grand staircase, and Felix and the porter appeared from some hidden entrance, carrying the luggage. "It was lovely to meet you, Lady Wright."

"You as well," she said, lying through her teeth, and I took my leave of her, intent on seeking out Charles and telling him what had happened with Lady Wright. I made it as far as the door that would take me to the garden when I was stopped by a clearing of a throat and turned to discover that James had found me.

We looked at one another for a few long moments, and then he spoke, considering me with clear dislike. "How was London?"

"Perfectly lovely, thank you," I said, surprised that he had so quickly confirmed my suspicions about why I had been called back, but not letting on that I was caught off guard. Whatever game he was playing, I knew I could outwit him. "It was nice to get the opportunity to defend a client in court, even if it was sooner than I had anticipated. How has your summer been since you were here last?"

"Fine," he said with the sort of voice that told me that it hadn't been fine, that he had no doubt spent the last few months planning on how he could get back at me for being the reason he was driven out of the house earlier than he had anticipated. He stepped closer to me, his hands in his pockets, and cocked his head to one side. His attitude now, arrogant and entirely aloof, spoke to someone who still thought they had the upper hand, and I wondered if he had been working as hard as Charles and I had been over the last few weeks. "I heard something when I was last in town."

"Oh?" I asked, and immediately I was struck by a feeling of nameless dread. "You were in London?"

"I spoke with Mr. Garretty," he said, and the dread grew a name. "He was quite surprised to hear that you were working as Lord Ashford's private solicitor, particularly as he had been fired from the same position. I wonder why you didn't disclose that information to him when you were in town working on your case."

"I'm hardly Arthur's solicitor," I said, even though I knew exactly where this was going. If I was correct, James had just cost me a job, the only one I'd had since I'd left university. "Working with him on the poaching case is nothing more than repayment for allowing me to stay here this summer."

"I'm sure," James said. "And yet I still think you'll receive word soon enough that your services are no longer needed by Mr. Garretty. It's a shame, isn't it? That your interference here would lead to such an outcome."

I suppose he expected me to break down and cry, to tell him that he had done something terrible, and yet… at the idea of losing my job with Louis Garretty, I had felt nothing but immense relief. I had been struggling with it all summer, since the knowledge that Garretty had been instrumental in carrying out the blackmail case against Arthur had come to my attention, and the thought of not having to return to that oppressive office with a man whose morals were so obviously against my own was freeing. "Would it be such a shame, though?" I asked, and I could tell my answer had caught him off guard. "After all, you and I know exactly what transpired here last summer. Perhaps I had been thinking in my own way that I could no longer work for a man who so willingly engaged in blackmail."

"Blackmail," James repeated, and I could see from his face that he had not expected me to know about the details of what I was working on. Perhaps he thought that I knew only of the poaching case, that I had not spent the summer investigating every last aspect of what had happened as soon as James had meddled in the Ashford affairs. "So you know about that?"

"You told Mr. Garretty I was the Ashford family solicitor without thinking that I knew the details of the case?" I had the upper hand again, and job be damned; James's attempt to sweep my legs out from under me had backfired, had only made me more determined than before to see justice done for the Ashford men. "You truly have no idea what I've been working on this summer." I gripped the knob of the door to the outside, ready to take my leave. "I'll see you at dinner, James."

He gripped my arm, preventing me from going out to the garden. I was suddenly aware of his mouth at my ear, his voice low and threatening. "Do you think I don't know?"

"Know what?" I asked, turning and pulling my arm out of his grip; I was not a man to be threatened. "Spell it out for me."

"That you replaced Rudolph, you sodomite," he said, and the vitriol with which he said the word almost made me laugh.

Instead, I just looked at him, unwilling to give him any sort of satisfaction. "You are quite the conspiracy-minded man," I said, searching his eyes and finding only hatred there. "Why do you want so badly to destroy Arthur?" Even as I said it, I knew the reason: jealousy, sheer jealousy, whether it was because of Arthur's status or his looks or even his sexuality. "Spreading these rumors gains you nothing, James."

"It gains me satisfaction," James said, taking a step back. "I can continue to play this game as long as it takes, Thomas."

"That's fine," I said. "I've come to realize that you have no idea what kind of man I am, James. You have done all of this with the assumption that I will play by the rules you've been raised with. That I will do what Arthur did and simply keep my mouth shut to avoid rocking the boat." It was my turn to grab him, gripping the collar of his shirt and staring him in the face. "If I have no career when I return to London, then I only have time to spare when it comes to ensuring that you cannot cause another person harm. I will do whatever I can to reverse the harm you've done to those I care about. Now leave me alone."

I dropped his collar and turned, this time getting outside without his interference. Shaken but not deterred, all I could truly do was consider what I had just learned. James clearly thought that Louis Garretty had put my termination papers in the mail, and I could reliably believe that; I had worked with Garretty long enough to know that he had undoubtedly seen my work with Arthur as a betrayal, regardless of whether that work had been done to undo his own sabotage. I had enough in savings to comfortably survive for some time, but I would need to begin to make inquiries in town about another position.

Or I could take Arthur up on his offer.

The idea of doing that sent chills down my spine—prolonging our relationship? opening myself up to heartbreak?—and I decided to set it aside until I had the time to seriously consider the implications of accepting a job as the Ashford family lawyer. I also had no way of knowing if the offer still stood, and the idea of turning back to Arthur and admitting that I was willing to risk his comfort for a paycheck was disgusting to even myself.

# 24

"IT LOOKS quite nice," Charles said, tucking the edges of my cravat into the deep navy blue vest of the suit he had ordered for me. "You're sure to have quite a few dances tonight, Tom. Hattie's already told me several times she can't wait."

"Isn't she already being courted?" I asked, the fabric tight around my throat, uncomfortable in a way I wasn't used to; I raised my fingers to pull on it and gain some breathing room, but Charles caught my hand and tugged it away. "I just have to choke all night?"

"It's fashion, Tom. It's meant to be uncomfortable." He gripped me by the shoulders, squeezing gently. "You seem nervous."

"I am nervous," I said, looking at him. "I've never been to anything like this." Carriages had been coming all day, dropping off guests before their drivers pulled around the side of the drive to make room for the carriages that came after. Servants were bustling everywhere; even Felix was too busy to have done more than give me a cursory greeting that morning. The gardens were filled with lanterns, ready to be lit as soon as the dark settled, and the ballroom had been scrubbed from floor to ceiling, perfectly set up for mingling with tables around the walls. Guests had been rerouted to one of the atria to have afternoon tea as they waited for the festivities to start, and I could hear the band tuning up through my open balcony door.

"You are going to do just fine," Charles said, offering me a smile. "Tom, you're the best friend I've ever had. There's nothing you need to do tonight other than have a good time. Who knows, you may find some woman who ends up being your wife."

"Who knows," I said, although I will admit my agreement was little more than tepid at the thought. I certainly wasn't seeking out a wife, and in fact all I could think about was the prospect of having to spend the entire evening apart from Arthur. Things had been so busy that I hadn't even been able to tell him about the threat James had made the day prior, and I was going into the evening with an intense sense of dread percolating once again. "Perhaps *you* will."

"I already have my first dance promised to Ida," he said, smiling. "I didn't want her to be embarrassed."

"So gallant of you," I said, jumping as a knock came at the bedroom door. It was Rudolph on the other side, wearing a suit that was even finer than my own, his curls effortlessly beautiful, and an aura of sheer charm about him. He looked at me, eyes flicking briefly from my head down to my toes, and I was struck by the momentary, obvious hunger in his dark eyes.

"You look nice," he said finally before looking past me at Charles. "You… I don't think anything could fix you."

"How kind of you," Charles said, waving his hand. "Are we beginning?"

"Arthur would like everyone downstairs, yes," he said, and Charles headed into the hallway. I began to go, too, and Rudolph stopped me, offering Charles a small smile. "Go ahead. We'll be along in a moment."

Charles nodded, heading off down the hallway, and I looked up at Rudolph. "What?"

"What's going on?" Rudolph asked, still blocking me in the room. "You've been acting strangely since yesterday."

"I no longer have a job to return to in the city," I said. "And James informed me that he believes I'm your replacement and will not stop until he proves that my relationship with Arthur is not one of friendship. I am desperately afraid that I've failed to help Arthur in any way and have only made the situation worse for everyone."

Rudolph looked as though he was seriously considering this, his dark eyes thoughtful as he mulled it over. "Do you really believe that?" he asked. "That none of us are better off for having spent the summer with you? I certainly don't feel that way. I'd hazard a guess that neither Charles nor Ida nor Felix feel that way, either. I also believe that genuinely, deep down, you don't feel that the summer has been a waste."

I didn't, but I was a little upset nonetheless that he had read me so easily. "Have I satisfied your curiosity?" I asked, sarcasm dripping from my words. "Will you allow me to attend the ball now?"

"I suppose," Rudolph said, and he let go of the door jamb. We walked down the hallway together in companionable silence, and I was unsurprised to find that Charles had waited for us at the top of the grand staircase, his hands in his pockets as he peered down at the Great Hall, which was abuzz with activity. "If you're looking for Ida, you won't find her," Rudolph said, patting Charles on the shoulder. "She has every intention of being fashionably late. Mentioned to me that she was hoping to impress a beau."

Charles hit Rudolph lightly on the stomach in return, but the blush that crept up the back of his neck revealed that he had in fact been watching for Ida. "I was waiting for you two and your secret conversation," he said, beginning to head down the stairs. "Come along. Arthur will be fit to hang if we don't arrive with some time left."

I followed him downstairs into the ebb and flow of a human tide, the volume unlike anything I'd ever experienced outside of the opera. Finding my way to the ballroom was simple, and once inside it was as though I was being exposed to every facet of pleasure available to man. The replacement band, who had come highly recommended, was playing a lively waltz as guests entered and were shown to their bespoke tables; wine and champagne were flowing freely. I found myself immediately in possession of a champagne flute and took a sip, peering around the hall for any familiar faces. I spotted James, Lady Wright, and who I assumed was the current Lord Wright, James's brother, sitting at a table across the dance floor. Hattie was talking to a tall, handsome man who must have been the marquess she was wooing. Charles had been lost in the throng, Rudolph speaking easily to a group of men who looked about his age and who I assumed were friends he had not seen since he'd been in France.

Alone and admittedly overwhelmed, I sipped my drink and considered what I was supposed to do next when someone touched my arm and I turned to find Arthur. Immediately my anxiety eased, my stupid traitorous heart doing a flip at the sight of him. "Well?" he asked, amusement visible in his bright eyes. I realized that at some point I had become capable of reading him as easily as I could read a book, and the thought frightened me. I had made mistake after mistake since I'd arrived at Ashford Hall in June: involved myself in a case that had almost certainly lost me my job, allowed foolish feelings to override my natural judgment, hidden my true self from Charles, from Ida, from everyone.

I had stupidly fallen right into a trap that millions of people had before me: I had fallen in love with the wrong person, and there was no redemption at this point.

"It's quite something," I said, hoping I hadn't taken too long to answer, caught up as I was by the idea that I had been lying to myself about my ability to let go of my feelings after a set time limit. "Are there this many people every year?"

"Yes," he said with the air of a man who was long-suffering. "If it was up to Charles, we'd have even more. I convinced him that two hundred was quite enough, but he's under the impression that we can hold even more in the future." He looked at me, a softness around the corners of his eyes. "Are you all right?"

"I'm fine," I lied, smiling at him. "Now, what brings our busy host over to talk to a mere commoner like me?"

"You're not a commoner," he said as though I had hit a nerve, glancing over his shoulder before turning his gaze back on me. "It's a shame we can't dance," he murmured, this time low enough that we wouldn't be overheard. "I'll have to see what I can do about that."

I felt my cheeks flush, unable to keep myself from grinning at the thought of it. "Stop," I said, although I really didn't want him to. "Why did you come over here?"

"To look at you," he said before raising his eyebrows slightly. "I want to introduce you to someone."

I furrowed my brow, puzzled, but followed him as he set off across the floor, walking with far more confidence than I expected from him in this sort of situation. I wondered if he had to force himself to hold himself with such poise, especially since he had made it abundantly clear that being the center of attention was not something he enjoyed. I looked across the ballroom and found Charles watching us; he gave me a small, encouraging wave and I waved back, taking another sip of my champagne and wishing I had something stronger. Arthur came to a stop next to a table filled with people, but it was an older, impeccably dressed man who he turned his attention to, offering him an actual *smile*. "Mr. Hughes," he said. "Do you recall me telling you about Mr. Thomas Whitmore?"

"Lord Ashford!" the man said, rising to his feet and shaking Arthur's hand heartily before turning and doing the same to me. "And this is Mr. Whitmore? Of course I recall our conversation. You're the young lawyer who defended that fraud case in London a few weeks ago. Masterful work, and Lord Ashford says you've only been a lawyer for a few years. Quite impressive."

I was genuinely flabbergasted, shaking Mr. Hughes's hand in return and looking to Arthur for a brief moment. "Thank you for the praise," I said, finally catching myself before I was rude in not answering the man. "Did you see the trial?"

"I was lucky enough to see your closing arguments," Mr. Hughes said. "My brother was the magistrate who oversaw the case and mentioned that he thought you were quite the talented lawyer. I have to admit I agree. When I heard that you were acting as Lord Ashford's lawyer, I reached out to ask if you were possibly looking to leave Mr. Garretty's employ."

I couldn't stop myself from glancing at Arthur again, finding that he was looking at me as well, clearly amused. "I'll leave you two to talk," he said, touching Mr. Hughes's shoulder lightly before taking his leave.

I recovered quickly, sitting in the chair that Mr. Hughes indicated was free, and spent the better part of an hour discussing my career with the man. It turned out that Mr. Hughes was in fact Matthew Hughes, a prominent London solicitor whose name I was quite familiar with. He had been so impressed by my performance in court, and by the rumors that I was working for Arthur, that he had asked if I would be attending the ball and, if so, if I could be pressed upon to speak with him about a job. While I was thrilled at the offer—and it couldn't have come at a better time if James's threats were to be taken seriously—I was far more touched by the fact that Arthur had put his neck on the line for me.

My feelings for Arthur were intensifying by the day. First the letter I had found in his desk, a clear confession that he had feelings for me beyond just base attraction, and now this display of genuine thoughtfulness. Returning to Louis Garretty's offices had been a misery I could not fathom, and here was a way out of it, a new job after I had rejected Arthur's offer to be the family lawyer. There was a bittersweet cast to everything, however. I was actively seeking ways to leave, to ensure that I could not allow myself to fall further for Arthur or try to have him fall further for me, and all I could hear were Rudolph's warnings that I was facing a relationship with a man who could not love me the way I wanted.

And yet his actions spoke to a man who was perfectly capable of love if one knew where to look. Had Arthur not cared for me, he wouldn't have set up this meeting. He wouldn't have let Charles buy me the suit, nor let Rudolph pick me up from London, nor would he have so quickly allowed me access to his legal files to work on the poaching case. I was a coward, a fool, running from someone who was trying his hardest to open up to me, and the dread I'd been feeling all day seemed to suddenly have crystallized into an obvious issue: I was the one who was refusing to be loved and to love in return.

Had Arthur shown his love this entire time, and I had just been too foolish to recognize it?

I spoke with Matthew for a while longer, and by the end of it he was quite intent on me coming to his office in London when I returned and interviewing for a position at his firm. I readily agreed, glad that my double cross of Louis Garretty was not going to be the end of my career after all, and was equally glad when Ida appeared at my shoulder, apologizing to Matthew for stealing me away for a dance.

I went with her after thanking Matthew again and promising I would set up an appointment with his secretary. On the dance floor, Ida immediately engaged me in a rather lively waltz, looking at me with the same dark intensity that her brother usually exhibited when he had figured me out. "Did Arthur set up that meeting?" she asked, peering up at me, and I nodded, seeing no reason to hide it. Her eyes swept the floor behind me, clearly seeking out Arthur, and when she found him, she studied him briefly before turning her attention back to me. "When did this start?"

"It's just repayment for the work I've done this summer," I said, but she narrowed her eyes in a way that clearly said she didn't believe me. "Ida…."

"I'm not a fool," she said. "I knew about Rudy and Arthur long before the blackmail began, and I can see what's happening here. You two obviously care for each other. Or… perhaps not obviously, but obvious enough if you know what you're looking for. You care for him quite deeply, don't you?"

"Yes," I murmured, unable to lie as I turned her around easily, glad that I had at least kept up with the dances that were fashionable this season. "But I told him that I only wanted a relationship until I returned to London. Your brother made it quite clear that Arthur would not give me what I was looking for."

Ida snorted, shaking her head as though it was a ridiculous statement. "There is a reason they didn't work, and they wouldn't have worked even if James hadn't intervened. Arthur shows his love for a person through subtle acts and small gifts, and Rudy very much believes love should be a fairy tale. What do *you* want? Take my foolish brother out of the equation."

I knew what I wanted, had known since earlier that evening when I had first seen Arthur in his perfectly tailored suit with his perfect hair and perfect eyes and perfect smile. Wanting it and taking it, however, were two entirely different things, and as I swept around the dance floor with my hands on Ida's shoulder and waist, I realized that despite acknowledging my cowardice, I was not going to be able to overcome it. I was no longer worried about Rudolph, and I don't think I even doubted that Arthur cared for me—rather, after everything he had shown me since I'd returned to Ashford Hall, I was convinced that he *did* care for me. This was the crux of the issue, the true root of my growing fear, and I recognized that since the start of all of this, I had never been afraid of Arthur *not* loving me.

I had been afraid of him doing just that.

Quick relationships in gentleman's clubs were one thing, but the idea of opening my heart up and allowing a man like Arthur Ashford in was frightening in a way that I had not been able to recognize before. "How did you know you were in love with Charles?" I asked, and her eyes widened imperceptibly. "Don't look at me like that, Miss Nelson. You aren't the only one with eyes."

She sighed, shaking her head and looking up as the song ended, a new one beginning. A young man approached us, and she smiled at him but politely declined his offer to dance, staying with me so we could continue our conversation. "I knew someone would realize. Does Arthur know?" I nodded and she groaned. "Felix?"

"Of course Felix knows," I said. "No offense, but you two weren't being particularly covert."

She stared at me before something seemed to click into place. "That night in the garden when Charles thought he heard something," she said. "It was you?"

"Well… it was myself and Arthur," I admitted, and she groaned again. "We were quite busy, though, so we didn't hear very much."

"This is dreadful," she said, her face flushed. "You must think so little of me."

"Of course I don't," I said quickly. "Ida, I'm hardly one to throw stones. What you do is your own business. I just want to know… well, how you knew."

"I'm not sure," she said. "I never…. Arthur and I never intended on our marriage being a real one. We had been betrothed for so long that it just seemed the right thing to do, but I knew about him and Rudy, and I had never loved him, not as a wife would. Charles, though… it was just so easy. He's younger than me, but he had always been so close, and I think I just realized after calling off my betrothal with Arthur that I had only kept up the pretense as long as I had because I wanted to be close to Charles. I'm comfortable with him in a way I am with no one else."

I considered this, considered the way I felt when I was with Arthur, the easy companionship that had built between us since our first tumultuous week together. There had been many days of us sitting together in the library working on different projects, and the comfort of that silence had been unlike anything I'd felt outside of my relationship with Charles. How I felt about Arthur, though, was decidedly different. "I see," I said, frightened at the creeping realization overtaking me.

"You need to tell him," Ida said, clearly having come to the same conclusion I had. "If you know how you feel—"

"What if he feels differently?"

"Then you can at least move on," Ida said. "Do you want to spend the rest of your life wondering what if?"

"No," I said, and I meant it. I could have kissed her, a mixture of nerves and relief washing through me, and instead I settled for pressing my forehead briefly to hers in a show of gentle affection. "Thank you, Ida."

The waltz ended and I left her on the dance floor, looking around the ballroom for Arthur; he was on the far side of the room, standing with a few beautifully dressed women I did not recognize, and I began to make my way across to him when I was grabbed by the arm. I turned to find Charles had a hold of me, the look on his face one I had never seen before, at least not directed towards me.

Rage.

# 25

"COME WITH me." Charles had already begun to move before he said those words, leading me through the ballroom and towards the large glass doors that led outside. There was a note in his voice that was genuinely frightening, an anger he was desperately trying to suppress, and nausea flooded me as I followed him, not that his iron grip on my arm would have allowed me to do anything differently. He didn't say another word until we were outside, a good twenty feet from the doors of the estate, and he finally let go of my arm, pacing back and forth in front of me.

The night air was cool and pleasant after the humidity of the ballroom, but a fine cold sweat had broken out over my forehead and my neck, making me far chillier than I should have been on a summer night. I crossed my arms over my chest, watching him walk back and forth, his fists clenching and unclenching at his sides as though he was struggling terribly with some inner turmoil. I knew then that something had happened, that I was too late to do anything to repair this. "Charles," I said, and he stopped pacing, turning to look at me fully. For a moment, I genuinely thought he was going to hit me and I took a step back, Charles watching me briefly before he went back to pacing.

"James came up to me tonight," he began, and my chest twisted up into a tight ball. "After I'd danced with Ida. He pulled me aside, and he said… he said that he needed to talk to me, but that it wasn't something he could discuss in polite company. I didn't trust it, but he produced a letter with my brother's signature on it and said that it was a necessity."

A letter.

*The* letter, undoubtedly, the one I had stolen. The one I had left stupidly in my room, my unlocked room, where anyone with a passing knowledge of the layout of the estate could enter and find my things without trouble. James had undoubtedly taken the onset of the ball to do just that, to rifle through my papers in search of something incriminating, and he had found something so damning that I could hardly breathe thinking of it. "Charles—"

"Stop!" he snapped, continuing to stalk back and forth, voice thick as though he might cry. "Stop it. Let me finish. We spoke in the sunroom. I listened because I thought I would be able to refute his claims. I knew he was targeting you because you were working on the poaching case, and I knew that he was behind you being called back to London. I'm not a fool, and I thought if I knew his accusations, I could defend you." He stopped, turning to look at me fully. "Until the end I was sure I could defend you, but… the letter, Thomas. My brother! Do you have any idea?"

"Please, just listen," I said, my voice trembling despite myself; I had never had to defend my sexuality before, and to have to do so against my closest friend, the one person I had always been able to rely on, was making me sick. "I never intended for this to happen."

"I invited you here," Charles said. "I trusted you, and you just turned around and threw it back in my face. My brother, Thomas? Do you know the scandal this would create if it were to get out beyond these walls?"

"Charles, please, of course I know," I said, swallowing a wave of nausea down. "I was going to end it when I left for London again. I've never intended for it to be long-term and certainly never intended for it to bring shame on anyone."

"Shame?" Charles shot back, and I could tell he was only getting himself more upset. "No, this is not *shame* I am feeling. It is *disgust*." He turned his gaze back on me, and I could practically taste it radiating off him, the terrible crushing weight of his disappointment and his betrayal, a Shakespearean mixture of rage and regret that he had ever let me into his life. "I have trusted you my entire life. We've shared beds, Thomas. I defended you against every sort of insult imaginable about your upbringing. And I… I bring you into my home so you can what? Debase yourself for my brother?"

I was still reeling from being called disgusting, my arms uncrossed now, a weight settling on my shoulders. I could recognize when I was backed into a corner, could see that I was not going to change his mind. Decades of friendship gone, swallowed by my own rash adoration for Arthur, and the worst part was I could not even defend myself properly because I had not recognized the depth of my feelings until this very night. I stared at him, waiting for him to continue his tirade. Instead, he reached into his coat pocket, pulling out a crumpled piece of paper.

My eyes flicked to it before returning to his face, brow furrowing in confusion. "What is that?"

"It's the damned letter," he said, clutching it in his fist. "Consider this a last kindness. I stole it back from him to prevent any word of this getting out. You can take your cursed letter and leave the estate this very hour. I will not have this continue, Thomas." He stared at me searchingly, and I wondered what he saw in my eyes looking back: the fearful gaze of a cornered creature or the defiant gaze of a man who would not apologize? While I desperately wished it was the latter, I knew just from the way his lip curled in disgust that he had seen nothing human in me. "I trusted you," he said finally, throwing the letter on the dirt at his feet and stalking back into the estate.

It took me several minutes before I could move again, walking over to the discarded letter and bending down to pick it up. Writing that had filled me with butterflies for days prior now left a lead weight in my chest, and I looked at it unfeelingly before slipping it into my pocket and glancing around the garden. If it was my last time here, I wanted to remember it as it was in the moonlight, softly lit and fragrant.

When I finally came to my senses, I realized Charles had given me an order to leave. Undoubtedly he had already alerted Felix to my impending departure, although I doubted he had given the servant the truth of it. As though in a fog, I made my way to the servant's entrance to the estate, avoiding the ballroom doors altogether although I could still hear the music, lively and loud. I'm not sure how long it took me to reach my room, only that it felt like an eternity, and when I arrived I found that a maid was already packing my things.

"Lord Charles says he can ship anything you've left behind," she said politely, avoiding my gaze, and I wondered how many of the staff had figured out the truth of why I was leaving already. I merely nodded at her statement and gathered my traveling bag with shaking hands, putting together enough to get me back to London comfortably. I was cognizant of the maid stealing glances at me, so was perhaps less thorough than I should have been in collecting my items, as later there were several boxes delivered to my London flat, but I needed to get out from underneath her scrutiny.

Bag packed, I left the room and began to make my way downstairs, only for Felix to come flying up the grand staircase. He looked dreadfully disheveled, his red hair askew and his face flushed with exertion, and he grabbed the banister, steeling himself as he stopped me from going further. "What has happened?" he asked, sounding genuinely upset. "Charles has just told me to prepare a carriage. What's going on?"

"Have you prepared one?" I asked, surprised at the composure of my voice, an icy quality to it that sounded foreign to my ears. "I need to leave."

Felix stared at me, his eyes huge with disbelief, and when he spoke again it was nearly accusatory. "Thomas. What on earth has transpired? Charles looked as though he was about to cry. If you've had a fight, you shouldn't just storm off like this. It can be fixed."

"No, it can't," I said. "Charles has made it abundantly clear that I'm no longer welcome here and that my mere presence disgusts him. I have no desire to impose any longer."

"But Arthur—"

"Felix, if you are truly my friend, you need to keep my departure to yourself until I am well out of the county," I said, looking at him, and something in my eyes must have struck him because he took a small step back. "Now let me go."

He pressed himself against the banister to let me pass, his chest heaving before he managed to speak again, this time barely audible. "This is a mistake," he said, beginning to follow me. "Tom, if you leave now, you might not be able to fix this. Arthur will be crushed."

"He will recover," I said, continuing down the stairs. "I am not going to try and change Charles's mind."

"He won't recover, you know that," Felix said, the words a dagger, and yet I still didn't stop. "Please, this can be fixed!"

I stopped short on the landing, turning to face him and bringing him to a halt as well. He was three steps above me, looking down with a panic in his eyes that I had not seen there before, and I could not stop the dreadful words that came pouring out of me next. "Stop it, Felix. You need to learn your place."

I knew as soon as I'd said it that I'd hurt him terribly, another blow I'd inflicted against a friend that night. He stared at me, panic fading and replaced by anger, and he gripped the railing so tightly his knuckles turned white. "Learn my place?" he echoed. "I know my place. Do you? Do you have any idea how hard Arthur worked to set up that meeting with Matthew Hughes? How anxious he was that it go well? Now that you've made your connections and gotten what you want, you're leaving.

You're no better than any other leech that's come through these doors. Perhaps you're worse, because you made each and every one of us think that you cared!"

I had no retort, no rebuttal, because I could see that from Felix's position it looked as though I had taken the easy way out. I had accepted Arthur's connections without complaint and now was not willing to fight to stay, but he had not heard what Charles had said nor had he seen the look in his eyes. The idea of staying at Ashford Hall and facing the anger that Charles had for me was impossible, and I knew that I had to go.

I did not answer him, turning back around and hurrying down the stairs. A carriage was waiting—Felix was good at his job, and I felt another twinge of terrible regret—and I hoisted my travel bag inside, the young driver at the reins giving me a nod of acknowledgment as I tapped on the door to let him know we could leave. I settled into one of the plush seats, realizing for the first time that my heart was beating uncontrollably, my breathing short and shallow. I rested my head against the back wall of the carriage, closing my eyes and trying to calm myself, seeing only Arthur there against the back of my eyelids.

I took small comfort in knowing that the bridges I had burned tonight were for him. Charles's disgust, anger, betrayal: with me gone, they might disappear, might allow him to continue to love his brother. Felix's worry about his lord: if I left, there was no risk of a scandal, no fear I was using Arthur simply to advance my career. And Arthur… despite what Felix said, he would recover. We had agreed to a summer affair, and we had enjoyed a few weeks of just that. I would fade from his memory, although I doubted he would fade from mine, and things could return to normal.

I'm not sure how long we had driven before I heard the sound of hoofs approaching. I opened my eyes, sitting up straight in the carriage and recalling my return to Ashford Hall earlier this month. Was Charles riding us down to deliver some parting insult, some ultimatum? The thought that I had betrayed him so thoroughly that he would do such a thing made my nausea return and I clenched my fists against the seat, willing myself to calm down.

Abruptly, the carriage stopped. I heard muffled voices for a moment and considered opening the carriage door when it opened on its own and Arthur entered. If Felix had looked disheveled, Arthur looked positively frantic. He had clearly ridden hard to catch up to us, his curls a mess and his clothes in disarray, his riding coat only half-buttoned and one shoulder showing from where his shirt had undoubtedly been caught on a branch and torn open. Already there was a thin thread of blood on his collarbone where the skin had been cut.

"Arthur!" I managed, so surprised at his appearance that I nearly fell out of my seat. My surprise was almost immediately replaced by guilt, however, and I quickly composed myself. "What are you doing?"

"Felix came and fetched me," he said, panting softly from exertion. He tugged on the shoulder of his shirt to move it back into place, looking at me with clear misery in his green eyes. "What are you doing, Thomas?"

"Leaving," I said, trying to harden my heart against what was to come. I knew that I was going to hurt him, but I had hoped like a coward and a fool that I would have been able to get away with not having to hurt him to his face. With that option gone, I needed to do what I could to get away, but I saw a path open up in front of me. Charles's hatred of me did not need to extend to his brother. I had still had a single piece of ammunition in my arsenal, and I would have to use it. "Please, just let me go without causing a scene. The driver will hear."

"I told him to stand with my horse until I am finished," Arthur said, regaining some of his usual composure, although he was still visibly flustered. "You intend to steal away in the night like a thief? What could have caused this?" A darkness passed over his face. "Did James do something?"

"No," I lied, because of course Arthur was right. James had turned Charles against me before I could even begin to stop the events from playing out, and he had no doubt meant to do the same to Arthur. "No, James said nothing. I just took advantage of your distraction with the ball to leave."

"But *why?*" Arthur insisted, and he reached across the carriage, seizing one of my hands and drawing it to his chest so I could feel the rabbit-fast beat of his heart. "I rode like a madman to catch you. I think that I deserve some sort of explanation."

I withdrew my hand almost as quickly as he took it, willing my face not to flush at the touch, the feeling of his skin on mine a balm to my anxiety that I could not allow myself to indulge in. "What aren't you understanding?" I asked, barely capable of keeping my voice from shaking. "I'm leaving, Arthur. That's all. I have nothing more to say."

"I don't believe you," he said, getting up from the carriage seat and moving so he was sitting alongside me instead, his presence overwhelming. I was seized by the desire to tell him everything, to beg him to take me back to the estate and tell Charles everything in the hopes he would understand, but I knew that what I was doing now was the best thing to do for both of us. I was mad to think that I could have a relationship with a titled man, mad to think that there would not be repercussions. I just hadn't expected them to come from Charles, nor had I expected them to seem insurmountable. "I saw you earlier this evening. I saw the way you looked at me. The way you are *still* looking at me. You can't hide it from me."

"I'm hiding nothing," I said, reaching into my breast pocket and removing the crumpled letter. Immediately his face changed, his eyes flicking to the paper then back to me. "I intended to blackmail you from the start," I said, the lie coming to my lips unbidden. "I used your feelings for me against you, and tonight I went into the library and I went through your desk in the hopes of finding evidence." I shoved the letter at him and he took it, and I was sick to see that his hands were trembling as he did so. He opened it, saw which one it was, and the color drained from him. "I found it. I was fully intent on using it against you, but Charles intervened before I could. He told me in no uncertain terms that I had to leave."

He was still looking at the letter. The letter I had stolen, not because I ever wanted anyone to see it, but because it had filled me with so much love and adoration that it had been impossible for me to not want to read it time and time again. I had memorized it, the looping curves of his handwriting and the way his nib had pressed too hard into the paper as he had been overcome by emotion. To hand it back to him and claim that the words written there were only important to me because of what I could gain materially....

When he spoke, there was a chord of devastation in his voice. "I don't believe you," he said, but I could tell that he was *beginning* to believe me, that my performance was convincing enough. He would not find out about James Wright, would not find out about what Charles had said. He would return to the estate, and he would continue his life the way he had lived it before I had come along, and we would both be happier for it. "What possible reason would you have to blackmail me?"

"Money," I said, and his eyes flicked up, alarmed. "Do you truly believe that a man of my standing would have had a friendship with Charles for so long if I didn't want this in the end? I saw an opportunity and I took it."

"I would have given you money if you needed it so badly," Arthur said, my heart cracking straight down the middle. "Money, jewels, prestige… I would have done anything. Do you… did you not realize? Should I have said it out loud?"

"I've tricked you into feeling whatever way you do," I said, although I did not believe a word of it. My feelings for Arthur—his feelings for me—were genuine.

"Say it," he said, and it was my turn to look surprised. He grabbed my hand again, leaned forward, peered at me closely. "I will only let you leave if you tell me to my face that you never cared one whit for me, Thomas. Say it!"

I hesitated, teetering on the precipice. If I said what he wanted, there was no recovery. But I could not return to Ashford Hall anyway, and if this was a clean break, perhaps he would move on. Felix was certain that I would wound Arthur, but I had wounded him already. The only way forward was through this insurmountable agony. "I never cared for you," I said, and it was the final blow, his expression crumpling. The man I had for months seen as stoic had finally revealed his face to me, and in that revelation I had learned how to see his misery as plain as anything else. "I saw what you were and I used it against you. You were right about me from the start."

He rose from the carriage seat, crushing the letter in his right hand, and I willed him to hit me, yell at me, show anything to tell me that he would be all right when the anger and betrayal had dispersed. Instead, he merely opened the carriage door and went out, his back to me, and his retreating form and the terrible look on his face were the last I saw of him before the driver returned and we began our departure from Ashford Hall.

# Part Four—1854

# 26

I STEPPED out of the law offices of Hughes & Murphy onto a bustling London street, the sweltering summer heat pervasive, suffocating. My dislike for this time of year had grown from a mere annoyance to a serious hatred, and all the light fabrics in the world could not prevent me from overheating as I made my way down the packed sidewalk, carriages clopping past as I went. The city was growing, always growing, buildings slapped on top of one another to the point where they looked nearly comical, and Hughes & Murphy, with their offices so close to the city core, had become ever more difficult to reach in a timely fashion since I had begun with them three years prior.

I flagged down a hansom cab and climbed inside, undoing the top button of my work shirt. Thankfully finished for the day, I had only a quiet evening at home to look forward to, no personal engagements pressing upon me. Since starting with Hughes & Murphy, I had become a lawyer much in demand, and a day where I could do nothing but lounge about my home was a good one.

Three years was a long time for a man to grow. I had fully expected to turn up to the interview with Matthew Hughes and find myself no longer wanted, Arthur having put an end to that after my terrible betrayal, and yet I found him just as cordial and interested as he had been at the ball. It had taken me hours of agony to even decide to take the meeting, and I was eventually glad I did, as it severed the ties I had been unwillingly keeping with Louis Garretty and moved me to a law firm of much repute. For the first time in the entirety of my life, I found myself on equal footing with my coworkers; they did not care about my background as much as the Garretty cohort had, and my education was enough for me to stand on.

I had moved from my small flat to a nicer two-bedroom home on a quiet tree-lined street, only fifteen minutes by cab from the offices even during the crush of traffic that came with the workday ending. I had been in the paper a handful of times, was well-liked, well-paid, well-adjusted by nearly every measure, and yet I was possibly more miserable in this new life than I had ever been before.

I had not spoken a word to Arthur or Charles since that terrible September night. There had been moments over the last three years when I had heard, through some avenue or another, that Charles was in London, frequenting one of the places he liked most, and yet I had never sought him out. He had also never come to visit me, even though my change of address was well known to those friends we had in common. I combed the papers every day for any word of an engagement between himself and Ida Nelson, finding none; in fact, for the past three years, there had been hardly any news in the papers regarding the friends I had made that summer. The most I had been able to glean was that Rudolph Nelson had returned to France for a short time but quickly made his way back to England, and that was hardly newsworthy.

No letters were exchanged, no surreptitious meetings. I had hoped, foolishly hoped, that I had severed my affection for Arthur with my cruelty, and yet I had only seemed to intensify it. There were nights I would wake up in tears recalling the look in his eyes when I had delivered that final blow, and I could only ease my pain through a mad desire that my words had at least salvaged his relationship with his brother, that Charles had not come for him with the same malice he had shown me on that dreadful night.

To put things in the simplest of terms: I was a man who was still in love and without recourse. I knew that Arthur would have been a perfect match for me, had I allowed myself to see that he loved me before I convinced myself he did not, and it was this loss that continued to consume me even now. Growth had taken place at some point, and in hindsight I could see every misstep I had taken, yet I could not even begin to understand how to rectify what I had done.

The hansom driver clucked his tongue and shook his reins, the horses coming to a stop in front of my handsome little house. "Here, sir," he said, and I paid him from my coin purse and stepped down onto the cobblestone. I knew that I owed my current affluence to Arthur, that by some grace he had allowed me to work with Hughes despite the way I'd treated him, and that made it all so much more bitter.

My house lay behind a wrought-iron gate, and I let myself through, greeting the small black kitten that had taken up rat-catching duties in my garden over the summer with a pat on his little head. I had barely made it up the front steps when Elke, the German woman I employed as a housekeeper, threw the door open. "Herr Whitmore!" she exclaimed, her English still not perfect, although it was improving all the time. "There is a man!"

I blinked, thoroughly startled, and pulled my planner from my pocket to check I had not forgotten some meeting. The evening was blank, and I turned my attention back to Elke. "A man? Where?"

"I have put him in the parlor," she said, glancing over her shoulder at the room in question. "He comes here around one this afternoon, insists he must speak with you. I say again and again, you are at work! Does not matter. Rude gentleman, most rude."

"I'm sorry, Elke," I said, too bewildered to do much else except apologize. "Perhaps he's looking to hire me." Even as I said it, I knew it couldn't be the truth; any client would have naturally come to the office. I removed my traveling hat and hung it from a peg at the front door, contemplating who the stranger could be. My friends all knew I would be at work, and there was no one I could imagine would burst into my house so suddenly. "What does he look like, if you don't mind me asking?"

"Short," she said without hesitation. "Red hair, very red."

A chill went through me and I looked at her. "Red hair?"

"Yes," she said, nodding. "And freckles."

Something close to hope flashed through me and I had to force myself to exhibit composure; after all, there had to be thousands of short red-headed men in England. "I see. I may have some idea of who it is, then. You're free to leave as soon as you've done your work, Elke. Your payment is in the kitchen as always, and feel free to take home the rest of the bread on the counter. I doubt I'll be able to finish it all before it goes moldy in this heat."

She gave me a suspicious look when I admitted knowing the stranger but relaxed at the offer of the bread; I knew she had several small children at home and did my best to "accidentally" purchase too much food to help her feed them in turn. "Very well," she said. "If he tries to murder you, Herr Whitmore, just scream."

"I will," I promised, turning up the cuffs of my shirt and stepping into the parlor.

Felix was sitting on the loveseat, reading a translated version of *Candide* I had been lucky enough to purchase, and despite how our farewell had gone, when he looked up at me I could see the same soaring joy at being reunited that I was currently experiencing. He set the novel aside and lurched to his feet, and I grabbed him by the torso, pulling him into the tightest hug I feel I have ever given someone. He hugged back with gusto, and when we pulled apart he didn't let go right away, looking up into my face. "You're going gray," he said, touching the dark hair at my temple that was admittedly beginning to streak with silver, and I swatted his hand away gently, too pleased with his appearance to fuss over his comment.

"What are you doing here?" I asked, so caught off guard I could hardly believe what I was seeing. "I can't imagine what business you have in London."

"Business?" Felix repeated, letting go of me in order to settle back down on the loveseat. I took a seat on the armchair across from him, my body thrumming with happiness. "You're my business, Tom. Did you not see the news in the paper today?"

"News?" I repeated, frowning and picking up the *Times* I'd left discarded on a side table that morning after having my breakfast. "I check the announcements every day and saw nothing."

"It wouldn't have been in the announcements," he said. "Check the obituaries."

My joy was replaced by fear, tempered only by the recognition that he would not be in such a bright mood if someone we cared for had died. I quickly leafed through the paper for the obituary section, scanning the page before my eyes settled on a short section near the very bottom, abutted on either side by other military obituaries.

*JAMES EDWARD WRIGHT, 1817-1854, killed in combat in Crimea.*

I had not seen it during my cursory scan of the page earlier in the day, and as I read it now, I was struck by a sensation of strange sorrow. James had not been a good man, had not been kind, but to die so far from home in the dreadful war being carried out in Crimea at the time was not something I would have wished on even him. I looked up from the newsprint, locking eyes with Felix. "He's dead?"

"Yes," Felix said. "As soon as we received word, Charles dispatched me to fetch you."

"Charles sent you?" I asked, setting the newspaper down on the table again and marveling at the chain of events that had led to this point. "What possible reason would Charles have to send for me? He's the one who sent me away to begin with, and it had hardly anything to do with James."

Felix stared at me, clearly perplexed, and tugged at a satchel that lay at the end of the sofa. "That damned fool," he murmured, shaking his head. "I've been wondering what he said to make you stay away for so long. No wonder…." He unearthed an envelope from the satchel and gave it a cursory glance before holding it out to me. "He gave this to me in case you needed convincing. I suppose I didn't think it would be necessary."

I took the envelope, checking the seal and finding it was Charles's done in a deep navy blue wax, a color that only served to remind me of the suit he had gifted me for the ball. What could possibly be written within to undo the hurt that he had inflicted upon me? I slipped my finger under the seal to pop it out of place, removed a few sheets of paper from the inside, and unfolded them to read.

*September 13th, 1851*
*Dear Thomas,*
*I write this in the aftermath of your departure,*
*so that when an explanation is due I can give you it as*
*freshly as it has happened. The words that lie here are*
*the truth, the absolute truth, of why I drove you from*
*the house this evening. I suppose some background is*
*necessary and I hope you will hear it out. Perhaps by*
*the end of this missive I will have explained in some*
*depth and eased the hurt I caused, and I can only hope*
*that this letter comes before we are both old men and the*
*time for reconciliation has long passed.*

*I came to you with disgust and anger, betrayal and*
*hatred, but those emotions were not directed at you nor*
*were they born out of anything other than abject fear.*
*I have always suspected your attractions, and perhaps*
*you will recall the terrible fight I initiated with Percival*
*Harbour in our seventeenth year; I bloodied his nose*
*and blackened his eye because he was spreading such*
*rumors about you and I never wanted them to reach*
*your ears. The truth is, I have never cared whether you*
*love women or men. It is simply not an aspect of you that*
*I worry about, because my love for you is as deep as it*

*is for my own brother, and it is that love that pushed me into my treatment of you that night.*

*It was before dinner on the night of the ball, while you were distracted with Matthew Hughes, that James approached me. He asked me to meet him in the sunroom, knowing it would be quite empty, and fearing some repeat of his prior poaching scheme, I listened. I found him armed with the letter I ended up giving you, along with half a dozen more that he had stolen from Arthur's desk in the library. They were clear declarations of love, irrefutable evidence, and James said he had others in his possession, even more explicit than the ones he carried with him then.*

*His demands were simple. If I did not drive you out of the house, force you to drop Arthur and the poaching case both, he would have you arrested for sodomy. I knew the letters were enough. He had Louis Garretty in his pocket for the blackmail issue, and if he could levy some of that weight again, there was no question he would have carried out this vendetta. A monetary demand was made as well, but that was nothing compared to the idea of your execution. The idea of having you cut from my life was better than the idea of having you lose your own, and so I agreed with no reticence.*

*You know what happened after. I cannot apologize enough. I am not disgusted by you, nor do I want you gone from my life. I write this now in the hopes that I can rectify this at some later date, hopefully soon. I know nothing of what you said to Arthur, except that it has convinced him; he returned from chasing you down and has not left the library since. Whatever dreadful thing I made you say, I am sorry.*

*Yours (truly and without pretense),*
*Charles*

*Addendum (August 16th, 1854): James is dead. Telegraph has come from Crimea and our aunt has*

*informed us of his passing. Have dispatched Felix by*
*train to fetch you and will give you a proper explanation*
*in person. Far more developments than contained in this*
*writing.*

I devoured the letter as quickly as I could read it, my heart twisting in my throat. Never once had I suspected that James was behind Charles's actions that night, that he was acting out of anything other than his own disappointment and disgust, and I suppose that was the point. Charles knew me well enough to know that I never would have left if I had suspected something was amiss with James. I could see, too, why Charles would have reacted with such fear; if I was drawn up on such charges, Arthur would be soon to follow me to the gallows.

I looked at Felix, stunned. "Did you know any of this?"

He shook his head vehemently. "Not until the word came about James. When Arthur returned that night after chasing you, he was practically mute. Locked himself in the library, did not even see his guests out after the ball. And the next morning… he was back to normal, except he refused to talk about you. Rudy, knowing nothing of what had happened, asked after you at breakfast and I truly thought Arthur might cry, but he quickly made it clear you were not to be mentioned. I could not begin to understand what had taken place, and it remained a mystery until the other day. Charles produced that letter you hold in your hand, had me read it, and cried for what felt like an eternity. We immediately made a plan to fetch you."

"And Arthur?" I asked, loath to hear the answer.

"He has no idea you're coming," Felix said. "He thinks I've come to town to see my married sister. Truthfully, we've no idea how he'll react. That night, I remember what you said to me. That he would forget and recover, and that he would eventually move on. He acts as though he has, but he has not been the same, Tom. There is this look in his eyes that never goes away. The same damned look you carry with you now."

To think that Arthur had suffered the same scars as I had was untenable, and yet I knew by looking at Felix that it was the truth. "What if I can't undo the harm I did?" I asked, and Felix shook his head.

"There are no more secrets now," he said. "Not from Charles, not from myself, not from you. If we all tell the truth, this can be fixed. I know it can."

"I was only with him for a summer," I said. "We have been apart for ten times as long. It is impossible to believe we could pick up where we left off."

"There is no reason to believe that things won't be different," Felix said. "But that doesn't mean you can't form something else. This has to be rectified or you and Arthur will be caught in this in-between for the rest of your lives. I know you don't want James to have that power over you."

"Of course I don't," I said, looking at Charles's letter again, spirits raised by the sight of his familiar handwriting. "Fine," I said, and his entire face lit up. "But I need the evening to prepare. Someone will need to look after the house, and I need to talk to Mr. Hughes and ensure that I can leave on such short notice."

"Oh," Felix said, turning pink. "You don't need to speak to Mr. Hughes. He's been telegraphed already by Charles and given his permission for you to go. It seems you're quite a favorite of his."

"Charles," I said, unsure if I should be annoyed by my friend's meddling or touched by the knowledge that he was as rash as he had ever been. "In any case, the house will need looking after." I removed my watch from my pocket, glanced at the time, and nodded. "Very well. You and I will go to dinner, we'll stop by a friend's house and see if he'll do me the favor of keeping an eye on things here, and we'll depart in the morning." I looked at him, my gaze softening. "I hope you know I meant nothing I said the night I left. I was so upset by Charles's words that I simply had to leave by any means necessary."

"I know," Felix said, rising from the loveseat and offering me a hand. "I've never thought differently, Tom. Now come along. I simply must see if London food is still as unwholesome as I recall it being."

## 27

FELIX AND I caught an early train from Paddington with our destination Taunton, my friend having promised to keep an eye on the house and to ensure that any services I'd employed were halted while I was out of town. I cannot begin to describe the joy I felt at having Felix in London, his mere presence bringing me back to the way I'd felt that summer so many years before. We spent the evening at a pub not too far from my house and then chatted for hours once we finally returned, but Felix was reticent to explain anything that had transpired after I had left; like the postscript on Charles's letter, he would only admit vaguely that a lot had happened since my departure.

We had a private carriage on the train, the journey only a little more than four hours in length, and with no pressing business remaining in London—and a note left for Mr. Hughes despite Felix's assurance that Charles had taken care of it—I readily settled in for the trip. With the rails now reliable and relatively affordable, taking an uncomfortable carriage was no longer the most fashionable form of transportation. "When was the last time you were in London?" I asked Felix as the train began to move, the city starting to slip by.

He looked thoughtful, tilting his head back against the plush headrest of the bench. "I suppose it would have been… six years ago? When my sister had her oldest. I don't much care for the city."

"No?" I asked, looking out the window at the sprawling city, smoke rising from buildings and the bustle of everyday life visible from the rails. "I suppose if you didn't grow up here it might not have as much charm. You'll need to come back for a true visit when things have settled down somewhat."

Felix laughed, shaking his head. "You'll be lucky if Charles lets *you* come back to London after this is all said and done, Tom. When he admitted everything to me… I've never seen him cry that way, not since his mother died at least. He was physically ill the night that you left. I don't think you realize just how important you are to both of the Ashford brothers."

"I can't imagine Arthur will be pleased to see me," I said. "You and Charles must be prepared for that outcome. Whatever happened that night, it was a chain reaction of misery. I took it out on you and Arthur, and the things I said to him were beyond reproach." I sighed, looking down at my hands. "I want nothing more than to reconcile with him, and I know that I need to face him so we can move on, but I don't think there will be a happy ending after what took place."

Felix shook his head. "After what James did to all of us, I think you should have some optimism. Besides, I can tell you without a doubt that Arthur hasn't moved on. Have you?"

"No," I admitted, recalling my three years of celibacy; before Arthur, I had been a frequent member of such gentlemen's clubs that catered to men like myself, but since leaving Ashford Hall, I hadn't indulged in anything of the sort. "But I wouldn't blame him for being distrusting of forming another relationship. I told him I was blackmailing him."

Felix started at this admission, looking at me with wide eyes. "You said that to him?"

"I wasn't going to tell him that Charles was driving me out," I said. "There was no use in destroying two relationships, so I convinced him that I had stolen a love letter and Charles had caught me."

Felix brought his hand to his mouth, chewing distractedly on a hangnail. "Charles was wondering why Arthur hadn't blamed him for your departure. Thomas… your quick thinking may come back to bite you."

"I know," I said quietly. "I took the thing he was most frightened of happening and used it against him. I would not be surprised if he never forgives me."

Felix shook his head. "No," he said finally. "No, this can still be fixed. I think neither of you realizes the impact you've had on one another." He was quiet for a moment, considering me, and then abruptly smiled. "Anyway, there's no use considering what *might* happen. I feel like everything will work out, but we won't know for certain until we arrive. Now, I swore to Charles I would tell you nothing of what he's been up to since you left, but I can at least tell you what *I've* been doing."

"I assumed you went back to being Arthur's manservant," I said, surprised. "Your father *did* return from Essex, right?"

"He did, but he decided that he was past the age where he could be of much assistance to Arthur. He and my mother now seem to devote much of their time to gardening. So I'm still head butler, just permanently now. Although from my understanding, the leeway Arthur gives me is atypical of what's usually received by people of my standing. Being raised alongside him has made him more fond of me than I realized." He shook his head, refocusing. "Anyway, my employment isn't the important part. What have you heard of the Nelsons?"

I hummed softly at the question, thinking. "Not much at all," I admitted. "I read that Rudolph had been back to France but nothing further than that. We have few friends in common."

"So you saw that much," he said. We had passed out of London now, the city left behind for the more sparsely populated suburbs, and in no time at all we would be into the countryside. "I have a confession to make."

I looked at him, wondering what exactly he was getting at; Felix was not a man who talked much about himself, a trait I had noticed in those who had been raised to believe that they were meant to serve, and for him to do so now was a clear indication that he had something important to admit. "You can tell me anything," I said without further hesitation.

"The summer before last, I was doing my nightly rounds when I came upon Rudy in the parlor. From what I understand, he had been drinking and playing games with Charles and Ida, but they had retired and left him alone. He asked if I'd play whist with him, and I agreed. One thing led to another, we both had too much to drink, and…." He was turning pink now, a flush creeping over his cheeks and throat. "We fell into bed."

Shocked was an understatement when it came to the emotion that flashed through me at the admission. I was quiet for a long time after he said that, contemplating the confession, but at the end of every train of thought was the same terminus: that it honestly made some kind of sense. Rudolph was boisterous, confident, loud, and Felix was steadfast and collected. They made a strangely fitting pair, and it wasn't as though Felix had anything to worry about when it came to good looks. He was as handsome as Rudolph, freckled and blue-eyed, and I could easily see how Rudolph would have allowed himself to succumb to temptation.

"Say something," he said, and I laughed, unable to stop myself.

"So you slept with him," I said in response, and I could see from the way the tension ebbed from his shoulders that he had clearly been expecting something other than acceptance of what had taken place. "Why would I judge you for that? You've known the man for years. It's not as though he was a stranger."

"No, and to be quite honest, he's flirted with me before," Felix said. "I thought I was imagining it and he was just being friendly, but he confirmed it for me." He paused, rubbing at his jaw before continuing. "Anyway, after that first night it became, well… a habit. A habit I quite liked, to be honest. I don't think either of us were expecting it to be anything serious. He is quite my superior in terms of class and status, so I assumed it was just a way to pass the time for him. After all, I knew of his relationship with Arthur, which ended poorly, and I knew he'd attempted, however halfheartedly, to court you. I thought I was the latest in a string of romances."

"You thought all of this, but the way you're speaking tells me you were proven wrong."

"That's the thing," Felix said. "Ever since they've returned from France, Rudy has been talking about using some of his money to buy a home there. He'd like to winter on the Riviera, and last November he decided he would go down and see about procuring some property. He had no sooner left than I fell terribly ill. I've never been so sick in my life. It was pneumonia brought on by overwork, and Arthur quickly fetched a doctor and I was prescribed bed rest. However, there were times where even the doctor thought I might not pull through. I had my relative good health to thank that I did not die. That isn't the important part, though."

"His brief visit to France," I said, the puzzle beginning to fall into place.

"Yes. I'm not sure how word got to Rudy, but someone must have mentioned my poor health to him, even if it was just in passing. He immediately cut short his business there and returned to England, returned to *me*." Felix was fully red now, his gaze averted as though looking at me would embarrass him too fully. "I had assumed until that point that I was a convenience, that there was no love involved, but he returned from another country to be by my side when I was barely even conscious enough to know that he was there."

I had always been a romantic at heart, and Felix's story was making me genuinely emotional, my hands clasped in my lap as I leaned forward on my seat and looked at him intently. "You and Rudolph have fallen in love. Actual love!"

"Yes," Felix admitted, looking at me finally, the barest smile on his lips as though showing too much emotion would be even more embarrassing. "Yes, we have. I don't understand how it happened, only that it seemed very quick. It's the strangest thing. I knew I was capable of loving a man, but I never in my life thought I might love Rudy. He has always seemed to me, well… boorish, I suppose. There's a strange kindness underneath it, though, and he has no patience for any sort of class issue that might arise."

"You're positively giddy," I said, entirely touched by the fact that Felix had confided in me about this. "Have you told Arthur?"

"It doesn't feel right to tell him that Rudy and I have fallen in love when I know how much he's struggling with losing you," Felix said, looking at me. "I know you think he is strong enough to rebound, but he's not *right* now. He's not been right since you left."

"Do you truly think he'll be happy to see me?" I asked, my nerves at arriving at the estate unannounced and uninvited by the actual lord of the manor beginning to rise again. "You and Charles seem sure that he will be pleased, but I can't imagine he'll forgive me."

"I'm sure he's going to be happy," Felix said, reaching across the space between us and squeezing my hand. "Even if it takes him some time to realize it."

"I hope you're right," I said, squeezing his hand back gently. "Who will be meeting us at the station?"

"Harry, I believe," he said, settling back into his seat.

"Really?" I asked, pleased despite myself. "I've missed him as well."

"He's a good man," Felix agreed, and with that our conversation naturally turned to other topics, the remainder of our time on the train pleasant despite my growing anxiety that Arthur was not going to be at all excited to see me back in his home.

When we finally arrived and stepped off onto the station platform in Taunton, we were quickly greeted by Harry, who gave me a near-fatherly hug before leading us to the carriage. From the station to Ashford Hall was not that much longer of a ride, and my nerves were now frayed, the conversation dried up as I focused instead on what I would say to Arthur when I saw him.

Would he even speak to me? Perhaps he would be so angered by the mere sight of me that he wouldn't even let me set foot on the drive. Thoughts of this nature occupied my mind until the familiar gate appeared, the trees right up to the wall of the estate and as beautiful as ever, and I was overcome by the desire to wander them again, to return to that easy companionship that had developed during my first sojourn here.

Felix seemed to sense my apprehension in some way, as he kept quiet once we passed the gate and entered the manor proper. Despite how beautiful the weather was, how picturesque Ashford Hall remained, a great dread was growing in my chest, an awful and heavy weight on my shoulders. I could only sit and wait as we drew closer to the source of my misgivings, the idea that Arthur would be terribly unhappy at my presence almost all-consuming.

As soon as we reached the roundabout drive that led up to the front door of the estate, I could see that Charles was already waiting for us, a figure pacing back and forth on the top of the stone steps. He stopped as soon as he saw the carriage and hurried down the steps towards it, and the moment we had come to a full stop, he had pulled the carriage door open and grabbed me by the wrist. "Charles!" was basically all I had time to say before he was hauling me out of the carriage and hugging me with rib-crushing force.

Immediately my anxiety about Arthur was replaced by an overwhelming surge of sorrow as I hugged Charles back. I'd missed him terribly; this was by far the longest we'd been apart since our friendship had first formed, and for two men who had been essentially inseparable for decades, three years of separation was far too much. I grabbed him by the back of his blouse, holding on for dear life, and when he finally pulled back, I could see that his eyes were full of tears. "Tom," he said, sorrow absolutely oozing from his voice. "I knew you'd come back. I'm so, so sorry for everything that happened. I never meant any of it, not in a thousand years. Did Felix explain what he could?"

"Yes," I said, still holding on to his shirt and looking up at him, utterly relieved to find him mostly unchanged from what I remembered. "Charles, I had no idea he had done that to you. If you'd said something—"

"It would have made everything worse," Charles said. "Trust me. So much more happened after you left that Felix doesn't even know about yet." He squeezed me one last time before letting go completely, looking at Felix with clear relief on his face. "Thank you so much for going to get him. I was sure you could get him to listen."

"I'm more than happy to help," Felix said, helping Harry get my luggage off the back of the carriage. "Where's Arthur?"

"The library," Charles said, glancing over his shoulder at the front door of the house. "I have a feeling he might be growing suspicious that *something* is taking place, but he certainly doesn't know exactly what is happening. I haven't told him anything about what James did."

I looked up at the manor, the pit in my stomach growing wider and deeper as I thought about what Arthur would think when he saw me. I was still convinced there was no recovery to be had when it came to our relationship, that the damage that had been done was the equivalent to a fatal wound. There was no time to wallow, however, because a moment later Ida and Rudolph came around the corner of the house, having clearly heard the carriage and come to look. "Tom!" Ida said, so surprised she came to a full stop. "What are you doing here?"

"Ah," Rudolph said, a smug look crossing his face as he nudged his sister. "I told you."

"The thing about James?" she asked, composing herself and continuing to approach. "Is it true, Tom? You were being blackmailed? Rudy's been insisting on it since you left."

"Yes," I said, figuring Charles could fill her in later, although when I looked at my friend, he was not looking at Ida. I realized that I had failed to ask Felix about the status of their relationship, too caught up in the information I could glean from him about Arthur, and wondered if their relationship had somehow not survived what had taken place all those years ago. "I have Charles to thank for bringing me back, as I don't think I'd have come on my own."

She finally reached me and pulled me into a hug, as warm and gentle as before I'd left. "I'm so, so glad to see you again. We were all upset when you left. Several times I've been in London and thought of coming to see you, but I wasn't sure if you'd have been happy to see me."

"I'm always happy to see you, Ida," I said with the utmost conviction. As soon as I let go of her, I was pulled into a hug by Rudolph as well, the clear joy the siblings had at my return making me feel worse about my trepidation. I had already spent three miserable years without Arthur and without my friends. If I had to have the latter without the former, it was my own fault. "You've both been well?"

"Of course," Ida said, squeezing my hand as Rudolph let go of me. "I can't believe you've come back."

"Honestly, I'm having trouble believing it as well," I said, starting slightly as Charles lay a hand on my shoulder.

"I promise I'll give you all time to catch up with him later," he said, his gaze not leaving Ida; surprisingly, she turned away from him and focused her attention entirely on me. "I have to clear some things up with Thomas before I want Arthur to know he's here."

At that, both Nelsons exchanged a look before Rudolph spoke, clearly disturbed. "Arthur doesn't know?"

"No," Charles admitted. "I swear I have my reasons for not telling him, but I need just an hour or two with Thomas before he can find out. Please trust me."

Ida finally looked at him, and I wondered what had transpired between the two of them since the night of the ball to give her such an icy cast when it came to Charles. "Fine," she said finally, glancing at the house. "But go quickly, because Arthur's sure to realize something soon."

"Thank you," Charles said, his hand slipping to my elbow as he hurried me up the front steps and into the house.

# 28

WE ENDED up in a seldom-used parlor in the west wing of the house which had been aired out solely so Charles could use it as his makeshift headquarters, and the moment we were behind closed doors he hugged me again, squeezing me so tightly I thought my ribs might buckle under the force. "I'm sure you have so many questions," he said, letting go and beginning to pace as I took a seat on a sofa. "Felix will bring tea soon. I'm sure you're tired from your journey, but you need to have all the information before you face Arthur."

"Before you begin," I interjected, undoing the top button of my blouse in order to reach some semblance of relaxation. "What has happened between you and Ida?"

"What do you mean?" Charles asked, but he did not look at me, instead raising his right hand to worry fretfully at his collar. "Nothing has happened."

"Charles, you may be able to lie to anyone else, but I've known you for far too long," I said. "Besides, well…. Arthur and I caught you in the garden one night."

"No," Charles breathed out, less a denial and more a refusal to believe it. "Oh, damn it, Tom, I knew I wouldn't be able to keep that from you. I was planning on telling you before everything went so dreadfully wrong."

"It doesn't matter now," I said, waving my hand. "She certainly wasn't looking at you like a woman in love."

Charles sighed, tilting his head back to look at the ornate ceiling. "Fine. You already know what took place between James and I at the ball. Ida saw me approach you that night and followed us outside, unbeknownst to me. She heard everything I'd said to you. After you left, she confronted me, and the fight we got into was absolutely terrible. I could not admit to her the truth for fear that she would make the situation worse, and she was rightfully furious that I had treated you in such a way. I had given her a ring a few weeks prior as a promise that I would marry her when I had sorted things out, and she gave it back."

Another relationship utterly destroyed by the actions of a single jealous man, and I knew Charles well enough to know exactly what he had done in the face of Ida's anger. "You took it as penance."

"I did," Charles said, looking over at me, and he seemed relieved that he had not had to say it out loud. "I had torn you from Arthur. It seemed only right that I had Ida torn from me in return."

"You have to fix things with her," I said, leaning forward to look at him more closely. "I have the letter with me. Show it to her and explain yourself."

"Perhaps," he said. "But more has happened than I wrote in that letter. That night, I thought that removing you from the situation would ensure that both you and Arthur were safe. That was at the forefront of my mind and the reason for my actions. I knew James was being serious, and I knew that he was on the brink of telling his mother what you and Arthur had been getting up to. If he told Joanna, then there would be no stopping the avalanche. I got you out of the estate, and I set about seeing if I could retrieve the letters he'd stolen. I paid the first of the blackmail demands out of my yearly salary and worked towards righting what had happened."

"You paid him?" I asked, sounding surprised. "How much did he ask for?"

"The number of pounds I receive a year is public knowledge, and James is not so stupid as to leave me dirt broke," he said. "He took enough to keep himself satisfied but to not have me come off as any worse for wear. I grew suspicious, though, as time went on, particularly the Christmas after you left. Lady Wright came to visit, quite out of the blue, and as Ida and Rudolph were not here, it was just myself and Arthur to entertain her. She was in quite bright spirits despite historically being a woman who rather loathes seeing our estate as she believes her side of the family should have received it, and the reason for her visit became clear soon enough. She expected Arthur to marry Hattie."

"Hattie?" I echoed, eyes going wide. "Your cousin? I thought she was marrying some marquess or other."

"I thought so as well, but it turns out that the Wrights have nearly no money and the marquess was disturbed by this discovery. It seems he was willing to overlook a lot for the sake of love, but not the burden of looking after his betrothed's mother and brother for the remainder of his life."

"And marrying Arthur would solve the issue," I breathed out, collapsing back against my seat in disbelief. "What did he say?"

"He said no, of course," Charles said, stopping his pacing and turning to look at me fully. "So she said she would get James involved and gave me quite the meaningful look. I knew then that she had been in on the blackmail as well. I doubt she knew the specifics, as even Lady Wright is too proud to marry her daughter off to a man like Arthur, but she knew that it was happening. Honestly, I was stunned. I desperately wanted to reach out to you at that point, because on my own I'm quite useless, but help came in a very unexpected way."

I pondered this for a moment before hitting upon the most likely answer. "The war."

"Yes," Charles said. "James was called off to deal with the Russians and with his departure, the immediate press of blackmail was relieved. I made it my mission to retrieve the letters and to ensure that no one could blackmail me, Arthur, or you again. I had to make this right. The biggest issue I found myself facing was getting into the Wright estate. Lady Wright, Hattie, and James live together in a home that belonged to the late Lord Wright and that James's brother continues to allow them to use as their personal home. I made a meeting with Lady Wright under the pretense of discussing the possible engagement with Hattie, and I'm sure I led her to believe that I was going to try and change my brother's mind. Once I was inside the estate, it wasn't difficult to find James's room, and from there the letters."

He glanced at me as if to ensure I was still paying attention and then reached into his pocket, removing a small and well-worn notebook. "I stole the letters back from him, and I stole something else from alongside them." Charles's face was flushed pink now, clearly overcome by what he had found. "There's a reason I waited until I knew he was dead before I sent for you, even with the letters in my grasp." He flipped the notebook open and read from it solemnly. "I know that what I did was wrong, but I did not do it for the money. Let them think I did, and I will not correct them, but it was never motivated by material gain, and even if I lose the ability to blackmail those involved, I will not stop. I did all of this for love."

"For love?" I asked, realization dawning across me before I even truly realized what he'd said. "Charles, you're joking."

"I'm not joking," Charles said, looking at me directly. "It goes on in detail." He tossed the notebook on the table in front of me and I picked it up, leafing through its contents. It was a journal of sorts, some written in shorthand and some written in full length, James's writing small enough that most entries took up only an inch or so of each page. It was clear he had carried it with him for a long period of time, and I realized he had only left it behind when he was deployed because he had filled it.

A cursory glance revealed that Arthur's name filled the pages, mentioned across entries and over years. "My God," I said, furrowing my brow before I looked back up at him. "Have you read all of this?"

"Yes," Charles said. "He was a madman, Tom, obsessed beyond anything I've ever seen before. What he's written in there is years of obsession."

"Does Arthur know?"

"Arthur has no idea," Charles said. "I haven't told anyone. I was afraid of what would happen, so I kept it to myself with the full intention of confronting him when he returned. I thought if he was faced with the fact that I knew, he might stop." He came and settled down alongside me on the chaise longue, gripping one of my hands tightly. "Now you know exactly what I know. I swear to you, I've regretted the night I sent you away since I did it. You have to know that I only did it because I thought it would keep you safe, and I… whatever you said to Arthur, whatever kept him from turning his anger on me… I will do whatever I can to undo the harm you caused on my behalf."

"I told him I was the blackmailer," I said, turning my hand over to grip his in return. "It was the only thing I could think of to prevent your relationship with him from being destroyed, and I… I thought that if I was going to leave him that night, he wouldn't have been able to handle it if he hadn't had you at his side still."

"*You* took the fall?" he asked, visibly surprised at the admission. "Thomas…."

"I told him I had stolen the letter to use it against him," I said, my voice barely above a whisper. "I told him I wanted money, and he told me that he would have given it to me, but I… I told him I cared nothing for him, Charles, and I made him leave. I don't think that what I did is something that can be repaired."

"I refuse to believe that," Charles said. "If it takes me the rest of my life, I'll restore what you two had."

"What about you and Ida?" I asked. "I can't believe that you would just let her think you some kind of monster. Surely you could have leaned on her during these past three years."

"I knew she would try and intervene, and I was afraid of what James would do," Charles said. "Everything that's happened, everything that's taken place… it's all been out of fear. I never knew what a coward I was until I was faced with the thought of your imprisonment." He was quiet for a moment, and I could tell there was more that he wished to say. "Why didn't you tell me, Tom?"

I was quiet in return, leaning against the cushioned seat and letting go of his hand so I could cross my arms over my chest. "I never planned on telling you," I said, and I could tell from the way he averted his eyes that I had hurt his feelings, but it was the truth. "I need you to know that I really never intended for anything to happen with Arthur. I thought him handsome but nothing more. It wasn't until I returned from London that summer that I realized the depth of my feelings. And I…. Charles, you are my best friend, but there is no easy way for a man of my precarious standing to admit his sexuality."

"I should have said something to you when I realized," Charles said. "But I didn't think it was my place."

"It wouldn't have been," I said. "And I think it would have scared me. I genuinely believed your reaction that night, Charles. I was wholly prepared to accept that you were so disgusted by who I was that you would drive me away."

Charles breathed out hard, looking at me. "Do you still care for my brother?" he asked.

"Yes," I said, because there was no other way to explain why I had spent the last three years avoiding my previous haunts, overtaken by a celibacy that really would have been unheard of in my previous life. "Truthfully, Charles, I think of him so often that I fear I'm mad. Three months should not account for three years of longing, and yet…."

"He's not the same either," Charles admitted. "I don't think any of us have been. Listen. If you swear to me that you will try and resolve things with Arthur, I will do the same with Ida. You have all the information you need to make your argument now. I've given you the evidence I've accumulated. I can't believe that Arthur would have closed his heart off to you forever."

I was still not convinced, but the story that Charles had pieced together over the years was a compelling one. Never once did I assume that James was motivated by anything other than monetary greed, and to know that he was in fact so consumed by hunger for his own cousin that he was driven to the acts he'd committed was eye-opening. I tilted my head back to look at the ornate ceiling, avoiding his gaze. "Do you know how much I've missed you?" I asked, hearing him sigh softly. "Even after I thought you'd said those terrible things in earnest, I wanted to write to you."

"I've missed you too," Charles said quietly. "We spent nearly every waking moment together as boys. To be an adult and suddenly not have you to turn to…. I lack the words to describe that sort of misery." He retrieved my hand once again, squeezing it gently. "This can be fixed, Tom."

"I hope so," I said, sitting there in silence for a few moments more before I screwed my courage to the sticking place. "Arthur's in the library?"

"He hardly leaves it these days," Charles said. "He is…. Outwardly, he seems fine. But his habits have changed, and he looks withdrawn at times, as though in a fog. Your influence on him was monumental."

I forced myself to get to my feet, gripping Charles's hand for a few more brief moments. "I'll go talk to him," I said, deciding to do what I could with the courage I had mustered. "If he's the one to drive me out of the house this time, I apologize."

"Go," Charles said. "I'm going to think about what I should say to Ida."

I let go of his hand and left, every step that took me closer to the library heavier than the one before. I had almost reached the hall and the staircase that would lead me upstairs to where Arthur was when I was grabbed by the arm and dragged into a small, dusty side room that looked as though it hadn't been touched in years. In the dim light coming in through a single window, I could see Rudolph looking at me, an intensity about his dark eyes that was not entirely unusual for him but was unexpected. "Rudolph," I said, surprised that he had manhandled me. "What's going on?"

"I have been in London a dozen times since that summer," Rudolph said, and I was surprised to find that there were clear tears in his eyes, unshed but still present. "I always stopped myself from visiting you because I thought that there was a reason you no longer wanted to be around us, but I was on the brink of seeing you every last time. To know that you were utterly without a friend and that I was playing into James's hand by not seeing you…. This entire business makes me sick. I *told* Ida that there was something happening, that there was blackmail afoot, but she was sure that you would have told us, at least written to us. That it was Charles being blackmailed and not you…."

"Rudolph," I said, reaching out and gripping his arm. "You couldn't have known. I didn't even know what had happened until today. There's time to rectify this."

"But the amount of unnecessary suffering…."

"It can't be taken back, but we can fix it," I said. "I need your help, though. Everyone has come out of this worse for wear." I paused, raising my eyebrows at him. "Aside from you and Felix, it seems."

He looked at me, clearly unamused. "He told you about that, did he? And what do you think?"

"I think you're a good match," I said. "Is that enough to convince you to help me?"

"I was already going to help you," Rudolph said, pulling his arm out of my grip before looking at me again. "You really think we're a good match?"

"Yes," I said, rolling my eyes. "Now go convince your sister that Charles is a good match for her."

"Good luck with Arthur," he said, and I realized as I walked away that I felt as though I truly did need it.

# 29

How could I even begin to explain to Arthur what had taken place? As I headed for the library, I knew that I would tell him the truth, but would that be enough to convince him? I had to prepare myself to be turned away, rebuffed, returned to London with my friendship with Charles restored but Arthur lost to me forever. Even with the threat of that hanging over my head, closure would be better than being stuck in a limbo where I simply could not move on.

I reached the library and dithered outside the door for a few moments, regaining my nerve before I knocked briskly and waited for a response. "Come in," he called, and hearing his voice after this length of time made my heart race uncontrollably. I entered the room, closed the door behind me, and found that he was sitting at his desk, looking down at something in front of him. "Charles, I've told you a dozen times you don't need to knock. This is as much your house—"

He had looked up mid-sentence and frozen, the color draining from his face as soon as he saw me. When he next spoke, his voice was trembling. "Thomas?"

"Arthur," I said, drinking in the sight of him. He was as handsome as ever, unchanged aside from a slight bit more maturity in his face. I briefly wondered how different I must look to him before shrugging off that thought, recognizing that he undoubtedly was unhappy to see me.

"What are you doing here?" he asked, placing his hands on the desk and pushing to his feet with such force that he nearly knocked his chair over. I had been expecting anger, but to be proven right stung me deeply regardless. "Is this where Felix has been?"

"Yes," I said, not intending to hide anything no matter how poorly I came off for it. Before he could throw me out or tell me off, I launched into an explanation, running through everything Charles and Felix had told me and what I had filled in on my end. To Arthur's credit, he allowed me to speak, although he did not take his eyes off me and stayed by his desk as though having it between us would somehow protect him from my words.

"Why are you telling me this?" he asked as soon as I finished, and it was the last thing I was expecting him to say. I stared at him, momentarily rendered mute, and he continued. "You say Charles was being blackmailed, but that night…. That night, you didn't know any of that."

"I didn't," I agreed, beginning to recognize where he was going with this line of questioning. "But even if I didn't know, I still—"

"You still said to me the worst thing you could have said," Arthur shot back. "You knew I was afraid of being blackmailed, and yet you said you were doing just that. I begged you to tell me the truth, and instead you lied to my face and told me that you cared nothing for me, that my trust in you had been misplaced, and I had once again entered a relationship that would end only in my absolute misery. You had no reason to put me through that!"

"I thought… I thought that if I didn't do something, you would lose Charles too," I said, although now that I was facing Arthur, his cheeks pink with clear distress, the excuse felt weak. "What he said to me that night was a nightmare, and I thought if I had repeated it to you, you would have lost Charles that night as well. Everything he said applied to you as well, and I couldn't put that back on you."

"So instead you have allowed me to spend the last three years in absolute certainty that I was a damned fool for trusting you. And you spared me what fate? I may not have 'lost' Charles, but our relationship has not been the same. I resented him for bringing you here. I'm sure he resented me for opening him up to blackmail to begin with. I can count on one hand the number of conversations we've had since you left, Thomas."

Hope was slowly being squeezed out of me, my fears that I had permanently closed myself off to regaining Arthur's trust coming true in front of my eyes. I had no argument that would convince him, nothing that I could say to him that would undo the harm I had done. In my haste to leave and my attempts to shield the brothers from the reality of the situation, I had undone my own chances. "I'm sorry," I said, and he folded his arms over his chest; I was disturbed to see that his fists were clenched. "I've told you what happened, and all I can say now is that I'm *sorry*, Arthur. I acted rashly, and I've had three years to think about the mistakes I made that night. I had been so stricken by

Charles's words that I could think only of leaving and preventing more damage from being done."

"I need you to leave now," he said, looking at me, and something must have flashed across my face because he quickly spoke again. "Not the estate. The library. I'm sorry, but I desperately need to be alone."

I didn't argue, didn't attempt to overstay my welcome. He watched me go, his brow furrowed and a nearly panicked gleam in his eyes, and for the first time since coming here, I thought that my attempts to reconcile might have caused more harm than they did good. After closing the library door behind me, I once again stood there in thought, although now I was not considering how much I wanted to see him. Instead, I was contemplating my own role in all of this. Arthur's accusations had been fair and true. I hadn't known that Charles was being blackmailed, and everything I had said had been based on my own faulty understanding of the situation. Worse, I had purposefully chosen to say things I knew would hurt Arthur to force him to return to the estate and let me leave.

Any hope I had regarding our reunion had been thoroughly dashed by that first meeting. I left the library hallway slowly, ruminating on the sight of him as soon as he had seen me. He had seemed like he'd laid eyes on a ghost, like there was no part of him that was happy to see me there, and that alone was disheartening. I was not a man who gave up easily, however, and even before I had reached the stairs, I had made up my mind that I would give Arthur the time he needed to process my reappearance, but I would not pretend I was no longer interested in him.

Everyone in the house I cared about knew now: the Nelsons, Charles, Felix. The four of them would be invaluable allies going forward, and I would work just as hard to help Charles regain Ida's trust as I knew he would work for me to reclaim Arthur's. I had known the moment I'd stepped into the library and seen him that I was still in love with him, still sick for his affection, and I would not allow it to be torn away from me because of a series of terrible events. If it took fifty years, I would show him he could trust me again.

I spent the rest of the day in something of a fog, focusing on getting back to the routine of being at Ashford Hall. Felix had my old room ready for me, and he said with some seriousness that the suite had been untouched since my departure. I found that this was the absolute truth, some of my less important papers still on the desk, and I set about ensuring that everything was back to my liking, organizing the space.

I composed a telegraph to Mr. Hughes to inform him I would be working from the country for a time, although I doubted he would kick up much of a fuss. Even this simple missive to my boss made me wonder why Arthur hadn't gone to him the night of my departure and asked him not to provide me with the opportunity to work. He could have easily undone the introduction and yet he hadn't, a fact that pointed to some lingering softness despite how horribly I had erred. With the administrative tasks over, I headed for the garden, intent on whiling away the time before dinner, although even the logistics of that were making me nervous. Could I sit at the same table as Arthur? Could he sit at the same table with me?

I walked until I reached the lake that lay on the far side of the garden, where I'd first realized how much I was attracted to Arthur, and was surprised to find that I had inadvertently come across Ida. She was standing in the shallows, her dress hiked up around her thighs as she skipped stones, and I watched her for a moment before approaching. "Ida," I said, and she looked over her shoulder at me briefly before going back to her pastime. "Do you mind the company?"

"I'd rather you here than Charles or my brother," she said. "Unless you've come to try and change my mind as well?"

"No," I said, too tired from what had transpired between myself and Arthur to even think of trying to convince her of anything. "Are you hiding from them?"

"I suppose," she said, leaning over to pick a rock up from the water and skipping it. I watched it ripple across the still water before slipping my shoes off and walking into the lake behind her, glad for the cool water. "Have you truly forgiven Charles?"

I considered that briefly, coming up alongside her. "Yes," I decided. "But I've had an extra day to think things over already. It's fine if you don't forgive him right away."

"I'm furious with him," she said, looking up at me. "Genuinely furious. It's been three damned years of sorrow for everyone because he was too afraid of that fool James to tell anyone he needed help. And what he said to you that night, Tom…. My god."

"I know," I said, because the anguish that had been caused by that fight in the garden had been a raw spot, nightmares of being called disgusting plaguing me for months afterwards. "But I took what he'd said to me and turned it onto Arthur. Neither me nor Charles were blameless that evening."

"Arthur," Ida said, sighing softly. "You've talked with him, then?"

"I explained what had happened and apologized, but I doubt he'll be forgiving me anytime soon," I said. "That night, I said things that I knew would hurt him deeply just to make sure that he wouldn't try and get me back. I never assumed that I would have the opportunity to return here, and… well, I suppose that even if I had hoped that, I didn't think that I would still care for him as deeply as I do."

"I've long thought that you and Arthur would be an ideal match if you could overcome your lack of confidence and he could overcome his lack of trust," she said. "It seems you've gained some confidence in the intervening years. Do you think that what you said will make it so Arthur will never grow to trust you again?"

I considered this, leaning down and grabbing a flat stone from the water. I rolled it in my fingers and then tossed it, the rock only skipping twice before sinking, and then looked at her again. "No," I said finally. "No, I'm going to do everything I possibly can to ensure that he trusts me again, and if he reaches that point and decides that he really can no longer love me… I can accept it then. But now? Losing him because of events set in motion by James? I am not going to let that happen."

"Good," Ida said. "Don't tell Charles, but I feel the same way. Underneath all this anger. I have no desire to lose out on a marriage because I was too stubborn to forgive him for being a damned fool."

"I'll keep it to myself until you decide you can talk to him," I promised. "Do you really think I'm more confident?"

"I did until you asked that," Ida said, but she laughed at the indignant look on my face. "You do. You seem steadier, as though you're no longer trying so hard to prove your worth. The new job suits you?"

"I feel as though I'm finally in a place where I am seen for my abilities as a lawyer, and not my background or upbringing," I said. "At Louis Garretty's office, I knew that I was seen as lesser. The cases I was given were often ones that were seen as unwinnable or ones where the defendant did not have the money to mount a reasonable defense. There was always a sense that I was separated from the men who had better backgrounds than I did, and now that I know that Louis was actively blackmailing clients… it makes sense that he would keep affluent men closer to him and would have little use for me. Mr. Hughes, however, has proven himself a fair and intelligent man to work for and seems to genuinely appreciate my skills. There's been talk of him making me a partner before the decade ends, and that's not something I ever thought would be possible for a man of my background."

"Oh, Tom, that's wonderful," Ida said, sighing softly. "It must be so nice to finally be recognized as a good lawyer. I… well, I was worried that Arthur would remove the opportunity when you left. But I've had time to think about it since, and it really seems to speak to some lingering affection for you, doesn't it?"

"I've thought as much myself," I admitted, hefting another stone in my hand. "That perhaps he did it out of a sense of protecting me, just as I did for Charles that night. But I think it was my way of comforting myself, and not any true feelings on his part. Ida…. When I left that night, I told Arthur that I had been lying to him from the start. That any love I'd shown him had been because I was gaining his trust for blackmail and that I wasn't actually falling for him. He doesn't trust me now, and I can't blame him for it."

"If he didn't trust you anymore, if he was completely convinced that you were a bad person, he wouldn't have let Matthew hire you," Ida said. There was something in the way she said it, the total surety she had that Arthur would not have allowed Matthew to go through with bringing me on if he had really lost all trust, that I couldn't help but feel that little spark of hope again.

I skipped the stone in my hand—again failing to get it more than two skips before sinking under the water—and looked down at her. "You seem sure that I'll be able to win him back. I just don't see how that's possible."

"He didn't trust you when you first came here, and you convinced him otherwise. You just need to do the same thing again. How long are you staying?"

"I haven't decided yet," I admitted. "I don't have to be back in the city until the middle of next month to appear in court, and I sent a telegraph to Matthew this morning to ask that my work be sent here in the meantime. I really don't intend to leave until I convince him to either trust me again, or he tells me to my face that I need to leave."

"You sound like an insane man," Ida said, but she was clearly amused. "Speaking of insanity, did you hear about Felix and Rudy?"

"I did," I said, laughing. "Honestly, I'm quite surprised that it took them this long. They seem particularly well-suited."

"They do, don't they?" She twisted the skirt of her dress around her hand and looked out at the lake. "I'll do what I can to help you, Tom, but I think the bulk of the work will need to be done by you. There's only so much that I can say that will influence him."

"I know." I had torn down the relationship I'd built with Arthur, and I would need to take the time to build it back up brick by brick.

# 30

So began the most difficult work I had ever undertaken.

I had crawled out of the lower class, had kept perfect grades at school to facilitate scholarships, had clawed my way into a respectable career as a lawyer, and yet winning Arthur Ashford back would prove to be a thousand times more difficult than any of that, a Sisyphean sort of torture that seemed destined to last forever. First, there was the fact that he hardly left the library, and that if he saw me when he did, he would rapidly leave the area. Several times I had come upon him in the garden, only to have him turn and flee in the opposite direction, and Felix had told me in no uncertain terms that I had been forbidden from the library.

I was finding that despite my optimism that I could eventually wear him down, this was impossible if I couldn't even speak with him. Still, I could be stubborn too. I kept at my work, repaired my relationship with Charles, wrote small missives to Arthur every day as he had done when I was in London. There was nothing life-changing in these notes, just that I still loved him and would continue to do so until told otherwise, but I did not keep them in the bottom drawer of my desk; rather, I slid them under the library door, had Felix put them on his breakfast tray, left them where I knew Arthur would find them.

Summer was giving way to fall, the nights beginning to grow a little colder and the grass frosty when I woke up most mornings. I was standing on the balcony with a cup of tea, watching the sun glisten on the frozen dew that carpeted the lawn, when the sound of carriage wheels, faint but still audible, reached my ears. I had heard nothing about a visitor, but the thought that it was a telegraph or the mail overrode any actual speculation as to who it might have been. I had effectively put it out of my mind when a rapid series of knocks came at the suite door.

I had barely turned to look at the door, let alone given my permission to enter, when both of the Nelsons were in the sitting room. Ida was in only a slip, her hair cascading around her shoulders, and I had never seen her look so disheveled; Rudolph was not much better, his shirt too tight.

The longer I looked at him, the more I was sure that he was wearing Felix's blouse, but any curiosity about where the siblings had spent their mornings was quickly replaced by concern as they hurried into the room. "What's going on?"

Rudolph closed the door behind him, turning to look at me with wide dark eyes. "It's Lady Wright."

I stared at him, uncomprehending, before it dawned on me exactly what he meant. "The carriage? I thought it was mail!"

"So did we," Ida said, hurrying over to my balcony, although she didn't step out onto it, simply looking out into the garden. "Thank goodness Felix was paying attention. He fetched Rudy right away."

"I'm sure that was easy to do when you were in his quarters," I said, and Rudolph shot me an exasperated look before moving to stand by his sister. "Why would Lady Wright be here?"

"We think it's to do with Hattie," Rudolph said. Abruptly, they moved back from the doors. "I knew they would go outside."

"Arthur loves to walk and talk," Ida said, and I went to stand with them, still holding my tea and peering out at the garden. Arthur and Lady Joanna Wright were walking towards the hedges, their backs to us, and I could tell that he had offered her his arm, his head bowed towards her in deep conversation. She was dressed extremely fine for a woman who was just on a social call, and something twisted up in my stomach as I realized exactly why she had come wearing her best clothes.

"I thought Arthur had already told her no," I said. Still, I was haunted by the idea of him saying yes. His continued disinterest in me combined with the appearance of Lady Wright indicated to me that perhaps he had reached out to her to accept her terms, that perhaps what I had done had made him swear off love and instead agree to a marriage of absolute convenience. "My God, what if he says yes?"

"Calm down," Rudolph said, helping himself to one of the scones on the tea tray I'd been brought that morning. He crouched down by the door even though there was no way we would be able to hear the conversation, sucking his teeth in frustration. "You should have brought your opera glasses, Ida."

"I apologize for not knowing in advance that we would be spying from a distance," she shot back, looking up at me. "He's not going to say yes to her, so don't start down that road."

"But what if he invited her here?"

"Arthur, invite someone like Lady Wright over this early in the morning?" she asked, and I had to agree that the odds of him taking a meeting before noon was almost unheard of. "No, she's arrived solely because she thinks she'll have caught him on the wrong foot at this time of day. He's not even wearing his nicest coat."

"How can you tell?" I asked, peering at the pair as they drifted in and out of view between the hedgerows. Arthur's overcoat, long and a deep brown, looked the same as any coat I'd ever seen him in before.

"His nice coat is black," Rudolph offered. "You said Charles believes she had a hand in the blackmail?"

"Yes, he thought so," I said. "Do you think she's here to follow up on it?"

"I'm sure she's been putting her case together since news of his death reached us," he said darkly. "This will be her last attempt, I think. There's been rumors that Hattie is being courted by a merchant from Glasgow. Lady Wright really needs to accept that she will need to go and live with her eldest son, and not here at the hall."

I considered this, leaning against the frame of the balcony door and keeping my eyes on the garden. The sadness of the situation wasn't lost on me, the idea that the Wright family had been trying for years to infiltrate the Ashford family despite having their own title and their own home. It was the sort of social climbing I had never been able to wrap my mind around, the minute differences in reputation and wealth that were beyond my ability to comprehend, but armed with the knowledge that James had committed his terrible acts out of a misguided desire to bask in Arthur's warmth, that Lady Wright was here now to attempt to reclaim the house where she had grown up, I could see how desperation drove these people onwards.

I was pulled out of my pity for the Wrights by yet another invasion of my suite, this time by Charles, who was inexplicably bearing a tray of tea. I must have given him a strange look because he shook his head as he set the tray down on my sitting table. "I passed Felix and had this foisted on me," he said. "He said we would need refreshments for spying. That *is* why everyone is gathered here, isn't it?"

"Yes," Ida said, looking up at him. "Did she tell you why she'd come?"

"You saw her?" I asked, surprised, and Charles nodded, stepping aside as Rudolph made a beeline for the tea. "When?"

"Arthur and I were having an early breakfast to discuss, uh, matters," Charles said, glancing at Ida, and I very quickly realized what the matter might have been. "Lady Wright interrupted us, said she had an urgent matter to discuss with Arthur. She seemed hesitant to talk to me about it." He shook his head, walking towards the balcony but staying out of sight; Arthur and Lady Wright were far enough away that I'm sure they wouldn't have noticed us, but the risk didn't seem worth it. "I fear she realized that I had been up to no good when I visited the house and stole James's notebook."

"Ida and I think she's here to convince Arthur to marry Hattie," Rudolph said, settling on the sofa in my suite, clearly finding it unnecessary to be next to the open door when there was nothing to be overheard. "Did you get that impression?"

"Oh yes, that would make a lot of sense," Charles said. He looked at me. "Is that why you look so miserable?"

"I'm not miserable," I said, even though I could not shake the fear that Arthur would somehow be compelled to agree to the marriage. "When you visited Lady Wright, where did you leave the conversation?"

"Hm," Charles said, peering out at the garden. "Well, I made no promises to her. I told her I wanted to hear why she thought that Hattie and Arthur would make a good match, even though I knew that she had no reason other than the fact that marrying Arthur would ensure Hattie would be rich and that she and James would be well looked after. I told her I would take what she said back to him."

"And what did she say?"

"That Hattie was pretty, that she would be a fine mother and a good woman to have in charge of the house. To be honest, I was hardly paying attention to her when she was telling me her reasons. I was too busy thinking about how I could get to James's room and go through his things." Without even looking down, he offered Ida his hand to help her to her feet, having clearly noticed her beginning to grow bored. "Have some tea," he said. "Felix insisted it was for you all."

"I'll keep watch," I promised her, and she laughed and went to join her brother. In all truth, I was watching more to assure myself that Arthur would give some sign that he was not listening to Lady Wright, that I would be able to read on his face or in the way he held his shoulders that he was simply hearing her out before he turned her down. I crossed my arms over my chest and peered out at the garden, a slight fog beginning to rise from the frosted grass as the sun melted the dew.

I was beginning to realize how lonely I was. Felix and Rudolph were clearly happy together, Charles and Ida were reconciling rapidly, and I had made no progress whatsoever with Arthur. It seemed I never would, that he was incapable of loving me again, and my anxiety as I waited for any sign of what was happening outside only grew the longer I waited for them to return. I did not truly believe that he would say yes to marrying Hattie, but I hated that I could not be sure of it. We hadn't been able to speak about the proposed match at all due to his avoidance of me, so I had no way of knowing how he felt about it. Was he as anxious as I was? Was he nervous or confident, annoyed or angry? I had no way of knowing, and that alone was driving me near mad.

I'm not sure how long they talked in the garden, only that by the time they began to return the sun had risen above the forest that surrounded the estate. Ida had finished her tea and had rejoined me, and we were sitting on the balcony where we wouldn't be seen by anyone in the garden below when we heard voices approaching. Arthur was barely audible, his tone measured and gentle, but Lady Wright was speaking in a loud, harsh voice and was therefore easy to hear as they drew closer. "I do not understand why you're being so unreasonable," she said. "It is not as though you have an excess of potential wives to choose from. After your engagement with Ida was broken, the rumors that have abounded make you a most unpleasant choice of a husband. I'm offering you Hattie because I'm concerned about your reputation, Arthur. Perhaps you should be too."

They were close enough now that we could hear Arthur reply, Ida and I essentially holding our breath as we leaned forward on the balcony. "As I've said, your concern is touching but unnecessary. I believe I'm capable of making a decision regarding my own marriage, and as upsetting as it may be for you, that decision is not one that includes Hattie. I'm truly sorry for what happened to James, but you have another son who has offered many times for you and Hattie to stay with him. You should consider doing just that."

Relief swept through me at hearing his denial voiced out loud, and I knew Ida was looking at me to see my reaction, but I couldn't help the smile that crept across my face. This was quickly undone, however, by Lady Wright's next words. "James told me, you know. About that lawyer you keep on retainer. He said the man was a sodomite, and that was why he left so quickly after the ball. I thought you'd cut ties, but rumors are that he's returned to the hall. Do you have any idea what sort of shame that would bring on your family if word were to get out?"

There was a moment of silence before Arthur spoke again. "No more shame than that which would befall your family if it became known that James was a blackmailer," Arthur said, measured in his anger. "Lady Wright, I have been patient with you because you are my aunt and because I thought, perhaps, that you were not going to sink to the same level as your son. If you release information about Thomas Whitmore, I will release everything I have regarding James, and I can promise you now that what comes out about him will far overshadow anything that would come out about me and mine. You've made your argument, and I have told you my answer. If you continue to push, you will not like what I have to say."

Ida and I exchanged glances, and I wondered if Lady Wright was foolish enough to continue to push him. Arthur's tone suggested that he was reaching his limit with her, a darkness in his words that only came from a man who had been doing his best to reach a polite end to an unpleasant experience and was finding himself rebuffed. "I have never been spoken to in this way," she said, but there was something in her voice that said she was disturbed. "What would your mother think?"

"My mother would think it repulsive that her sister had sunk so low as to threaten blackmail upon her nephew," he said. "Joanna, I've been patient today. You've invaded my home without invitation, have argued with me for nearly an hour regarding something I simply do not want to do, and now you are threatening me. I believe you've overstayed your welcome."

"You're making me leave?"

"I am," Arthur said without a moment's hesitation. "I need you to go. And if I hear a word against Thomas, I will know where to go to find the source."

There was the sound of boots on cobblestone, presumably Lady Wright storming away from the conversation, and then silence. Ida and I were about to launch into a debrief of what we'd just heard when Arthur spoke again, this time louder. "I know you all have been listening."

Ida and I startled and glanced at the balcony door, where Charles and Rudolph had been eavesdropping, and it was clear none of them were going to speak up. Nervous but recognizing that we had to say something, I clambered to my feet before walking over to the railing. Looking over the edge, I found that Arthur was standing there with his head tilted back, his arms crossed over his chest. "Good morning," I said, and I could have sworn he nearly smiled before he got himself under control and straightened his face out again. "In our defense, it does seem like you manufactured the conversation to take place just beneath my balcony."

"Pure coincidence," Arthur said. "Can you come down here?"

My heart stuttered in my chest, and I gripped the railing a little more tightly. "Me?"

"Yes," Arthur said. "Leave your co-conspirators behind and come down here. And I will not have our conversation overheard if it settles you any to hear it."

"All right," I said. "I'll be down immediately." I left the railing, darting into my room with Ida at my heels. "My coat," I said, finding it hanging over the back of a chair and shrugging it on. "Ida, what could he want from me?"

"I have no idea," she said, seeming just as flummoxed as I felt. "You better hurry, though. Whatever he wants, I doubt procrastinating will make it any better."

31

ARTHUR WAS waiting underneath my balcony when I finally made my way downstairs, Ida having quickly subdued my unruly curls and ensuring that I no longer looked like I had just rolled out of bed. Without saying a word, he began to walk deeper into the garden and I followed, a little afraid that he had realized this morning that he was no longer going to put up with anything he didn't want to, whether that be Lady Wright or my continued presence at Ashford Hall. Still, there was something about the way he was holding himself that didn't speak to him being sick of me or that he was even still angry. The silence between us was not strained in the way I thought it would be, and as I walked alongside him I was struck by the urge to reach out, to take his hand, to walk with him as we had all those summers ago.

I kept myself in check, however, sating my desire through stolen looks at him. Even if he wasn't in his nicest coat, Arthur looked terribly handsome. He was beginning to truly come into his own in terms of maturity, and at this distance I could see the fine wrinkles around his eyes, the gray just barely beginning to creep into his hair. The aquiline slant of his nose, the slight pout of his full lips, the stubble that dotted his jaw as Lady Wright's appearance had undoubtedly disrupted his morning routine. I hadn't been in this close proximity since I'd returned, at least not for this length of time, and to have the chance to truly drink in the sight of him....

"We should be far enough that they can't see us now," he said, coming to a stop in a small alcove of the garden, shielded from the main house by a hedgerow. There was a stone bench there and I was reminded of the first night after we had confessed our feelings for each other, a brief burst of heat flushing to my face as I recalled the depths of debauchery we had indulged in. "Come sit down."

I settled on the bench as he sat beside me and the silence persisted. I knew why *I* was being quiet—I was afraid that I was about to be told that he had realized he would never love me the way he once had—but I couldn't think of a reason why *he* would be afraid to speak. I couldn't shake the feeling I had gotten earlier however, that he had been about to smile at me, a softness in his face that had been absent since I'd come back. There had been *affection* there, and I didn't think I had lost my ability to read him; I could still see what he was feeling underneath the stoicism he liked to present to the world.

"Thomas," he said, leaning against the back of the bench, his arms crossed over his chest. "You heard what I said to my aunt?"

"Yes," I said, looking over at him. "And I heard what she said about me. I suppose the extent of her role in the blackmail is clear now." I paused, frowning at my hands. "It seems James was leaving an insurance policy in his mother's hands. Do you think she'll say anything?"

"If she does, I'll release what we have on James," Arthur said. "I don't think she'll say anything. I made it abundantly clear to her that I have no interest in marrying Hattie and that she does not have a place in this house. My mother would not want myself or my brother to allow someone who clearly dislikes us both so much in our home even if it is her sister."

"I appreciate you sticking up for me," I said, unsure what else I was supposed to say. Truthfully, I wanted to grab him by the collar of his coat and beg him to tell me what was on his mind already, the idea of sitting in this silent agony for much longer driving me absolutely mad. Why had he called me out here if not to put an end to my torment? "Arthur." I looked at him, my brow furrowed. "If you're going to say it, please just say it."

"What do you think it is that I'm going to say?" Arthur asked.

"That you have no desire to have me here anymore, that I've overstayed my welcome, that whatever change I was hoping to enact is not a change that is coming," I said, and he looked at me in return, his jaw set in a hard line. "I would rather you just tell me right to my face than let me live in this agony any longer. I am out of ideas to get you to talk to me, Arthur. I have tried everything I know how to do."

"And you think that your attempts have been in vain?"

"Yes," I said before the oddity of the question struck me. I looked at him, confused. "Have they not been in vain?"

"At first I was annoyed by your persistence," he said, and that crushing hope reignited in me, a swell of optimism that I simply couldn't tamp down. "I was impossibly angry when you first reappeared because I couldn't understand what you were doing here. Even your explanation meant little to me, because at the time all I could see was what you had said that night, the cruelty you had visited upon me. I didn't think you had returned in good faith."

All I could do was listen to him, my hands folded in my lap, as he continued. "You made up with Charles quickly, but I still couldn't fathom forgiving you." He sighed softly, looking out at the garden, which was beginning to fade as fall began to settle over us. "A week or two after you arrived, Charles came to talk to me in the library. He told me the entire story from his side, but I was going to dismiss him as well until I realized that what you had said to me that night…. You weren't protecting *yourself* when you fled the estate. I was convinced that you had been acting in your own best interests when you left us, that you weren't thinking of me in the slightest. But you were, weren't you?"

"Yes," I said quietly. "All I was doing was thinking of you. I didn't want James to hurt you, Arthur, but I also didn't want you to lose Charles if you had to lose me."

"And when Charles came to talk to me, I realized it for the first time. I believe that's when my feelings began to… well, change." He looked at me, his eyes soft. "And then your foolish letters, smuggled into every last nook and cranny…. Did you have the entire staff on your side?"

"Yes," I said again, embarrassed but well aware that the hope I had kindled was not in vain. "You wouldn't let me talk to you."

There was a long pause, Arthur looking down at his hands. "When you returned, I was sure that you were here to break my heart again. I didn't want to believe that… that I had a second chance, I suppose."

A second chance. While I had been agonizing over Arthur, he'd been agonizing over me in a different way, had been attempting to justify allowing me back in. After all that had transpired, he still wanted me enough to try and sort things out on his end. I knew that Arthur was a man who took everything into consideration, who would not make a decision until he was certain it was the best course of action, and that he was here today telling me what he was telling me… it pointed to the choice he had made.

"Why did you choose today to tell me this?" I asked. "Was it your aunt?"

"I was planning on telling you soon, but Lady Wright's visit sped it up," he admitted. "The thought that I had lost three years of my life to hating you because of them… the idea that she still thought she could scare me into marrying Hattie. I simply couldn't live like that anymore. The truth is, Thomas, I think I never stopped loving you. The anger and betrayal I felt were the mirror image of the love and trust I had in you that summer. If I hadn't cared for you that much, if you had *truly* meant as little to me as I tried to convince myself, then I wouldn't have been so miserable without you."

My chest was tight with emotion I could not understand or properly put into words, hope and trepidation and love all intermingling in a way that would have sent me crying if I hadn't been there with Arthur. I looked at him and found that he was already looking at me, his cheeks flushed pink with more emotion than what I was accustomed to seeing from him. It was incredible to imagine that three months had affected us both for so long, and yet I knew that he was feeling everything I felt, that we were overcome with the same level of adoration.

"Arthur," I said quietly. "I cannot apologize any more than I already have for what I did to you, what I put you through, and all I can say at this point is that I will spend the rest of my life making it up to you if I have to. Because I love you, I really do, and I have spent the last three years in abject misery without you at my side. I have never felt this way about anyone before and I don't think I'll feel this way about anyone else. I *love* you."

"I thought when I ended things with Rudolph that I would never again have an opportunity to be loved," he said, a quiet fervor in his voice that spoke to how difficult it was for him to keep his emotions in check. I hadn't seen him like this, and it was taking everything I had not to reach out and grab him by the hand, to profess my feelings for him all over again. I had never had a true first love, not really; my relationships had always been flighty and fleeting, dalliances that weren't meant to last long. Arthur was the first man I had truly looked at and loved, and three years hadn't changed that. "I had opened myself up to you, but I was still afraid. Three years ago, I think you and I were still too far apart. I know you've talked to Ida about this. She told me that I was too untrusting, and you were still struggling to prove yourself. But I don't think that's true anymore. Now that everything has come to light… I trust you, Tom."

"I can work with that," I said, turning my entire body to face him, our knees pressed together on the bench. "Arthur, I don't care if you don't love me right this moment. I don't care if it takes a hundred years for you to love me as much as I love you. But I can work with trust, even if it's just a seed. I know I can take that, and I know that I can turn it into love."

He reached out, taking one of my hands in both of his and squeezing it tightly. "I do love you," he said, and I wondered how long he had been thinking about telling me that, the confession unexpected, but not unwelcome. "I know you read the letters I wrote when you were in London the last time, and those feelings have not diminished nor have they changed. The only difference is the man I am today and the man that you are, and I know that I can trust you. I know that I want you here and that the thought of having you return to London makes me sick, and if that isn't love, I don't know what is." He pressed my hand to his chest, his heart beating so fast that I could hardly bear to keep myself from kissing him, and looked at me with such obvious adoration that it was difficult to believe that this was the same man I had once thought so terribly stoic. "That's my case, as best I can argue it. I'm no lawyer, but I hope I've expressed myself eloquently enough."

"You've more than made your case," I said, and I could no longer hold myself back, leaning forward on the bench and kissing him with three years' worth of hunger. It was everything I had been dreaming of during our time apart, and I lifted my free hand to grip the side of his head, his lips parting to allow me to kiss him more deeply. He kissed back with matched fervor, letting go of my hand in favor of taking hold of my collar, and the emotion that exploded through me as I recognized that he reciprocated my love was nothing I had ever experienced before.

Love, hope, optimism… it was as though the last three years had been erased, and Arthur and I were finally free to face each other as equals. I had worked my entire life to reach a point where I was seen for who I was, and not how I had been raised, and I had found in Arthur a man who had been looking for someone who saw him at his heart too. I pulled back after what felt like a frozen eternity in that moment, resting my forehead against his and wondering if my own eyes were as unyieldingly adoring as his own. "Arthur," I murmured softly, not wanting to pull away entirely. "I don't know what the future holds for us, but I know I want to face it with you."

"That's all I could ask," Arthur said. "I want the chance to have a future with you."

I kissed him once more, running my thumbs over the apples of his cheeks and grinning at him, a giddiness I was unfamiliar with beginning to creep in. "Should we return to the others before they think that you've killed me?" I asked, Arthur's eyebrows raising briefly in amusement before he got to his feet, gripping my hand tightly in his own. We walked hand in hand back towards the estate, Ida the first to spot us from where she was hanging over the balcony.

"You made up?" she asked, and before either myself or Arthur could respond she was flanked on either side by her brother and Charles, the pair of them clearly wanting to see it with their own eyes. "Oh, I'm so pleased."

"Now we're brothers," Charles said, and I laughed despite myself, happier than I thought was humanly possible. Arthur's hand was a solid warmth in my own, and I knew that I was surrounded by people who loved me.

For the first time in my life, I had no question of whether I belonged.

Keep reading for an excerpt from
*A Shadow Comes Darkly*
by Lee Ohlson

Clark Wright had a theory that the bus at 3:00 a.m. was a liminal place, eerie and strange in a way it never was when he was heading to work in the afternoon. It was only after he'd gotten done with his shift and was heading home that it seemed sort of cursed. Like himself, every other rider seemed on the brink of exhaustion, but that made sense; they were night shift people too, and that allowed for a special kind of commute after the bars had closed and the streets were mostly deserted.

Clark rarely paid attention to his fellow riders, too tired from his work as an emergency room nurse to do much more than stare out the window, but tonight was different. The stop after he got on had seen a man get on board, tall and lean and clearly vampiric. It wasn't startling to see vampires out in the city anymore. Since the government had revealed their existence ten years prior, they had become commonplace, less afraid of persecution, and they were easy to spot if you knew what you were looking for. As a nurse, Clark had become proficient. Pale skin and visible veins was one indication, a golden corona around the eyes was another, but Clark found it was their aura that gave them away above all else. A chill accompanied them, and the man on the bus was no different.

He settled in the seat directly behind Clark, who was so dead on his feet he had paid the man little more than the most cursory attention until he felt the weight of his presence. It had been a long day, the ER always seeming way too busy for the amount of staff they actually had, and at this point in the night all he wanted to do was get back to his house and take off his shoes and scrubs, soak his aching feet, and indulge in a little takeout from whatever place was still open. He could tell the vampire was watching him, however, and wondered if the stranger was viewing him as a takeout opportunity in turn. He hated how close-minded he was, but being bitten was a frightening prospect. Even getting a flu shot made his head feel uncomfortably dizzy at the penetration of the needle, and the thought of a pair of those fangs digging into his neck… it made him feel sick.

"Excuse me, sir," the vampire said, and his voice was charmingly antiquated, like he'd been plucked from a 1930s flick about gangsters,

New York accent and all. "Do you have the time? I seem to have misplaced my phone."

Clark wasn't so impolite as to ignore a direct question, and he turned to look at the man, pulling his phone out of his coat pocket at the same time. "It's 3:10," he said, raising his eyes to meet the gold-laced ones of the vampire. Like most of his kind, he was ridiculously handsome, death having smoothed out any faults he might have had in life. The vampire sported curly hair that hung in ringlets over his forehead, such a dark brown it was almost verging on black, and had features Clark would have associated mostly with Italian-Americans: dark, deep-set eyes, thick eyebrows, and a mouth with a fairly pronounced cupid's bow. The only anomaly were the tattoos that wound up and down his arms, dark ink against his skin. All in all, Clark's first instincts about a 1930s gangster movie were proving pretty well-founded. "Are you heading home or just going out?"

"Heading home," the vampire said, a slight surprise in his eyes at the question, as though he'd never been asked something so inconsequential by a human. "I bartend in the Annex," he continued, referencing the section of the city popular with tourists and locals alike thanks to its high volume of bars and restaurants. Carthage sat on the California coast, the most affluent part of town sitting on the cliffs that directly overlooked the horseshoe bay that Carthage had been named for. Like most sprawling cities that had sprung up after the gold rush, there were particular neighborhoods that seemed to fall into certain archetypes, including the tourist-flooded Annex. "Do you work at Mercyside?"

Clark nodded, not surprised that the vampire had figured out the hospital he worked at so quickly; it was the only one that sat on this particular bus route, and his bag was covered with various pins he'd picked up from employee appreciation events over the years. "In the emergency room, yeah," he said, before awkwardly sticking his hand out toward the vampire. "I'm Clark."

With true amusement now, the vampire took Clark's hand in a firm grip, and a thrill went through Clark, starting in his neck and shooting straight down his spine. The vampire's fingers were cool but not unpleasantly cold, which answered Clark's question about how long it had been since the vampire had eaten. They had vampires in the emergency room sometimes that hadn't fed for ages, whether out of guilt or stubbornness or lack of prey, and their skin was always like ice. This vampire's touch was pleasant, almost human. "Alessio," he said, and Clark smiled. "What?"

"That name just suits you, is all," Clark said, letting go of the man's hand and letting it fall back into his lap. "I figured you were Italian, and I like being right about that stuff. Makes me feel better knowing that even if I'm exhausted, I can notice those details."

Alessio smiled lopsidedly, a hint of fangs visible when he did. "I get the feeling that you would easily outdo most people in noticing those details even if you were half asleep," he said quietly, an arm draping over the back of his seats as he leaned back. He was dressed simply in jeans and a black T-shirt, everything about his aesthetic minimalist, but even without any gaudy accessories, he was one of the most handsome men Clark had ever laid eyes on. Clark could see his clothes were designer, a mark of money, but he had never known a vampire who had a job out of necessity and not just because they were bored. "After all, you're the only person on the bus who's figured out I'm not human."

"Perk of being a nurse," Clark said. "I'd be pretty bad at my job if I couldn't tell a human from a vampire." The bus announced its next stop, and Clark glanced at the ticker, frowning. "That's my stop," he said apologetically, getting unsteadily to his feet as the bus began to brake. "It was nice to meet you, Alessio. Hopefully we run into each other again."

"I have a feeling we will," Alessio said, still smiling, and Clark felt a strange little tug in his chest at the words, a genuine glimmer of hope that he was telling the truth. At least he wasn't so tired that he couldn't still get passing crushes on random men. "Have a good night, Clark."

Clark smiled in return, unable to think of anything to say that was as smooth as what Alessio had just said, made his way to the back door of the bus, and pushed it open with one hand. He hoisted his work bag up over one shoulder as he stepped off into the night, the streetlight that was supposed to illuminate his stop out as always. It was a cold night, November giving way to December, and he was glad he'd thought to put on his corduroy jacket before he'd left the hospital, even though the aesthetic didn't particularly match his scrubs and Sketchers. While this bus stop was the closest to his house, there were still a good few blocks to walk, and he popped an earbud in and put on a podcast as he began the trek.

His house was just on the cusp of the wealthy part of town, an invisible line and a hill separating the small bungalow from the mansions that lined the cliffs. The Heights were populated almost solely by doctors and millionaires, but Clark's street was safely middle-class, although he had a feeling it was gentrifying; just last year a vegan cafe had opened up on the block over from his own. All this to say, he'd never had a reason to worry while walking home at this time of night. He rarely saw anyone else walking, and when he did it was almost always someone whose dog had decided it was a great time to go out for a piss. Clark had lived in sketchy areas, and where his house was now was far from a sketchy area.

So when he passed a guy in a leather jacket walking the opposite direction, he didn't think much of it until there was a hand around his throat.

Clark froze, his fight-or-flight reflex refusing to kick in the way he needed it to, and it was this momentary hesitation that allowed the stranger the opportunity to throw him back onto the pavement. Clark fell hard, sharp pain jolting through both elbows as he slid back on the sidewalk, and it was this pain that shook him out of his shock. He twisted to the side so he could get back to his feet, bracing the ball of his foot against the concrete like a runner ready for the starting gun, and the guy grabbed his ankle, dragging Clark back toward him. He was strong, way too fucking strong, and Clark knew instinctively that he'd just run into his second vampire of the night. Palms bloody from where he'd failed to find purchase on the sidewalk, he opened his mouth to yell for help. Cold fingers closed over his mouth instead, cutting off any sound.

"I'll break your neck if you scream." The voice was soft and low in his ear, and Clark didn't doubt the truth of the words, his heart beating rabbit-fast in his throat as he was pulled closer. The vampire was basically on top of him from behind, pinning Clark down against the sidewalk, and for a moment Clark wondered if the guy really had blood on his mind or something worse. He had to fucking get away. Scanning the sidewalk, he realized the guy had ambushed him at a spot where there was a house under construction, surrounded by hedgerows—no one was going to see what was going on.

The vampire grabbed him by the shoulder, hauling him over so he was facing his attacker head-on. Clark found himself looking into dull blue eyes flecked with gold, blond hair buzzed short. Handsome but gaunt, a Bowie wannabe.

A skinhead vampire. Great. "I won't kill you if you're good."

Clark doubted the truth of *those* words, and he raised his hands, gripping at the vampire's arms and bodily heaving himself upward to get the man off him. He didn't even flinch, straddling Clark's thighs to keep him pressed against the asphalt and using the hand over Clark's face to shove his head back against the sidewalk. The asphalt scraped along his cheek, but the vampire didn't seem to care about that, pressing his hand hard against Clark's skull to keep him pinned and exposing his throat.

Jesus, this was happening.

Clark stared up at the cloudy night sky, breathing, hard and panicked, through his nose as he tried to stave off the sheer terror overtaking him; as much as he wiggled and squirmed, he couldn't get the vampire to let go, and the fear of having his neck broken was intense, but not as crushing as the knowledge that he was about to be bitten.

Scan the QR code below to order

Lee Ohlson's earliest literary memory is laying on her back in her bedroom listening to *The Hobbit* on audiotape while reading along in a mass market paperback to make sure she didn't miss a word. Early forays into fanfiction – self-inserts into *Lord of the Rings*, of course – and an ongoing collaboration with a middle school friend introduced her to writing for fun. After twenty-five years of ups and downs, including an entire 300-page manuscript lost to flooding during Hurricane Ike, she has finally reached a point where she can start working on publishing romance novels for a wider audience.

Lee Ohlson grew up in Houston, Texas, before returning to her home country of Canada in her early twenties. Outside of writing, she thrives on hiking, gardening, and swimming, as well as spending time with her two cats and two pugs. Her favorite holiday is Halloween, and she is an avid reader.

Some of her favorite books include *Pride and Prejudice*, *The Lord of the Rings*, *Lolita*, and *A Clockwork Orange*. Her favorite movies are *Fargo* and *The Thing*, and her favorite television show of all time is *Twin Peaks*. This eclectic mixture of media informs her works, and her adoration of different genres ensures that her novels are always fresh and compelling.

Lee's website can be found here https://www.leeohlsenauthor.ca/.

# A SHADOW COMES DARKLY

LEE OHLSEN

Clark Wright's life as an ER nurse is turned upside down when he's attacked by a rogue vampire and left for dead. Saved by Alessio, a snarky vampire bartender with an unsettling connection to him, Clark is thrust into a dark paranormal world. As they hunt down Clark's attacker, they uncover a series of violent vampire killings plaguing the city.

Bound by fate and a magnetic attraction, Clark and Alessio must unravel the mystery while confronting their deepening bond and the strange dreams connecting Clark to his dead twin. Time is running out, and survival isn't the only thing at stake—so is their fated love.

Dark, erotic, and hauntingly seductive, this is a tale of fated love, betrayal, and the gritty underworld that hides beneath the surface of the city.

Scan the QR code below to order

FOR **MORE**
OF THE
**BEST**
**GAY**
ROMANCE